Sherlock Holmes
and
The Great War

Richard Barton

Foreword

This book consists of four stories set in 1916, when Sherlock Holmes and Doctor John Watson would have been in their sixties. Three of the stories have previously been published on Amazon.

Sherlock Holmes and Doctor Watson are creations of the great Sir Arthur Conan Doyle.

CONTENTS

THE DETECTIVE AT WAR

London

I'd experience enough of war wounds to assess the young Captain as he walked into the ward: the way his left arm dangled as he moved told me instantly what had happened to him. I had seen other soldiers with conditions like his, but never one so young. His attempt to grow a moustache was only starting to succeed, and his pale skin looked as if it belonged on a schoolboy. He was tall but painfully thin although, of course, that might have been because of his recent suffering. When he spoke, he sounded as if he had just left the school choir.

"Doctor Watson?"

"I don't know about 'Doctor' anymore but yes, Captain, John Watson at your service." I had given up medical practice many years ago. My small success in publishing the tales of my illustrious friend meant I had been able to take a comfortable retirement some years earlier. My medical knowledge, already somewhat dated, had atrophied. But then the Great War swept over all our lives like a tidal wave and sitting at home reminiscing over past life and love seemed irresponsible. I was a volunteer at an auxiliary hospital called Challis House, assisting the medical staff where I could and doing small services for the patients: reading letters for those who could not see, writing letters for those who could not hold a pen. My most warmly welcomed service to this legion of heroes was to read to them from my books: a story was related most evenings in the mess hall.

The young man continued, "Captain Herbert Yates. I need to talk with you in private." It wasn't a request, it was given as an order, with a sneer that told me he felt demeaned at having to speak with an elderly civilian.

"With me? What about?" But already I knew there could be only one subject, one person that an invalided Captain would want to discuss with me. "Yes... the mess hall is usually quiet at this time of morning. Do come along." As we turned towards the corridor, I saw again the way his arm hung. Probably a bullet to the brachial plexus nerve, poor lad. But it had removed him from active service so here was another young man who would live to see peace eventually, even though crippled for life. Most of our charges at Challis House fitted the same bill: young men, cut down in their prime, here to be prepared for whatever they might be able to do next.

"A fine building you have here, doctor." He said this as though he had been planning and rehearsing a compliment, as though such an attempt at conversation did not come naturally to him. As compliments go, this was a pale one. No one would describe Challis House as

2

a fine building: squat, grey, leaking, even crumbling in places. Once it was the local manor house, and this corner of northwest London would have been countryside not long ago. Now it is an auxiliary hospital, set in a landscape of small factories and minor works which had once manufactured agricultural equipment. Now they were turned to very different purposes. Tin hats, mess tins, cooking equipment and other ancillary items for the national effort were the local product in 1916.

"Captain, forgive me if I intrude, but I perceive you have some experience of auxiliary hospitals?" He turned to me and looked me up and down as if I had said something abusive. He seemed to struggle for a moment, as if unsure whether to slap me down or answer me. Reluctantly, it seemed, he chose to engage in conversation.

"Since you ask, I do. I spent some weeks at the Red Cross Hospital in Aldeburgh. Do you mind my asking what your role is here, Doctor Watson?"

"Volunteer. My knowledge is too old, as am I, for me to be a medical practitioner. But I like to think I can help these young chaps get through what's happened to them and be ready for whatever comes next." We arrived in the mess hall. Weak early April sunlight filtered across the rows of trestle tables. At the farthest one, a few men sat around playing cards. They wore a mixture of uniform, dressing gowns and bandages. The smell of disinfectant was even stronger here than on the wards. Yates and I sat opposite each other at the table nearest the door, out of earshot of anyone.

"Surely you could do more for the war effort?" My

initially unfavourable impression of the young Captain was sinking lower each time he spoke.

"I think I am of the greatest service here. What more could I be doing?"

"You took part in the capture of the spy Von Bork –"

At this point the charade became too much and I laughed. "I drove the car! Von Bork was tricked, tracked and ensnared by Sherlock Holmes. That is who you have come to speak to me about, no? Why have you come to me? Why not go straight to Holmes?"

Captain Yates's expression went from serious to angry. Or was he afraid? Had something happened to Holmes? Had Captain Yates come to deliver terrible news? But the answer I received was almost more devastating.

"Sherlock Holmes is refusing to co-operate. We seek his help on a matter of national importance, but he will not engage with me."

I did not believe it. Holmes would not refuse to help his country at its most desperate time. I sat in dumbfounded silence. "What... What is it that you need his help with?"

"I cannot discuss that with *you*." His emphasis on 'you' further underlined his opinion of me as someone far below his station. "All you need to know is that I visited Holmes and explained my need of his assistance. I am aware you hold the man in high regard but I found his manner unconscionable. He was very clear that he was unwilling to co-operate. It's just..." the Captain struggled for a word to express his disgust. "It's tantamount to treason! I wanted to have him arrested but when I told Colonel Hooper about our meeting, he instructed me to come to you. I require you to visit your former associate and convince him to co-operate."

Again, it was an order, not a request. I left the army a long time ago but was quickly reminded of the type of officer I disliked in my regiment: abrasive, overbearing, relishing having found themselves in a position of authority over others. He had been sent to ask for help from Holmes, had failed, and was now being sent to ask for my help. He didn't like these duties, that much was clear. I did not like being treated in this manner but such sentiment is of no matter in the context of this war. "Captain, I will do as you ask although I cannot be certain of success. I take a day off on Mondays, so on Monday next I could take a train to Eastbourne and then…" But the Captain cut me off.

"Doctor Watson, I have my car waiting outside. We are to leave now."

The South Downs
The drive to Eastbourne took several hours. I had hoped we might stop for lunch but Captain Yates had instructed his driver to bring sandwiches, so we ate them as we crossed from Surrey into Sussex. I gave up trying to engage the Captain in conversation and tried to forget the cold by looking forward to seeing my friend. But I began to get worried. How would Holmes react to my arrival? I tried to call him on the telephone before we left but there had been no answer and Yates would not be delayed. Holmes would not be expecting me. I hoped he would be pleased to see me but when he learned the nature of my visit, would that change? He never showed much feeling, of course, but if he had refused to help the army, would he see my visit, on

their behalf, as a betrayal? Why would he refuse to help anyway? I could not think of anything more unlikely and that made my anxiety about the impending arrival increase.

The sun was low in the sky as we pulled up at the small farm upon the South Downs that had, for some years, been the home of the world's greatest detective. Silhouetted against a spectacular sky, just beyond the building, was a tall figure dressed in a long white cloak, bent over one of a row of beehives.

"I need to go into town to make some arrangements. I will be back in an hour. Make sure you have convinced that man to do his duty by then." The driver had opened the door for me, so I got out and the car drove away.

I turned back to look at the tall figure, standing with his back to me. I started walking across the grass towards him, wishing it was gravel or something that would make a sound and so herald my approach. I was planning the opening words I would use to announce my arrival when Holmes, without straightening up or turning around, said, "You're late Watson. I expected friend Yates would have got you here in time for lunch. Come and look at this."

He stood up, turned, pulled off his beekeeper's bonnet, and smiled. It was as if the decades fell away. My friend was just as tall and lean as ever, the eyes and chin just as sharp. The hair was now white and some wrinkles and liver spots marked his face but age and occasional rheumatism had not changed him, at least, not to me.

"Watson, my dear friend. It is, as ever, the greatest

pleasure to see you. Now look at this bee." He pointed into the hive. There were hundreds of bees crawling about while others flew in and out. It looked to me like random, chaotic movement.

"Is one of them the queen? Which one am I meant to be looking at?"

"See the one with a small dab of white paint on its back? Wear this and watch that one."

He placed the beekeeping hat on me, so the netting covered me down to my shoulders. I positioned my reading glasses underneath it, bent down and spotted one bee crawling around on the end of the comb, a small white dot on it. At first it seemed to be just one of many crawling about, but then I noticed the pattern.

"It seems to be following some kind of plan – like a figure of eight. And when it does the central part it's wiggling its thorax. Like a dance! Who knows what it can be doing that for?"

"I believe I know. It is a signal to its fellows."

"A signal? Signalling what?"

"I have placed a dish of sugared water over there." Holmes pointed to a folding chair placed on the lawn about twenty yards away. "I placed it there a few minutes ago and dabbed the drop of white paint on the first bee to find it. Now it is back with its fellows and wants to tell then where it found the feast. You will see it is in a direction about twenty degrees from the direction of the sun; the axis of the bee's dance is twenty degrees from the vertical. I have also found a strong correlation between the number of wiggles in the dance and the distance to the food source."

I watch the dancer a little longer. Other bees were leaving and many seemed to be flying directly towards the little dish on the chair. "Holmes, this is astonishing. How did you ever discover it?"

"A lifetime of looking for patterns and meanings. I have to say it has almost felt like solving a case to discover the language of the great but simple bee. I might draft a short monograph on the subject. But I might leave that to others – I believe we have other work ahead of us?"

"That's right, Holmes. The bee dance is fascinating but there are more important matters for us. I was driven here by an army officer..."

"Captain Herbert Yates of the Surrey Regiment?"

"That's right. He said he has work for you that is of national importance... but then he said..." I felt reluctant to repeat the accusation Yates had made.

"He told you I refused to co-operate and has driven you here to persuade me to change my mind."

Of course, I should have known that Holmes would already know anything I might have to tell him. "But – is it true? You're refusing to help the army?"

"No, I simply refused Captain Yates. What did you make of him?"

"I have to say, I did find him rather rude. Officious and demanding. It's true I did not take to the man, Holmes, but he has probably been through a great deal. He was injured in battle. I've been working with injured chaps and some of the stories they tell me about fighting in this war are simply horrific. We've seen bad things, you and I, but life and death in these trenches is something altogether different. I've never heard the like. But whether we like the Captain or not, he's come to us for help. We have to do what he asks if we can help the war effort."

"Of course we do, and we will. But we need to manage our friend Captain Yates. Let me close the hive, get these beekeeping things off us and go indoors. I have a rather fine Madeira I would like you to try."

The house was a large cottage. I was shown the fine dining room with a magnificent prospect of rolling hills leading down towards the sea. This splendid room had been turned into the untidiest chemical laboratory on the planet. We adjourned to the sitting room, which could have been very comfortable. Instead, gardening equipment, seedlings in trays, books and periodicals were spread over every surface. I recognised some things: by the fireplace was a solid iron chest which once held the Agra treasure; on the mantelpiece was a small black and white ivory box, sent to Holmes by Mr Culverton Smith and formerly armed with a spring-loaded poisoned needle; and above that, in pride of place, the photograph of Irene Adler.

Holmes poured us each a glass of red wine and sat in a leather armchair by the fireplace. I cleared some newspapers and gardening gloves off the opposite chair and sat down as well.

"Now, Watson, do you wish to deliver a rebuke for my failure to answer my country's call?"

"Of course not. I knew there must be an explanation."

"And you, of all people, deserve to hear it. You have seen many of my first meetings with clients. They have come to me wearing a mask..."

"The King of Bohemia, I remember it well. If I had not, the photograph above the fireplace could not fail to remind me."

"I do not wish to have a client who wears a mask even if he is a King. You will remember also, I have no doubt, that I was less than completely honest with Doctor James Mortimer and Sir Henry Baskerville when I told them I was unable to travel with them to Dartmoor?"

"So, Holmes, are you saying that you see the British army, currently engaged in what history will describe as the greatest war we have ever had to wage, as just another client?"

"As you indicate, probably the most important client I will ever have. All the more reason to get the terms right at the start. Captain Yates arrived here yesterday and told me to put myself under his command. He then started to recite a list of conditions and rules that I must follow. I heard him out then told him I would not accept his command nor any of his conditions. He did not know how to react, so he made a number of vague threats and departed. I knew that, if the need for my services was real, another approach would be made and so it has proved. Enjoy your wine, Watson. I will telephone a woman in the village who assists me with the housekeeping. She shall make up a bed for you for tonight and prepare a meal for us. When Captain Yates returns you can tell him that I will accept his case under my conditions, not his, and that we shall be ready to depart for any destination he decides at nine o'clock tomorrow morning."

After so many years of association with Holmes, I am accustomed to finding myself in situations which I do not fully understand. I have waited in an empty house watching a shadow in the window of our Baker Street home, just hours after Holmes had revealed himself as still alive and not, as all believed, dead beneath the Reichenbach Falls. I have waited in darkness in a bank vault with no idea how the mystery of the Red-Headed League had led us there. Once again, after so many years, I had the familiar sensation that I was lacking awareness of some vital truth. In the past, it worried me very little: I simply trusted that Holmes knew what was afoot and what to do, and that all would become clear eventually. This time, however, I had some concern: had Holmes delayed his service to his country by a day because of some minor argument between him and Captain Yates over who was in charge? I felt sure Holmes would have been able to negotiate a suitable understanding between them without sending the Captain away.

Perhaps Yates really was an impossibly unreasonable man. But he seemed polite enough when I went out to his car, on his return, and promised we would be at his disposal from nine o'clock. I mentioned that Holmes wanted to work under the conditions he had given to the Captain the day before. Yates simply nodded and said, "Yes, I should have thought it obvious I agreed to that," before wishing me good night and driving away to sleep at a local inn.

Folkestone

I had been to Folkestone once before. Many years ago,

my late wife and I had a short holiday there. I remember our pleasant walks together on The Leas, the wide strip of public park that runs along the top of the cliff. I hardly recognised it on my return. The Leas had become a vast army camp with men in khaki constantly coming and going. Captain Yates, Holmes and I had been driven to this part of the Kent coast after I had spent the night in Holmes's house. Yates said he would find Colonel Hooper and arrange a meeting. He suggested we rendezvous at a café at the top of the Old High Street at one o'clock. This gave us time to stretch our legs after the journey. We walked past the two great hotels, The Metropole and The Grand, once bitter rivals but now united in service, hosting military hospitals, officer accommodation and even, we were told, the Belgian royal family. Between the hotels and the cliff were rows of tents. Men from across the Empire were arriving, while those departing for France marched down the slope to the harbour. I saw regiments from England, Wales and Ireland. Soldiers from South Africa mingled with men from Newfoundland, troops from Scotland camped beside men from Bermuda and, everywhere I looked, there were Canadians.

Holmes and I must have looked out of place. We were far older than anyone else we saw. Holmes wore a Norfolk suit, tweed cap and one of those long neckties that became fashionable before the war. It was black with pink stripes and he said it was a college tie. I wore a dark suit with a bow tie and a brown trilby hat. Edwardian fashions would have been normal in a seaside resort just two years previously. Now the town was dominated by young men in military uniforms.

We arrived at the café on time. Waiting for us were Captain Yates and a man who had a look I had learned to recognize at Challis House: the laughter lines of a face that had once been jolly, but which had acquired a greyness and the haggard appearance of those who have known horror. The loose skin around his face and jaw spoke of rapid weight loss. This was Colonel Hooper and he brightened on being introduced to us.

"Famous chaps, both of you, very glad you've been able to come along. I can't say I've read the books myself but my butler had them all and said they were cracking. Now, you're a Consulting Detective and we rather need to consult you on a pressing matter. It seems the Germans have a way of knowing where our troops are. We had a corps of Australians go up the line and when they looked into no-mans-land, they saw a sign reading 'Advance Australia – if you can'. The damn Boche knew they were there and put that sign up to let them know it."

"Why would they do that?" I asked, "It seems a funny thing to do."

"Not funny as in making a joke, that's for sure," said the Colonel, "The Germans don't have a sense of humour. No, we think it was meant to scare the lads. As if to say, 'Look at our sign, boys! See how much we know! We're always one step ahead!'"

"Did the sign have that effect?"

"Hardly. The Boche can't know Anzacs very well. An undisciplined lot, by all accounts, but brave. A unit from Tasmania had prepared a sign saying, 'Don't worry, Fritz, we're coming' and were all for putting that up facing the German line, but they were ordered not to,

13

as it was seen as an unnecessary risk."

The waitress had arrived while Colonel Hooper spoke. We gave her our order before Holmes leant over the table to speak quietly. "Colonel, forgive me, but are you sure we should be having a conversation about such matters in a public café?"

"Oh, you don't need to worry about that. They're good people here. Belgians, refugees, forced from their home by Huns. No one more likely to be on our side. Doing very well here too. Besides, no offence, but we're not meant to allow visitors into our office. The real hush-hush stuff is there. Maps, orders of battle, all that twaddle."

"How do you know they are Belgian?"

"What do you mean? What else would they be?" The waitress returned and started placing saucers, cups, plates and cutlery. Holmes addressed her.

"Excuse me, Miss. I am told you are from Belgium."

"Yes, sir."

"May I ask from where, specifically?"

"From Leuven, sir – a little way east of Brussels."

"Leuven… It has a fine town hall, if I remember correctly."

The girl's face brightened. "You remember correct, sir, a fine building." Then her face darkened. "I feel sick at the thought of the godless swine who will be in it now." She suddenly remembered her station. "I am so sorry, sir. I did not mean to become familiar."

"Not at all, I quite understand your strength of

feeling." She ran away to fetch our lunch. "Well, well, I am sure you are right, Colonel, and that she is as Belgian as King Albert."

I felt compelled to ask how Holmes knew about the town hall at Leuven.

"I did not. But most Belgian towns have fine town halls. It was a reasonable supposition. Now Colonel: pray continue to explain your problem."

"Well, that's it really; the Germans know who they're facing across the line. What else do they know? How are they finding out? We can't have that. That's why we are seeking your help."

The conversation paused when the waitress returned. Perhaps the Colonel had decided he was speaking a little freely. She laid out a teapot, water, milk and sugar. Then she started pouring out each cup of tea and asking each of us in turn how we took it. The process lasted an inordinately long time. Finally, she left us and, as Colonel Hooper began to sip his tea, Holmes started his enquiries.

"I have a number of questions for you, Colonel. First, is the French army suffering similarly? Do the Germans know about their movements?"

"Goodness me, Mr Holmes, I have no idea. We don't discuss this sort of thing. I certainly would not tell my French contacts about our little problem, and I would not expect them to tell us if they have anything similar."

"I see. Then my second question. Do the men here know when and where they will be posted when they get to France?"

"Certainly not. Neither do the junior officers. Doubt

the senior officers either, come to that. Plans change all the time. Navy's in charge of sailing across, we go when the Dover Patrol gives us the go signal. Troops are then dispersed across the Pais-de-Calais and beyond. There's training and what have you until the orders come to move up the line."

"I understand. Therefore, information of troop movements is not being passed to the Germans from England?"

"Can't be. After all, the Australians didn't start from here. After giving the Turk a kicking, they landed in France down south – Marseilles, I believe. I would assume that some Frenchie down there was passing news east via Switzerland if that sign was the only evidence we had. But I'm afraid to say they seem to know who they are facing all too often. We send raiding parties over, they come back with a few prisoners for interrogation. Seems they know far more than we'd like. That's what we've got to find out: how much do they know and how are they getting that information?"

"Quite. Which leads me to ask – forgive me if this seems impolite – if this matter is of such great importance, why is it being addressed by a party of four in a café in Kent? Should this not be discussed in Whitehall or Westminster?"

The Colonel harumphed. "You're reputed to be the top man in England for this type of puzzle. But I understand your point. We invited the official intelligence services to look into it but they are not convinced that information is really leaking across to the other side. Besides, even if Germany has insight to our troop movements... it would be a matter of concern, of course, but it is not seen as making a difference." I was amazed at this pronouncement. If Holmes felt the same way, he hid it.

"Could you explain to us why such a possible lapse in security is not seen as significant?"

"Of course. Don't get me wrong, we want to find out if something is happening, how the Germans are getting their information and punish anyone who's helping them. But, as I have said, we don't see it changing the outcome of the war." The Belgian waitress delivered a dish of cutlets to each of us and the Colonel continued as he ate. "We have a big push coming. Oh, I know what you'll say, we've launched major offensives before and they did not bring victory. But this year will be different. We've got the biggest army yet. What you can see in Folkestone today is just a fraction of what we're building up. Then we have a new secret weapon. Now this is something I should not say out loud in a public place, so I'll just let you have a whisper: imagine steel bunkers, mounted with guns and motorised so they can drive across no-mans-land, across their trenches and across Germany!"

Holmes watched him carefully as he ate, and asked, "You are certain that the size of the army and these motorised bunkers will finally end it?"

"It's not just all that. Things are very different now from what they were even a year ago. The French have bled the heart out of the German army at Verdun. It cost them, mind, but they did it. The Russians are going to attack soon all along the Eastern Front and it's simply a question of numbers; the Germans won't be able to stop the Russian steamroller. Nothing will. Russia's also battering Johnny Turk from the north while we move on them from Mesopotamia in the south. The Italians started slowly against Austria but they've got the bit between their teeth now and are launching a series of hammer blows on the Isonzo; they're bound to break through eventually."

I was not sure whether to be inspired by this optimistic picture or horrified at his hubris. The idea that the war could be over in a few months was, of course, hugely appealing. I asked, "Colonel, can we really hope that the war will, this time, be over by Christmas?"

"Before then, Doctor Watson. My estimate is the end of August. Peace at last! We will raise a glass to those we have lost in bars along Unter den Linden." He was thoughtful for a moment, then continued. "There may be some mopping up to do here and there. Oh, and there's rumours of trouble brewing in Ireland, but there always are. It won't come to anything. But we still want to know how the Germans are getting news of our troop movements. That's the pressing matter. The question we want you to answer, Mr Holmes, is: how are they getting this information?"

Holmes took a bite of food and thought for a moment. "You have said yourself that the information cannot be coming from England. It must be coming from somewhere where there is information on the movement of troops arriving from here and those coming from the Mediterranean. Your information is being collected in France."

"Then you must go. I'll sign some chits giving you full authority to travel and make your enquiries. Captain

Yates will have to accompany you, you must have someone from the military with you at all times and I know you'll find him useful. So, will you go?"

Holmes took his final mouthful of food. The Colonel watched him eagerly. The Captain just looked furious. Holmes glanced at me. I nodded.

"Doctor Watson and I are happy to accept your case."

Holmes and I returned to our hotel – not, alas, one of the famous pair on The Leas but a pleasant enough establishment – and waited while arrangements were being made. It was late afternoon when Captain Yates called on us. He explained that he had all the documents and permits required and that we would be sailing the next morning if circumstances permitted it. Once we had gone through all these arrangements, Yates finally said what he had clearly wanted to say back at the café.

"I have to say, Mr Holmes, this trip to France is not what I expected at all. You are a Consulting Detective, is that not the title you have created for yourself? Then I should have thought it was merely a matter of consulting you here, getting your advice and instructing people, in France or wherever, on the actions to take."

"Sometimes I am able to satisfy my clients without leaving my home. On many other occasions I have found it necessary to travel to solve the problem that a client brings to me. This is one of those occasions."

Captain Yates looked as if he was having to chew his tongue to hold back what he really wanted to say to us.

"I never expected that we would have to go to France. I never... Well, don't expect it to be a holiday. I don't know if you were in France before but it's not as you might remember it. We shouldn't have to go."

Boulogne

We spent the night at our hotel. Captain Yates met us the next morning and greeted us with no more than "Follow me." We walked down the narrow, steep street to the harbour, which was thronged with troops, horses, vehicles and supplies. Everything was loaded with surprising speed onto the *SS Invicta*, a merchant ship converted to a troop carrier and painted in the strange 'dazzle' camouflage.

The voyage to France was uneventful. Our ship was packed with soldiers. Holmes spoke to some of them on the crossing, confirming that none knew where they would face the enemy, although rumours were rife. One man actually thought we were sailing from Folkestone to Archangel, to join with Russian forces there. But it was to Boulogne we sailed. Captain Yates was unwell during the trip. The ship's Captain invited Holmes and me to the bridge and offered us his hospitality. When his duties called him away, we were able to discuss the case in private.

"We've been involved in some serious matters, Holmes. The naval treaty, which was taken from poor young Phelps, for example. The loss of the Bruce-Partington submarine plans was presented to us as a vital international problem. Then there was that mysterious letter which you returned to Trelawney Hope's dispatch box. Those adventures aside, I don't remember another case which was of quite such national significance! What can you tell me at this early stage? How are we going to discover how the Germans get their information about our troop movements?"

"I do not consider the question of how they are getting it to be of great importance."

"Not important? But Holmes, the Colonel said that is the question they need us to answer!"

"How they get the information? Any number of ways. We are in the twentieth century, my dear Watson. For all we know, the Germans long ago laid a series of pipes under the French countryside and send messages through them by pneumatic pressure." He noted my sceptical expression. "No? Then perhaps they have an aeroplane that they fly by night, painted black. Perhaps it is quiet enough, or can fly high enough, so that no one can hear it. Every night it flies to a quiet field somewhere in France to be met by an agent who simply hands the news to the pilot."

"That sounds possible – do you think that could be how they do it?"

"It could be, or it could be any of a dozen other methods we could imagine before we disembark. That is why I do not think the matter of 'how' is of great importance. We shall find out, along the way, I have no doubt. But the question we must attend to is not 'how' but 'who'."

At this moment I was called away. Yates and several other men were very sick, although the sea was not rough. I had seasickness when I sailed out to Afghanistan, more years ago than I care to remember, but I recall just how awful one can feel. There was nothing I could do for those suffering, other than make them drink water, keep their eyes closed and their heads still, and assure them that their suffering would end the moment we docked.

And so it proved. Almost as soon as the gangway was in place, Yates summoned us and we disembarked. Saying something about making arrangements, he pointed us towards a long, low building that might have once been a Customs House but was now an Officer's Club. The staff made us welcome, once we had presented our credentials, and we were shown to a table with a fine view of the docks. Several ships were being unloaded. Cranes were lifting, from out of ships' holds, crates of supplies, artillery pieces and several bemused horses. Men were everywhere, swarming about the docks, some lining up for a parade or roll call, others overseeing the unloading of matériel from ships and its subsequent loading into lorries and the great trains which pulled up right along the dock. For a moment I could not identify what I was reminded of, as I watched the swarms of khaki figures. Thinking of the word 'swarms' reminded me.

"Holmes – it's like watching your bees swarming around in your hive!"

"Yes. If only one of them was marked with a white dot, we would be able to identify the man who is the source of the information being leaked."

"You don't think it's one of these men?"

"No. I think we are going to look much harder to find the spy we seek."

"Where do we start?"

Holmes watched the activity on the quay for a time, then said, "First I would like to get an idea of how troops are dispersed and what happens when they move. We need to find out when their destination becomes known, either to them or, what is more likely, I think, to those able to observe them. Next, we shall need to discover who can be observing them and drawing conclusions of their destination. Once we have that, we can trace the means of communication being used to collate the information that is being gathered, then perhaps we will be able to capture the enemy agents and put an end to their work."

While I am perfectly capable of understanding all of the words Holmes used, and the sentences he spoke made perfect sense, I was still entirely unclear about what we would need to do.

"You have a plan, then?"

Once again, a pause while we watched wounded men being loaded onto the ships for return to England. Some were able to make their own way onto the ship. Some led each other, crocodile fashion; those behind the leader had bandages over their eyes. Some were lying on stretchers, which were placed in pairs on pallets, then lifted into the ships by crane.

"I would not say I have a plan yet," said Holmes. "But I have an idea of the first step we must take towards developing one. Where is that man Yates? He must have recovered by now."

"He said he had to make some arrangements."

"Possibly. I think it more likely he needed a walk to recover himself after the voyage."

Captain Yates arrived shortly afterwards. The colour had returned to his face and, for the first time since I had met him, he looked almost cheerful. He ordered brandies for each of us and drank his in one. "Well, gentlemen, I have arranged accommodation for us on the Grande Rue. How long do you think we will need to stay here, before returning to England?"

"Captain, at this stage I have no idea. Although I doubt, very much, that we will be long in Boulogne; I believe our next destination will also be in France."

The sour expression which had always adorned Yates's face until just now swiftly returned. "Another place in France? I see. So where do you propose we go?"

"If we are to find out how the Germans are getting our information, we need to track that information from its source and seek points at which it could be being intercepted. So we start with this: where are the decisions made about which units will go where?" Captain Yates just stared at him, so Holmes continued. "I understand there are staff officers up at the Citadel." We could see the town's ancient fortifications from where we sat, crowned with the cupola of the basilica. "I suggest we take a walk up the hill and see what we can find out."

"Have you no plan? No design?" exclaimed the Captain. "I assumed you worked to a method and would be able to sketch out the steps of your enquiry. I understood that you have solved mysteries before and would have a good idea of how to crack this one, as well as how long it would take." He leant forward. "I thought you probably had a good idea already of what is going on."

"Data, Captain, I must have data! It is a capital

mistake to make theories before you have data."

This stirred a memory in my mind: "One begins to twist facts to suit theories, instead of theories to suit facts."

"Quite so," said Holmes. "You see Captain: Doctor Watson knows my methods. One has to trace the threads, untangle them and draw them together in order. When you have enough of them in your hand, you can begin to entertain possibilities, ruthlessly rejecting all that do not fit the facts, exploring further when there remain multiple possibilities, until just one hypothesis remains which fits. I have had the opportunity to work on a great many mysteries. While some of them have similarities to others, and many had no features of interest whatsoever, not a few were unique in the features of the puzzle they presented. Most of my work has been addressed at restricting the activities of the criminal classes, both in England and, I think, across five continents. This case is a matter of information being passed between great powers at war. I am most flattered by your presumptions of my foresight and ability, but I fear I must disappoint you. At this stage, we operate one step at a time."

I have no doubt that my face shone with admiration at this brilliant speech by a great man whom I am proud, beyond normal levels, to call my friend. But the young face of Captain Herbert Yates reminded me of the expression I have seen on the faces of many criminals at the moment when Holmes brought their careers to an end.

"Then I suggest, Mr Holmes, that we take the first step without further delay."

The climb up Grande Rue to the citadel is not far but is somewhat steep. When Yates pointed out the hotel to which he had had our bags delivered, I went in to borrow a walking stick. The Jezail bullet which wounded me in the second Afghan war was now causing stiffness after any great exertion. But the stick helped and soon we were at the mighty ramparts of the citadel, built to protect France from invading English, now home to Englishmen here to defend France.

We found an Adjutant and explained our need. I suppose the sight of a young Captain and two elderly civilians asking questions about troop movements would have raised anyone's suspicions. He gazed mournfully at us, looking at each of us, in turn, slowly. We showed him our credentials, which he scrutinised with great deliberation. I think he was deciding whether to have us arrested. But, after a time, he slowly said, "I think you had better see the General."

He led us through narrow streets which, while far from being deserted, seemed quiet and peaceful after the noise and activity of the port area. The people we saw were all British, most in uniform – army and navy, plus Voluntary Aid Detachment nurses. We arrived at a square surrounded by fine buildings: the Town Hall, the Courts and the Library. We were led to what had once been, I assumed, a smart hotel on a small scale. We were guided upstairs and ushered into a fine room, richly decorated and furnished, with dark oil paintings on the walls between windows which looked out onto a superb view of the square.

The General turned out to be an affable Scot,

General McStowe, who sat behind a large oak desk on which documents were arranged in columns. He was a large man with a florid face and untidy sandy hair. He listened, in some bewilderment, to the Adjutant's explanation for bringing the three of us to him. I don't blame him for being bewildered, as the explanation was long and rambling. But then we presented our credentials and the General's bewilderment became amazement.

"The Sherlock Holmes? The Doctor Watson?" He came round from behind his desk and shook Holmes's hand, then mine, then Holmes's again. "I've read all the books at least twice. Brought them over with me, I've got the full set in my quarters upstairs! Nice to bring along something familiar, I thought, although, I have to say, not had much time for leisure reading since I got here. But what tales! What adventures! 'Speckled Band' was always my wife's favourite, but I'd have to choose something like 'The Greek Interpreter' or 'The Dancing Men'. Whoever would have thought you would one day present yourselves in my office! Can I offer you tea or coffee? No? Well, never mind, let's talk about your adventures!"

Captain Yates was completely ignored. His face was white and he looked sickened. The General continued to talk about those adventures of Holmes and myself which are known to the public and seemed to have endless questions. "How was the man with the twisted lip able to disguise himself so well that his wife could not recognize him? Do you recall any of the funny stories which Mr Rucastle used to amuse the governess, what was her name? What became of Sir George Burnwell, the rogue who stole the Beryl Coronet (or part of it)?"

Holmes answered all his questions. It was the quantity of dirt which completed the disguise of Mr Neville St Clair. Holmes had never asked Miss Hunter about the funny stories. Sir George Burnwell was found dead in mysterious circumstances in Istanbul many years ago. I waited for the question which I knew must be coming, the question that all admirers of Holmes eventually asked. I did not have to wait long. "Ah, now, I tell you what," said the General, "What about that deducing all manner of things about a person just from looking at them? What can you deduce about me, eh?"

"General, I don't wish to presume. It can appear to be an invasion of privacy if I use my craft in that way."

"Don't worry about any of that. Have a go, I don't mind."

Holmes paused for a moment before saying "Other than the obvious signs of your preference for Turkish tobacco (although current hostilities have forced you to change to Burley), your skill at golf, your being right-handed and a violinist, I would surmise a liking for card games, bridge most especially, and former fondness for whisky, until you decided to give it up."

"I – ah – yes. Oh. I didn't think... you really are amazing, Mr Holmes. It, it was a viola rather than a violin but otherwise, I... Yes. Now. I have been taking up your valuable time and I... I am most glad to welcome you to Boulogne, Mr Holmes. Now, how can I help you?"

Holmes explained our mission. The General had heard that the German army was supposed to have advance knowledge of our troop movements. Like

Colonel Hooper, he did not think it would make much difference to the outcome of the spring offensive.

"Still, I think we need to find out what is going on. Plug any leaks. Root out any villains! Of course I would like to help you, Mr Holmes, be proud to. What is it you need from me?"

"May I ask you a series of questions? Firstly, where are the decisions made about which units to post on the front line?"

"General headquarters – that's GHQ in army lingo. It has just moved, as a matter of fact. They've set up in Montreuil, taken over a French military academy. About twenty miles south of here. That's where all the plans are made and orders issued. They're in charge of transporting supplies and equipment imported from England, they manage all the transport networks and even decide the construction of new roads."

"Do British military officials mix with French locals much?"

"Oh yes. I'd have to say relations between us and them are pretty good. It's tough for the locals of course."

"In what way is it tough?"

"Prices of everything have shot up. There's rationing and access to bars is strictly regulated for all. There's no street lighting and everyone has to cover their windows at night so no aircraft could see the place. It's called the 'blackout', but you know about that, of course, as Mr Churchill ordered it in our coastal towns and you have it in London now, I think. No one can enter or leave Montreuil after eight o'clock. But, on the other hand, the Tommies spend their money there and we put on various charity events and what not. I think the locals would be having a much tougher war if we were not there."

"Thank you. Now, once the strategists at Montreuil have decided a unit should move, how are the orders given?"

"A dispatch rider will deliver them. You see these chaps riding their motorcycles all over the country."

"You only use motorcycles? Would not a telephone message or wireless telegraphy be quicker?"

"We have telephone networks connecting GHQ with forward positions. From there, the infantry and the artillery have their own networks. We have wireless telegraphy sets too, 'radios' they call them now, but they are great big things, always going wrong. Besides, an order to move a unit isn't something you can put in a simple message by telephone or wireless. You need to send maps, orders of battle, dispersion diagrams, and we also send cypher books, so we can later talk by wire or wireless using terms that only someone with the corresponding cypher will understand." The General returned to the far side of his desk and sat majestically in a high-backed wooden chair that he could rotate as he sat. "Besides, anyone can listen in to a radio message and even telephone lines are not as secure as you might think. The cyphers and codes help but, in the end, the most secure system is to pack the bulk of the orders in a sealed bag and get them delivered by motorcycle. Then we use telephones and, at a pinch, wireless to direct and co-ordinate. You might ring a unit and say 'implement order 27A at H hour' or something like that.

They look that up in their documents and know what to do. Anyone listening in is none the wiser."

It brought home to me, listening to the General speak of motorcycles, telephones and wireless sets, just how much war had changed since I saw my service. Whoever could have imagined that there would be so many ways to deliver a message? In Afghanistan, orders were delivered by a man on a horse. I have lived through an age of unprecedented change. Modern science and industry have brought us many benefits. To see so many of them turned to destruction is tragic.

Holmes continued with his enquiries and, in response, the General explained how troops arriving from England were dispersed to camps across the British sector and occupied with training while numbers built up for the big push. He unlocked a cabinet and produced maps of the railway network, which formed the main arteries of military movement, and explained how lorries and trucks were being used for local transport. "Even London buses! If you noticed there are fewer of them on the street, it's because they are over here moving soldiers about. Mostly, though, it's Shanks' pony." I had to ask what that meant. "Marching, my dear Doctor Watson. We have regiments marching all over Flanders, Picardy and the Pas-de-Calais. Keeps the men fit, keeps them occupied and gets them about."

Holmes asked more detailed questions about movement of troops for exercise, dispersal or training, and how a unit moving to the front would differ from one moving to a camp. The General explained that troops moving to the front would carry full battle equipment and supplies, while those marching to a training area would only have their basic necessities. He asked about different trucks and trains and how they might be recognised for what they were. He asked about present locations of army units.

"All very hush-hush, of course. I wouldn't tell anyone but you and your party, Mr Holmes. You must keep it all under your hats until the war's over." He spread another map over the neat columns of documents on his desk. "We've got men everywhere as we build up. Just yesterday we sent the First Newfoundland Regiment to this area, northeast of Amiens. The day before we moved the 36th Ulsters here, to Bouzincourt, while the day before that we moved the 9th battalion of the Essex Regiment back to near Le Touquet for some rest."

Holmes looked up sharply. "The Essex 9th?"

"Yes, they were pulled out of the line three days ago. Why, do you know someone in that outfit?"

"I do. Well, General, you have given me a great deal to think about. If you will excuse me, I need some time to consider what I have learned. Perhaps you would indulge me with a further interview later, if it should be required?"

Not only that, the General also insisted we dine as his guests that evening. Arrangements made, we left his grand office and returned to the town square. Once we were outside, Captain Yates turned on us, managing (just) to contain his obvious anger.

"That man is a General in the British army, Mr Holmes."

"I deduced as much, Captain Yates."

"You questioned him as if he were a common

suspect in one of your murky criminal cases. You should show more respect. How did you trick him into telling you all that information? That's military intelligence, the German army would give half a division to know what he has told you."

"The German army does know what he has told me; or, if Colonel Hooper's fears are grounded, they will do shortly. That is why we are here. General McStowe has chosen to assist me and trust me. Indeed, he has trusted you as well, as you heard everything he told me."

The Captain appeared to be chewing back his reply. "I will see you both in the morning. Please be at breakfast at eight o'clock so we can plan the day."

"You are not joining us at dinner?"

"As one so famous for making minute observations, it must have been clear that the General's invitation was extended to you and Doctor Watson. I don't think he even noticed me. Besides, I have to prepare a report for Colonel Hooper. He wants to hear from me each evening."

With that, the Captain marched off, his injured arm swaying limply. Holmes and I started in the opposite direction and ended up walking the town ramparts.

"Well, well, so that was military intelligence, Watson? I think the term an oxymoron." We paused at a corner of the walls, looking down on the harbour. A locomotive was just steaming away from the docks, pulling a train of wagons.

"How many pipes will you need to solve this problem?"

Holmes smiled at the reference. "Just smoking pipes will not suffice to solve the problem. But I do need time to digest and consider. I must ask you to practise your great gift Watson – that of silence. Let us walk, we may smoke, but I beg that we do not talk for the next hour."

We met General McStowe, as arranged, in a restaurant just off the square. Our conversation began with Holmes having to explain his deductions to the General. While everyone knows that tobacco stains the skin of regular smokers, Holmes explained that the Turkish variety stains with a distinctive yellowness. The contents of the ashtray on the General's desk, however, could be identified as Burley at a glance. Holmes then asked the General to confirm he had been playing golf the previous Sunday.

"That's right! One has to have some recreation, even in these times, so I spent the afternoon at Wimereux. Not a bad course. A proper links. But how did you know that?"

"My hotel manager tells me that Sunday was a warm, sunny day here – the first really sunny day of the year. The weather since has been cooler. Your Caledonian skin caught the sun. But not on your right hand, which is pale. Some golfers, often the most serious players, wear a glove on their lead hand. Conclusion: you are a keen, right-handed golfer who played last Sunday."

"As you have been told many times, Mr Holmes, it does seem easy and obvious. But only once you have been told. I would never have worked that out. Now the viola playing – you saw the marks on my neck?"

"You show the classic pattern for a violinist. I have played the instrument myself, a little."

"Yes, yes, of course. But playing bridge does not leave marks on the player. How did you know I play the odd rubber? I looked over my room after you left – no cards, no card table, no clue at all that I could discover."

Holmes smiled. "That was something of a guess. But the layout of your documents on your desk made it a safe guess, in the circumstances. You have them arranged in columns, overlapping, to create a little set of paper stairways. It reminded me of the way cards are laid out in many games. Bridge seemed likely for a sociable and competitive man such as yourself."

"And the other thing? The – er – the whisky?"

"General, there is no need to feel awkward. I myself have a former habit with a substance much more malevolent than alcohol. Our vices leave their traces. It shows in your face. It could have been wine or beer or something else. I assumed a proud Scot would make the patriotic choice. However, I could see no sign of drinks in your room. There were some bottles of cordial in the cabinet and a pitcher of water. You offered us a hot beverage but nothing stronger. The wine list provided by the waiter remains at your side, unopened."

"You're right again, of course. I was drinking more and more in the years leading up to the war. People warned me about it and I always said I could give it up any time I chose. I just never chose to. Then, a year ago, King George promised that no alcohol would be had in the royal household until the war was over. That seemed to be the signal. I have not touched it since."

"I commend you on your willpower. An intelligent

move. Now, unless you have more questions about my little demonstration?" The General shook his head. "Thank you. First, then, I would like to summarize the case as I see it. Information generated in British army headquarters in Montreuil is finding its way to the Germans. The first possibility is that someone in Montreuil is their supplier."

The General looked aghast. "You can't be serious? A spy in GHQ?"

"I also find the idea unpalatable. But we cannot discount the possibility. Many German and English families are intertwined. Who is to say there is no one who has chosen loyalty to his German heritage over his British one? There is also the possibility that someone is being threatened: if an officer has family in Germany, who is to say that their empire has not threatened some harm to them unless that officer serves them?"

The waiter came over and we gave our orders. It did not take long, there was little choice available. General McStowe said, "One hears terrible things about what the Huns have done, in Belgium and elsewhere. But it seems hard to credit their High Command with threatening a chap's family."

"Indeed. It seems unlikely. As does the final form of betrayal from inside GHQ: blackmail. If an officer had been indiscreet... in a manner which would have serious consequences for him if found out..."

"Yes, yes, Holmes, I see what you are getting at. But would that drive a man to betray his country? After all, the penalty for treason is a great deal worse than what you get for a spot of... well, you know."

The waiter delivered our consommés and Holmes

36

continued. "On the whole, I think the scenario of a spy in GHQ is possible but unlikely. As well as the problems we have discussed, there is the matter of how a spy would get the information from GHQ to Germany. Montreuil is a closed community. People cannot simply come and go. Suspicious behaviour would be identified very quickly."

"I am glad to hear it. So if possibility number one is weak, what is the next possibility?"

"The next scenario is that the information is intercepted between GHQ and the units that receive the order to move to the front."

"Do you consider that more likely?"

"Dispatch riders could be opening their pouches and copying the information. But I understand there are very many of them. It is unlikely that they are all corrupt. Telephone and wireless messages can be intercepted, as you have said, but without the physical documents, such intercepts are not likely to provide Germany with the detailed information she seems to have."

The last of the soup was consumed and the spoons placed down with a clatter. The waiter was swift in clearing the bowls away. "Well then, Mr Holmes; what do you think is a likely possibility?"

"I consider that it is the actual movement of the troops that is being observed and communicated. You have told us that a unit destined for the front can be distinguished from one heading for a training or rest camp. They travel across the country by foot, truck and train. They carry regimental insignia and equipment related to their function. A small number of agents, perhaps based at main camps, crossroads and railway stations could observe and gather enough information for experts in Germany to piece together and determine much of the Allies' battle plans."

The waiter brought us fried sole, fried potatoes and spring salad. The General sat in thought as Holmes and I began to eat. "But, Mr Holmes, you're talking of a network of secret agents spread across the country. It would mean the Germans had dozens of men from Switzerland to Belgium, from the sea to the front."

For the first time during our meal, I saw an opportunity to speak. "When you have eliminated the impossible, whatever remains, however improbable, must be the truth."

"Quite right, Watson! In this case we have not had the luxury of eliminating the other possibilities entirely. So we can only cast the theory of a network of spies as the currently favoured hypothesis. It may not require such a vast number of men. But, like any hypothesis, it needs to be put to the test. And that, if I can have your support, General, is what I propose to do."

The General nodded. "You have my support Mr Holmes. But – what for, exactly? How do you propose to test your hypothesis?"

"I need a team of agents. People I can instruct and rely on to perform a search of likely locations in the way that is required. I only need half a dozen or so. I have an idea where I can find them, if I will have your permission to borrow them."

"Borrow them from where?"

"From the 9th battalion of the Essex Regiment."

Le Touquet

After dinner, arrangements made, we passed the night at our hotel on Grande Rue. I was woken in the night by the sound of someone screaming; it shocked me from my sleep, but then there was silence. I was not sure if I had dreamed it or not.

At breakfast we informed Captain Yates of the agreement we had made with General McStowe. Holmes had a contact in the 9th battalion of the Essex Regiment and the General confirmed they were currently out of action in the area of Le Touquet. The General had countersigned the documents provided by Colonel Hooper to, as he put it, "Give it a bit more clout." He did explain that we'd need the local commanding officer to agree to the loan of a working party but he thought that it should be forthcoming: "A name like yours, Mr Holmes, carries more authority than a room full of generals, eh? Besides, I don't think they will be needed for action again until the big push, and that's still a few weeks off."

Yates took all this information with no comment. He just looked miserable. It was not easy for him to manage the French breakfast one-handed. I offered to help him butter his rolls but he was clear (and somewhat sharp) that he had to learn to manage his condition.

As we ate, a messenger came from the General to confirm the address of a villa in Le Touquet that was acting as headquarters for the battalion. The messenger explained he was a driver and was at our service to drive us there.

The journey was only about twenty miles, but it took

two hours as the road was jammed with heavy traffic in both directions. The little roads of rural France were not coping well with the demands of mechanised war. Finally we arrived and an orderly ushered us into the presence of Lieutenant Colonel Bridge, commander of the 9th battalion. He was a serious man with dark hair, dark beard, dark eyes and a deep voice, although he spoke very quickly.

He looked through the credentials. "Mr Holmes; Doctor Watson; Captain Yates." He nodded to each of us in turn. "I have heard of you, Mr Holmes, of course. And I have great respect for General McStowe. He made sure we got a comfortable billet for now, although no home leave this time. We've had a bit of a rough few weeks. Now, it says here you are acquainted with one of our officers and would like the help of him and some of the men. Which officer is it?"

"Captain Lestrade. I am his godfather."

While my admiration of my friend Sherlock Holmes is as great as can be, he is sometimes infuriating. He has no respect for knowledge that cannot be applied to his work. That is why, very soon after our first meeting, I challenged him on his lack of knowledge of disciplines such as literature, philosophy, astronomy and politics. His assumption of the relative value of different schools of human endeavour meant that he would assume others, myself included, would have little desire for information that was not of practical value to them. In this case, I am also to blame: I had never, in all our encounters, asked Inspector Lestrade of Scotland Yard about his family.

It was not until that evening, when we sat together over a drink in an officers' club, that Holmes explained. "Terrance was born during your marriage. As you know, we saw less of each other in those days – I am not criticising you, Watson, I understand that Mary was your natural companion. The Inspector honoured me with the request to become godfather to his son. After your loss and our renewed friendship, the subject never arose. Indeed, it occurred to me that it might be somewhat insensitive of me to boast of being a godfather when your wife left us before you could start a family."

To return to my narrative: I sat dumfounded while a Corporal was sent to find Captain Lestrade. Meanwhile, Holmes explained his need: he wanted to borrow Captain Lestrade and perhaps half a dozen men to travel around the areas where British forces were, looking for clues.

"What kind of clues?"

"I shall give the men a detailed briefing on where to go, how to behave and what to look for."

"But how shall..." At this point the Lieutenant Colonel was interrupted by the sound of someone outside approaching at a run and then a hard knock at the door. Bridge had only started the word 'come' when the door flew open and in ran a young officer, who gave the fastest salute to his commanding officer before starting to shake Holmes by the hand with great vigour.

"Mr Holmes! Godfather! I could not believe it when Corporal Harris told me you were here! This is marvellous!" Lestrade was in his mid-twenties and had inherited his father's dark eyes, and more of his bulldog

41

features than those which, I recall, I rather unkindly described as rat-like. He was of average height and athletic with considerable power in his long limbs.

"It is good to see you too, Terrance. How fares your father?"

"He's well. Did you know he's been called out of retirement to help train Special Constables? They're a volunteer police reserve."

"And your father is training them?" Holmes's voice faltered but quickly recovered. "That is splendid news. I must write to congratulate him when I get back to England."

"Please do, he will be so happy to hear from you." He turned to me. "Doctor Watson! I know you by reputation and Mr Holmes has often spoken of you, always in the highest terms. Proud to meet you at last, sir." He turned back to Holmes. "We have so much to talk about, and you must tell me what has brought you both to France. But I have a comrade-in-arms who I know will want to see you as well."

"Is he here?"

"Yes, I sent Corporal Harris on to find him. Here he is now." Lestrade had left the office door open so he was able to see who had arrived outside. "Come in, Sergeant, and see our distinguished visitor."

A squat Sergeant with a cheery face entered the room, made his salutes and then took his turn in pumping Holmes's hand. He was aged about forty and I thought I recognised something about him, but I could not place him at first.

"Mr Holmes! So very good to see you, sir!" He

turned to me and shook my hand with great energy. "And Doctor Watson! I don't know if you will remember me, sir. I might have changed since you last saw me and my little band."

I was stunned. "Is it...? You're not... Can it be... Wiggins?"

At this point the Lieutenant Colonel, who was a patient man but needed to maintain the dignity of his rank, suggested we remove ourselves to continue the reunion, and asked Holmes to return to his office at three o'clock to go over the details of his request. Captain Yates, who had been ignored again, muttered his usual something about making arrangements, so the remaining four of us went for a walk along the promenade. I certainly needed some sea air to clear my head. Inspector Lestrade had a grown-up son. Holmes was a godfather. Wiggins was a sergeant. I tried to recall when I had last seen him: leader of the little rabble of London street urchins known as the Baker Street Irregulars. I concluded that it was when he and his team had been searching the Thames for the *Aurora* and Jonathan Small, although I then recalled that his band had also helped Holmes solve the Adventure of the Crooked Man.

"Why, Wiggins, no offence, but I can hardly believe the man you have become! What have you been doing since the days of the Irregulars?"

"I have a timber business out at Romford, doctor."

"You have a... but however did you raise the capital to start, or buy, such an enterprise?"

"Why, Mr Holmes..."

But he was interrupted. "Really, Wiggins, I don't think the good doctor needs to know intricate details of your business arrangements. Who is running the shop while you are here?"

"My wife runs it sir, along with a couple of the lads who were unfit for service, and my eldest, who is starting to be a great help."

"And business is good?"

"Booming, thank you sir, mainly because of the war. All war profits to the Red Cross, as we agree..."

But again he was interrupted. "Once more, Wiggins, we must spare our companions from the tedium of business arrangements. Now then: Lestrade, Wiggins; we have a case."

He had their immediate attention, and all thoughts of other topics were forgotten. Holmes outlined the problem we had been given as we walked up and down. I was starting to feel weary and wondered if there was somewhere we could all sit down, but I was not sure if there would be any venue at which a Captain and a Sergeant could sit at the same table.

"Then you say Germany has a small army of spies spread across northern France? However would such an organization have been created?" asked his godson.

Holmes paused to relight his pipe. "First, I do not say for certain that such an enterprise exists. At the moment, it is simply a plausible hypothesis which I mean to test. Second, I do not believe the network would need to be so very large. A small number of agents suitably placed could be all that is needed. Finally, it is clear, I think, that Germany always intended to drive through Belgium at the start of her next war with France. The two countries have been at war, on and off, since the Middle Ages. The attack from the north was clearly well-planned. Far from it being unlikely that agents had been placed in France, I would consider it unusually remiss of the German Empire not to have such an arrangement in place. It might have been small to begin with, but they have had eighteen months to build it. Now it is up to us to dismantle it."

"Just tell us what to do."

Holmes walked in silence for a minute or two, the three of us following and waiting. When he was ready, he rapidly gave the words that properly began our investigation. "Wiggins, I need you to find some volunteers. About half a dozen men. They need to be inconspicuous, observant, intelligent and willing to work just as the Baker Street Irregulars used to."

"Yes sir, Mr Holmes. I've got a number of pals who would be perfect. Let me round up the best."

"Very good. One more thing: they will need to be good cyclists. Next, Terrance: I need to make a detailed survey. I need you to gather maps. Pre-war and recent, roads and railways, whatever you can find."

"There's a good collection in the town library; they are all locked away now but I think I can get my hands on them. Battalion headquarters will have the military maps; we might have to go to them, I don't think they will let us borrow any."

"That is reasonable. Finally, Watson: my request is that you find Captain Yates and determine whether he has made accommodation arrangements for us. If so, find the man who drove us here and have our luggage

45

unloaded. If not, see what you can find for us. I think we might be here for a day or two so the car and driver can return to Boulogne."

I felt that my assignment was rather less important than those of the others but it was no time to question Holmes's allocation of tasks. "Very well, Holmes. What should I do when I have done that?"

He looked me up and down. "My dear friend, it is important that we have good quarters. We need to rest after our travels in order to be at full strength, or as full strength as men of our age can be, to face the adventures which I think are to come. When you have found our accommodation, please send word to me at the Lieutenant Colonel's office. I will come to you as soon as I can. Now, I am meeting Bridge again at three. That gives me time to make some telephone calls."

We dispersed to pursue our different missions. I found Captain Yates reading newspapers in an officers' mess. He had booked rooms for us at a small hotel that had been taken over by the army and had had our luggage taken up. He told me this in a few terse sentences then returned to his newspaper. I found the hotel, went up to my room and decided to lie down for a moment.

The next thing I knew, there was knocking at my door. I made some kind of sound and Holmes entered the room.

"Watson! What a puzzle this is! The best exercise for the intellect I have had for some years: having to think as the enemy think!"

"What? You – what have you been doing?" I sat up and checked my watch. It was almost five.

"We have our team of Le Touquet Irregulars assembled. Come and meet them."

We returned to the battalion headquarters where an upstairs room had been cleared and put at Holmes's disposal. Wiggins and five other soldiers stood up as we entered. Lestrade was also there and, sitting in a corner, Yates. I was furious to see he had brought his newspaper and was reading it, ignoring what went on in the room. Wiggins introduced us to his pals and they returned to the folding chairs which had been arranged in a row facing a desk.

"Welcome, gentlemen, and thank you for volunteering for our adventure. Now, has Wiggins told you why you are needed?"

They all shook their heads and Wiggins said, "I thought it best to say nothing, sir, until you were able to give us the full story."

"Quite right, Wiggins, thank you. Secrecy is vital. I must ask you all to tell no one about this case, what I am going to ask you to do, or what happens as a result, until the war is over. Do I have your agreement?"

They all agreed in strong terms. Holmes proceeded to outline the problem as it had been presented to us. They showed rapt attention and asked intelligent questions. "Captain Lestrade and I have spent the afternoon looking over maps to identify locations where the German army might want to have eyes. We are going to work out routes for each of you. Tomorrow morning, we will all meet back here, where you will be given detailed instructions on where to go, what to look out for and how to behave. It is vital that no one suspects you are looking for enemy agents, especially the agents themselves."

One of the men raised his hand. "Excuse me, sir, but if I find an enemy agent, I'm going to want to let him know I've found him all too well. I'll want him to meet my fist before I hand him over to be shot!" The other soldiers expressed their support for this action.

"I appreciate your enthusiasm for our mission, Private," said Holmes, "But catching just one agent is not enough. We need to net the whole gang. If just one gets away, he can tell his masters that the game is up. The leader of the enterprise could start to build a new web of agents. No, I need you to identify likely agents without them suspecting, for a moment, that you might have identified them as such. You report your suspicions to me, and we work to throw the net wide and catch them all, the leader most especially."

Another soldier raised his hand. "Excuse me, sir, what do we say if we're asked what we're doing? We're not allowed to go roaming around France like we're on holiday." A few titters greeted this, although it was another wise question.

"We'll give you chits to show any officer who asks your business. As for everyone else, including other soldiers you speak to, we're going to prepare a story that you are surveying the land for locations of more army camps. Soldiers are pouring into France right now, and you say your role is to suggest where they can be sent. We will have all the details you need on this as part of the briefing tomorrow morning."

A question occurred to me. "Holmes, will you and I

be part of this team, going around looking for suspicious fellows?"

"I am afraid we cannot, Watson. We are obviously not soldiers. I need our Irregulars to go where soldiers go. Our white hair and wrinkles would be hard to hide. Besides, we need to be here, so the Irregulars know where to find us when they have something to report. Any more questions? No? Then I wish you good night and will see you all here at seven-thirty tomorrow."

Our gathering broke up. I noticed Yates had already left.

Over dinner, Holmes enthused about the prospect of action. "The Lieutenant Colonel has been excellent, Watson. Not only has he loaned us the men and bicycles for them all, we also have the loan of a truck for the day so we can drive around dropping them off at different start points. That will save them all time. We've had a look at military maps but I found the pre-war maps more useful, as the Germans won't have known in advance where the army camps would be, or even where the front line would be. Terrance seems to have an aptitude for maps and has helped me plan routes for the men. They are a bright lot of lads, I am quite looking forward to playing schoolmaster for them tomorrow. I think we will be done by lunchtime and then they will be on their way. With any luck, we will have suspects by evening."

"Is there anything I can do at this stage?"

"The time for action is coming, Watson, and that is when I will need your presence, as I have on countless previous occasions."

After dinner I walked over to the town casino, which was now a hospital run by the Duchess of Westminster. I walked around the wards speaking to each man. Some were in talkative mood. Others seemed to have lost the power of speech. Some just wept when I spoke to them and one man only made strange noises like a wounded animal. Their injuries were various, plus there were cases of trench foot and fever. The nurses were unfailingly jolly when with the men, and all exhausted when in their mess room.

I was introduced to The Duchess. She showed me, with justified pride, the linen room and the X-ray equipment. She talked of problems with funding and supplies, and asked me to stay as long as I could to talk with the patients. When I explained (as far as confidentiality would allow) what I was doing in France, she prepared a 'first aid' kit for me to carry. We organized a reading in the main ward that evening. I related a story I have not published yet, about suspected vampires in Sussex. However, as at Challis House, I found these later, unpublished adventures with Sherlock Holmes were not nearly as popular with my audience of sick and injured men as the adventures I published in the last century. So I told them the story of the Adventure of the Engineer's Thumb and they were good enough to show their appreciation.

The next morning, I went down to the hotel's dining room for breakfast. Holmes was not there, but I spotted Captain Yates sitting alone, so I went to join him. He was eating bread and cheese and, at first, showed no sign of having seen me. So I tried a friendly greeting.

"Good morning, Captain. How are you today?"

He took another mouthful, so there was a long pause before he spoke.

"What are you doing here?" I found it a strange question.

"I was planning to have breakfast."

"No, Doctor Watson, I meant what are you doing here in France?" I found this even stranger.

"I am here to help Mr Holmes discover how the German army appears to know the movements of the British army." I managed to keep my voice calm, which did require some effort.

"How do you help exactly? Apart from writing the accounts of his work, what is your actual contribution to it?"

"I believe I have contributed in many ways. For example, I have often carried my service revolver when Holmes was on the point of confronting a dangerous criminal."

Yates took another bite and ate it slowly before responding. "Do you think he will need such a service from you this time? With thousands of armed men in France fighting Germany, do you believe Holmes may require his elderly friend with a Victorian firearm?"

"I have done much more. I have acted as his agent, messenger and witness. I once had to become, overnight, an authority on Chinese pottery to distract a villain while Holmes procured essential evidence. That adventure was just one of many when my medical skills were needed, as the villain had acid thrown in his face by one of his victims."

The Captain finished his meal. "Holmes has another team of agents now. I don't think knowledge of pottery is going to help here. And you yourself have said that your medical knowledge is now dated. So why has Holmes brought you along?"

"We're old friends. Talking things over with me helps him think. I provide the companionship of someone he knows and can trust."

The Captain stood up, said, "You can't trust companionship," and left.

I felt somewhat disturbed by this conversation, so after breakfast I went where I knew I could do some good – back to the casino hospital. Everyone there was pleased to see me return. I wrote letters for injured men and helped one fellow take his first steps since his injury.

I saw Holmes briefly at lunchtime. He told me that he had concluded his briefing to the men, who were now being driven off to start their hunt. "I hope we may have a clue by this evening," he said. I invited him to come to the hospital with me, but he said he had some more telephone calls to make and wanted to give the puzzle further consideration. "Besides, Watson, I don't have your skills of putting patients at ease. You will do that much better without me."

In the afternoon I helped change some dressings and fed a couple of chaps their lunch, as they were not able to do it for themselves. I moved men in various wheelchairs and bathchairs out into the square to enjoy some spring sunshine. Mostly I just had light conversations with them. They liked to talk about home, families and loved ones. I met a Gunner from Chatham, who knew Yoxley Old Place (where Mr Willoughby Smith was murdered) and a Private from Norfolk who knew Riding Thorpe Manor, the stage for the Adventure of the Dancing Men.

At dinner that evening, Holmes was preoccupied and downcast. The Irregulars had all telephoned, at the agreed time period between five and six o'clock, but none had any suspicions to report. Every time someone entered the room, Holmes looked up hopefully, only to be disappointed.

It was late in the afternoon of the following day that a soldier came running into the ward and told me that Mr Holmes requested my presence at battalion headquarters. I hurried over to Holmes's upstairs room. With him were Captain Lestrade and a tall, dark, middle-aged man standing by the desk, dressed in the uniform of a French officer. He had an intelligent face and sparkling eyes though a tendency to frown. Captain Yates sat by the door.

"Ah, Watson, we have a thread in our hands at last. One of the Irregulars, Private Harry Robinson, has telephoned in his report. There's a bar called Café Picardy in Amiens which has aroused his suspicions. We have just been discussing it. I think this could be what we have been seeking. Attia, how far to Amiens?"

The French officer answered in excellent English. "About a hundred kilometres, Mr Holmes."

"Then there's no time to lose. The Lieutenant Colonel has placed a car at my disposal, but we need a driver." He looked at me.

"Of course."

"Excellent. With Watson driving, we five can get in the car and... Hello... Where is Captain Yates?"

We asked a sentry outside the building who said he had seen Yates depart on a motorcycle a few moments earlier.

"He rode a motorcycle with only one arm?" asked Holmes.

"It can be done. It is not so easy but many people learn," said the French officer.

We found the car, climbed in and set off.

"Drive on the right, sir," said Lestrade, who was seated beside me. That correction made, we were on our way.

Amiens

Once we were out of Le Touquet, Holmes made introductions.

"Doctor, may I present Capitaine Louis Attia of the Deuxieme Bureau. Attia, this is..."

"Doctor Watson needs no introduction to me. Doctor, it is an honour."

As darkness fell and I became accustomed to driving on French roads the connection between Holmes and Capitaine Attia was explained. They met in 1894, when Homes was assisting the French government in the tracking and arrest of Huret, the Boulevard Assassin. That success earned Holmes a letter of thanks from the President of the Republic and the award of the Legion of Honour. Attia was a young gendarme at the time and they worked together on the case. It was the young Attia who actually clapped handcuffs on Huret. When the Deuxieme Bureau was reformed in 1907, Attia, by then a Lieutenant, was invited to join it.

"Once I had formed my suspicions, I telephoned Attia and sought his agreement to assist us. The British forces have certain rights in France but cannot make searches of a French citizen's property and have no formal powers of arrest. Having Attia in our party gives us proper legal coverage as well as the happiness of adding a fine officer to our team."

As we approached Amiens there were traffic delays. A lorry had come off the road at an awkward corner and horses were being brought to drag it out of the way. I made a comment that no traffic was likely to get into Amiens for a while.

"A motorbike could get past," said Holmes, which filled me with foreboding. At last, the obstruction was removed and we continued into the town. Holmes and I had passed through Amiens in 1891, as we zig-zagged from London to Canterbury, Newhaven, Dieppe, Brussels, Strasbourg and Geneva in the journey that ended so memorably at Reichenbach, but I could remember nothing of the town whatsoever. It did not help that it was 'blacked out'. Luckily, Louis Attia knew the way to the railway station. When I saw it, I suddenly remembered our visit there in detail, right down to the soup we had in the station restaurant. Private Robinson was waiting for us inside and he gave us his full account.

"Le Café Picardy is not two hundred yards down the road, Mr Holmes, sir. It's run by an American couple called Rien. The story is that they're of French ancestry so came over to do their bit. Ran a restaurant in Boston, they say, so it made sense for them to run one here."

"Did you speak to them yourself, Robinson?"

"No sir, Mr Holmes, as you instructed, I kept my distance. Besides, it's an 'officers only' place. I learned about it by casually asking around and listening in, just has you told us."

"Well done. Was there anything particular that has aroused your suspicions?"

"Well, sir, I heard an Indian Lieutenant telling his Sergeant that Mrs Rien had been asking him what he thought of the British and whether he supported home rule for India. Said she'd asked just a bit too much, if you know what I mean, sir. Mrs Rien sets up a little coffee stall in the station most days, which could just be more good work or could be a chance to see the comings and goings. I think what really did it for me, sir, was this afternoon. I was on the street watching a battalion of Buffs leaving the station and there, at an upstairs window of the place, is Mr Rien watching through a pair of binoculars. So I called in and said I'd wait here."

"Rien... Could be nothing, eh?" said Holmes, and everyone smiled, though I did not understand why. We walked along the road towards Le Café Picardy. The windows were dark because of the blackout but, as we got close, we could see it was more than that – there were no chinks of light and no one coming or going. The place looked empty.

"Let me go alone, Mr Holmes," said Capitaine Attia. "We are an unusual group, but I alone can be an officer looking for a glass of wine and not knowing the café is closed. That will not make anyone suspect. Besides, I have my revolver."

It made sense, so Holmes agreed. We four remained at a distance while the French Officer strode confidently to the door of the café and knocked. He waited but there was no answer. He tried the door; it was open and he disappeared inside.

We waited for a few tense minutes while Attia searched the building. At last lights came on in the café, he reappeared at the door and called out to us, saying, "It is safe to come in – there is no one alive here."

I hoped this was just a French way of saying the building was empty. When we got to the door, we saw Attia beckoning us into a back room, a kitchen. In there was a male body, face down in an enormous pool of blood. I stepped through it and turned the body over.

"That's him," said Robinson. "That's Mr Rien."

"Slashed through the left carotid artery," I said, "Probably from behind. A sharp knife. It would have been quick. The killer would have been covered in blood."

"You are sure there is no one else in the building, Attia?" asked Holmes.

"They would have to be hiding well, I think. I will have another look. Captain Lestrade, Private Robinson, you will assist?"

They went upstairs while I continued to examine the body. "I would say he has been dead less than half an hour. The angle of the cut suggests the killer was shorter than the victim. I'm sure the attack was from behind, so the killer is most likely left-handed." I looked up but I was alone. "Holmes?"

"I am listening, Watson. But also looking, and I have

found something." He emerged from a cloakroom carrying a woman's mackintosh which was dripping in blood.

"Hello, hello, what's going on?" asked another voice and I heard Captain Yates speaking as he crossed the café towards the kitchen. "Got here at last, have you? You took your..." He appeared at the door and caught sight of us, the body and the blood. "Oh God. Oh my God, oh sweet Jesus." He staggered back into the main café and was sick.

I found a towel which I used to wipe my hands and shoes and went into the bar where Yates was pouring himself a brandy. It was clear to me that it was not his first drink of the evening.

"Sorry about that," he said as he pulled himself together. "Wasn't expecting it, that's all."

"You must have seen worse."

He finished his drink. "Far worse, yes."

Holmes joined us from the kitchen. Lestrade, Attia and Robinson came down the stairs. They confirmed there was no one else in the building, dead or alive.

Holmes considered Yates for a moment, then spoke to him in a calm manner. "Captain Yates. Please tell me exactly what happened when you first came here."

"When I heard Robinson's report, I thought I would come and take a dekko. I could get here quickly and decide whether the people running this café were suspicious. I could save everyone time if they were legit and keep an eye out if not." He said this in an over-confident way, as if he were not really justifying his actions in the light of what had happened in the adjacent room.

"Never mind why you came; I need to know what happened."

"Well, I came in and asked for a glass of Burgundy. I asked the barman if he was the manager of the place and he said he was. So I started asking him where he came from, his background, that kind of thing. He seemed happy to talk, though his wife gave me a sour look when she looked in from back there. Don't think I said anything to alarm him. Just being friendly." But I could imagine Captain Yates asking his 'friendly' questions with a sneer and a knowing look.

"Did he answer your questions in a friendly way?"

"Yes he did. Well, at first. He talked quite happily about Boston, the little place he had there, how he and his wife had heard about the Café Picardy and made arrangements to come over. All sounded a little rehearsed to me. Sounded as if it was a planned story. So I told him I knew Boston and asked him the name of his place there and exactly where it was. I don't know Boston at all, of course. I'd never left Blighty before it all kicked off."

"How did he react then?"

"Got a lot less friendly, that's for sure. Said he was too busy to chat, though the place was pretty quiet. Started asking me questions, who I was, what unit I was with, why I was in Amiens. I though it seemed fishy." There was a pause. "The Burgundy wasn't good either, too new, hadn't been decanted."

Another pause, then Holmes said, "Please tell me what you said before you left."

The Captain poured another shot of brandy. "Now, look here, Holmes, I've been through some pretty tough times over here. Lots of chaps have. We've seen things... I didn't know anything like that –" he nodded towards the kitchen "– was ever going to happen."

"I understand, Captain. I am not seeking to make any judgement. You do not answer to me, I respect that. I simply require knowledge of precisely what was said."

"Nothing really. I only mentioned that they shoot spies, just to see his reaction." Again, I could imagine Yates saying this with a sneer and a smirk. "Well, he went white in the face. Disappeared into the back there. Heard them talking. Sounded like a blazing row done in a whisper. Finally, I heard him shout, 'No, enough. I've had enough. I'm not going to carry on with this.' A moment later, the wife appeared at the bar and said her husband was unwell and they had to close the café so she could take care of him. I drank up and left. Went over to the Carlton and phoned your man in Le Touquet to say they were almost certainly Huns or working for Huns. Had another drink then decided to see what was happening here. Found you."

Holmes kept his face impassive, though I wanted to knock the man down, and might have done if I had been a bit younger and he was able-bodied.

"Very well. Captain Yates and Private Robinson, you have both seen Mrs Rien. I want you to go to the railway station and ask if she has been seen there." Robinson nodded and left straight away but Yates asked, "Who should I ask? What should I ask them?"

"Ask at the ticket office. Ask if an American woman – you can describe her – has bought a ticket."

"I don't speak the lingo. A few phrases, yes, but not enough to have a conversation."

"Find someone who can translate for you."

"What if I can't find anyone to translate?"

"I can go with the Captain," said Attia.

"No, Attia, you are needed here. Captain Yates, please do what you can. See if you can trace Mrs Rien. If you cannot, please come back here." Yates looked around at us, got up slightly unsteadily and left.

"Attia, I think you should contact your local colleagues and inform them of what has happened here. Tell them it was a murder and that we have some knowledge of the suspect."

Instead of leaving the building, Attia started back up the stairs. He saw my puzzled look and said, "Do not worry, my friend, I am going to the telephone. There is one in the office room above."

"Is it normal for a place like this, in a town like Amiens, to have a telephone?"

He paused on the stairs. "No, perhaps not. We see the telephone as a toy for the rich. I believe there are fewer than half a million telephone sets in all of France, not counting the military ones. But a telephone is not as strange as the things on the roof."

Holmes had been going through a pile of papers he found behind the bar but at this point he looked up. "Why, what is on the roof?"

"I believe it is equipment for monitor of the weather. But I did not look at it close. It did not seem so material."

"Show me." The four of us climbed to the upper floor where there was a ladder to a skylight that led up to an area of flat roof. Attia had a torch which he found in the office but the battery was dying. There was just enough light to see a maximum-minimum thermometer, a rain gauge, an anemometer and a few other meteorological instruments. "These instruments have not been read in a while. The thermometer shows a high that has not been reached since Sunday and a low that was probably not felt here for several days. The rain gauge has not been emptied in over a week. If the Riens were amateur meteorologists, they have been neglecting their hobby."

We went back to the office, a small room with a window looking over the street that led to the station, although it was currently covered with a backout curtain. On the desk were heaps of papers, a pair of binoculars and the telephone set. Beside the desk stood an iron safe and a wastepaper basket. Holmes rapidly looked through all the papers on the desk, then those in the wastepaper basket. "Ah! A common mistake. Lock your secrets in a safe but throw your notes about them in the waste basket. Hmm... troop numbers as wind speeds perhaps; temperature and pressure readings seem to represent regiments; wind direction must simply be direction of travel. Clever – a simple enough system to convert military movements into climactic ones. Attia: please call the exchange and ask them to tell you everything they can about calls from this telephone, especially regular calls or anything unusual."

Attia picked up the telephone set, wound the handle and began. We heard people downstairs and a voice called, "Mr Holmes? Doctor Watson?" We left Attia to make his enquiries and returned to the bar. Robinson and Wiggins were there.

"We bumped into each other at the station," said Wiggins. "I called in my evening report from Doullens and they told me you were coming here so I cycled over. I didn't know where to find you, so I went to the station and there was Harry."

"I'm glad to see you Wiggins. Robinson, did you discover anything?"

"Yes sir. An American woman who could have been Mrs Rien bought a ticket for Paris shortly after the café closed. The ticket clerk was sure it was her; he has seen her at her coffee stall. He said she seemed scared and in a hurry."

"Then we must be on the next train."

"There is only one more train to Paris tonight, sir. Leaves in twenty-seven minutes, I checked." It was after nine o'clock. I had not realized it was so late but, now that I was reminded of the time, I felt tired and hungry. However, the idea of seeking food in the café kitchen was repugnant.

Attia hurried down the stairs to join us. "I have spoken to the supervisor and an operator at the telephone exchange. A call came from here to a number in Paris, every evening at about this time. Indeed, when I made the call, the operator expected to be speaking to Mrs Rien, who would want to be connected to her usual number. They are not meant to listen to telephone conversations, but the operator said it was all weather information – wind, temperatures, pressures – and that the French of Mrs Rien was very bad."

"Could they give you the address of the telephone she called in Paris?"

"No, just the number. They said Paris would know the address. They said that if an officer in uniform goes to the Paris exchange in Rue la Fayette, they are sure to be helpful."

"Then there is no time to lose," said Holmes. "Attia, call your local colleagues, if you have not done so already, so they can take over here. Then call Paris and have some of your colleagues discover the address of the telephone number, then meet us off the last train from Amiens. Wiggins and Robinson, I think you should return to Le Touquet and speak to your colleagues when they next telephone in. Tell them to look particularly for any establishment that has weather recording equipment. Wiggins, you can drive?" He nodded. "Then you can return the car." We all shook hands, made our farewells and the two soldiers left.

Captain Yates appeared at the door of the café. "I've asked around, Mr Holmes, but I can't find anyone who has seen Mrs Rien. She seems to have vanished."

Paris

We bought food at the station and I ate then slept as we rattled down the track to the French capital. I woke up at Chantilly, the final stop before our destination. Holmes, Capitaine Attia, Captain Yates, Captain Lestrade and I travelled together in one compartment. We steamed into the Gare du Nord just before midnight. Waiting for us on the platform were two men in the uniform I now recognised as that of the Deuxieme Bureau.

"I am sorry we cannot provide a greater force, Mr

Holmes," said Attia. "We are rather short of men at the moment." His eyes moved to a nearby platform, where a train was unloading. Dozens of men wearing the blue of the French army plus, in many cases, the white of bandages, were being guided out of the station. Some were told to wait, and they just collapsed, exhausted, on to the ground. More injured men, not able to walk, were being loaded onto trolleys and wheeled away.

We adjourned to a station bar. The barman was about to close but Attia handed him some money, so he shrugged and retreated to polish glasses behind his bar. The two Parisians were introduced as Lieutenants Dubois and Granvillain. They spoke no English but Attia acted as interpreter. Holmes asked if they had tracked the address for the telephone number that the Riens called each evening. The three Frenchmen discussed for a time, then Attia gave the answer.

"They think we have this wrong. The telephone number belongs to a very fine man called Monsieur Anton Marron. He is a famous patriot, because his family were refugees from Alsace after it was taken by Prussia in 1870. They were forced to leave their home when he was a boy and came to Paris. He has built an engineering business here and done very well. He is – *philanthrope*, you have this word in English? Gives money to good things. They think it cannot be he who is part of any conspiracy to assist Germany. They say he helps France. That is also why just two men have been sent: Colonel Dupont knows your name and respects it greatly but believes this may be a false lead."

"How does he help France?" asked Holmes. The French officers spoke together again and Attia reacted strongly to something one of them said. He turned to us with a smile.

"Very interesting. They say Marron provides weather forecasts. Dubois here remembers reading about him in a newspaper. He was an amateur weather forecaster before and now he uses his skill to provide weather information to *le Ministère de la Guerre* – the Ministry of the War. It seems his weather predictions are close to what happens on most days."

"Where does he live?" asked Holmes and the officers conversed in French again.

"He has a grand house in the 16th arrondissement. Dubois and Granvillain drove past it before coming here. He has a tall pole against the side of the house with his weather instruments on top, high above the houses so there is no interference with his measurements of the wind."

"Very good. Attia, please explain to your brother officers that we need to arrest Monsieur Marron and anyone else who might be in the house. They need to be brought to your headquarters for questioning and cannot be allowed to contact anyone outside the military and police forces as we make the arrest."

Attia explained this to his colleagues, then Holmes continued. "Warn them that it could be dangerous. If Marron is an enemy, he may attempt to fight rather than be taken."

I may not speak French, but it was clear that the French officers were not going to shirk in the face of danger. Attia spoke for them: "They say they are entirely behind you, Mr Holmes. They know you hold the *Légion d'Honneur* and will be proud to assist you in arresting any enemy of France."

We did a quick review of our weapons. The three French and two British officers all carried side arms. We were asked if we wanted weapons. I had not fired a gun in many years and would be a danger to myself and my colleagues. Holmes also refused, saying, "I am confident that we have enough firepower from you younger men."

Dubois and Granvillain had brought a truck with them. The three Frenchmen sat in the cab at the front and we four British in the back. The atmosphere was silent and tense. I heard a clock strike midnight. There was little traffic on the roads. We rattled along the streets as most of them are paved with stones and the truck had poor suspension. Because of this, I couldn't be sure if Yates was shaking from the motion or for some other reason. Terrance checked his revolver twice.

The truck had canvas sides, but I could see out of the back. Paris was not 'blacked out' but the streetlamps were off as a small-hours economy. Nevertheless, there was enough light from the moon, stars and the occasional lit window to see the city, once my eyes had adjusted. I saw the Arc de Triomphe recede behind us and, shortly afterwards, the Eiffel Tower across the Seine. Particularly after the past few days, the city looked remarkably tranquil. It was hard to believe that war raged only fifty miles away and that we were on our way to a possible confrontation with an agent of the aggressor.

Finally the engine was cut, the truck coasted to a halt and our French comrades joined us in the back. Attia pointed back down the road. About eighty yards away a road branched off from the road we were on, at an acute angle, making a 'V' shape pointed at us.

Straddling the apex of this V was a fine mansion in red brick with white stone at the corners and around the tall windows. It had three storeys, the top one in the form of a mansard roof. It looked archetypically Parisian except for the tall pole that ran up the side of the building and extended twenty feet above the roof. I could just make out instruments of some kind on the top. In front of the house, filling the tip of the V between the two streets and the building, was a triangular garden surrounded by high railings between stout brick pillars. To get to the house, one had to enter a gate in this fence and then approach the front door. It suddenly looked very secure to me, like a miniature fortress disguised as a home. All of the windows were dark.

"With your permission, Mr Holmes, we have discussed a plan."

"We are in your land, Attia. It is right for you to lead."

"Thank you. Dubois and Granvillain will go by the left-hand side of the house, to cover that side and see if there is access to the rear. Captain Yates, Captain Lestrade: can I ask you to do the same for the right-hand side?"

Terrance nodded but Yates intervened: "But it's the middle of the night! Would it not be better to wait until morning, we could get more men, surround the house properly?"

Attia shook his head and continued. "No, Captain, I think we must act now. The alarm raised at Amiens will have reached here by now. I think it possible that the birds have already flown the nest and we will find the house empty. But if not, we must act before they do escape. I will approach the front and say I have urgent need to consult with Marron. I will say we have heard there is a storm coming and we have the big action planned for early tomorrow, so we need his advice on the weather. If he is a true Frenchman, he will admit me to the house and I can speak to him. I can ask him to come with us. If he does not let me in, I will tell him I know him to be a German agent, that the house is surrounded and he must surrender peacefully or be taken by force. Are we agreed on this?"

"What about Holmes and me?" I asked. Perhaps I did ask rather forcefully, as the idea of staying away when action was needed did not appeal.

"We must wait here, John," said Holmes. I was struck by his use of my name. I realized afterwards that he used it to give his statement impact. "This action is for the young men. We will be called when we can contribute."

So the young men set off. Two French went off to the left of the house and two British to the right. The garden gate was also on the right and the tall figure of Louis Attia took his position there. I saw Terrance move down the side of the house to the far corner, where he could cover the side and the rear of the building, while Captain Yates stayed by the corner nearest to where Holmes and I sat in the truck.

It appeared that there was some kind of speaking tube, or one of those local telephone systems called an intercom, at the garden gate. We watched Attia having a conversation into it, though we could hear no words. Time seemed to stop.

Suddenly I heard Attia shout, "Grenade!" There was a flash and a bang, which I felt more than heard. I heard screaming and gunshots. My eyes had been confused by the flash and, when they recovered, I could see Attia crouched by a pillar in the garden fence exchanging shots with someone in the house while Captain Yates ran towards us, screaming, his right arm gripping his left, to stop it flapping. He hurled himself into the truck, between the two of us, and crouched in a ball against the back of the truck's cab.

"I can't stand it, I can't stand it – Peter, Peter, oh my God, no, no, no..." He ranted like this while Holmes and I managed to get him sitting on the bench. Occasional gunshots still rang out behind us.

"Who is Peter?" I asked.

"My friend, my dear friend. We knew each other all our lives, always best friends, through school, into the army. Half his head blown away, just one eye left to watch me, staring, accusing." He dissolved into sobs. "And the rest of them with him, the lads, the pals, in pieces. Poor lads, poor lads. I can't do it anymore, I'm a coward, I'm a shit, I'm sorry, I'm so sorry Peter."

The gunfire seemed to have stopped. "Captain Yates – Herbert," I said, "You don't have to do it anymore. You've done your bit, you were wounded fighting, you're a hero."

"No, no, I'm a coward. I stood up. When I saw them all, the pieces, Peter's eye watching me, I stood up above the parapet. I wanted to be shot."

"You could have been killed."

"I know, I didn't care. I wanted to be killed. I wanted

an end to it all. Bloody Germans, couldn't do it for me though, just got my shoulder, turned me into a cripple. More of a cripple than I was already. I can't go on. I'm sorry I've been such a cad to you both. I was terrified of having to come back to France. I want to go home. I want to die. I can't bear it anymore. Peter promised he would stand by me, be my companion through it all. But he's dead, they're all dead, and one eye looking at me."

There were more bursts of gunfire and Yates squealed. "I'm so sorry, so sorry. You were right to insist on Doctor Watson coming, Mr Holmes, I was wrong to try and order you about. You're both so much better than I am. Everyone's better than me, I'm a coward, I let Peter die."

"Doctor Watson! Come quickly, there's a casualty." It was Terrance Lestrade, he was running from the house towards us. "It's safe, it's over, you should come too, Mr Holmes. Is Yates all right?"

"He's not hurt," I said, though I knew that only meant he had no new injury. I still had the first aid kit given to me by the Duchess at Le Touquet. Holmes and I followed Terrance to the house while he explained what had happened.

"They were preparing to leave but were ready for an attack. They threw a grenade at Attia, luckily it hit the railings and fell below the low wall at the base. He's a bit stunned but unhurt. Well, with that we knew for sure that you were right and we had them. I went round the back and found their car, which was loaded ready for them to make their getaway. We got here just in time. They were going to shoot it out but Granvillain climbed a drainpipe and kicked entry to an upper window – you see all the lower ones are barred. Once they knew their defences were breached, they ran out at the back and jumped into the car. But I'd disabled it so it wouldn't start. They were shooting at Dubois and me but we got them."

We turned into the driveway at the back of the house and saw our three French comrades and a car that had bullet holes in its windscreen. An imposing man of about fifty with a magnificent walrus moustache sat upright in the driver's seat, quite obviously dead. A woman was lying on the ground bleeding profusely. The French officers were trying to stem the bleeding but they stood back when I arrived. I pressed wadding over the wounds in her chest but it was immediately clear that the exsanguination was catastrophic and she had just minutes left in this world.

"Mrs Rien, I presume?" said Holmes.

"The name's Ryan. And it's 'Miss'," she groaned in an American accent. "Who the hell are you?"

"My name is Sherlock Holmes. So the man you murdered in Amiens was not your husband?"

"Sherlock Holmes, the great detective. Well, I suppose I should be honoured, though I see no honour in meeting any English. No, Holmes, he was not my husband. Marron paired me off with him, thought it would look more natural if we were a couple. Anthony Mantels he was called. Tony. Supposedly of German heritage but you'd never know it, he was an oaf and a coward. He was getting more and more scared of what we were doing. He kept saying America will eventually join the French and British. He wanted to surrender, to go over to your side." She said this with all the contempt she could muster in her weakened state. "I told him I would kill him if he did. Tonight something happened. Someone came to the bar and as good as told him we were rumbled. He said he was going to hand himself in. So I killed him. It wasn't murder, it was the execution of a traitor, you must see that." She seemed to be pleading for our understanding of her appalling action, which I hope meant she felt some remorse. "I'd warned Marron that Tony was a weak link. I'd told him what might happen. For all I knew, Tony had already shopped us. So I followed the plan: get here and fly. We knew the game would be up sooner or later." She sighed, and the sigh turned into a groan. "If we had left ten minutes earlier, we would have been in Lausanne by sunrise. But we had to call the others, to warn them."

Holmes exchanged a look with Attia, who ran inside the house.

"How was Marron persuaded to betray his country?" asked Holmes.

"He didn't, he served his country."

"He is from Alsace."

"And Alsace is part of Germany! France invaded and took it by force but many families remember their prosperity under German rulers. Yes, Anton's family moved here in the 1870s and have done very well. But Anton was always German. For a long time, he simply kept quiet, it didn't matter and it was easiest to stay silent about his loyalties. But he stayed in touch with his fatherland and, when the need arose, he was ready."

"And Belgium?" asked Terrance. "Is that part of Germany too?"

She stared at him for a few seconds. "You British. You're all such hypocrites. You pride yourselves on your empire. All those countries you paint pink on your maps to show they are yours. Countries you have taken, stolen, invaded, occupied. Countries you drain and bleed. But if Germany should take Belgium, oh no, that is a crime, and you send your young men to die in the mud and at sea for a pointless little country that was invented less than a hundred years ago to please the great powers and give territory to a minor aristocrat."

Talking had sapped her remaining strength, but she looked at me and rallied. "You – you're the man Watson? You write the stories. I don't believe half of them. But write my story – write what we did, how we fought you. Will you? Will you write my story?"

I did not answer her, and after a minute more no answer would have been heard anyway.

Dover

The sun shone brightly on the white cliffs as we approached, two old men at the prow of a Royal Navy motor launch. We had spent a few days in Paris, resting after our adventures and helping the authorities complete their investigations. Louis Attia had contacted the Paris telephone exchange as Miss Ryan lay dying and got the numbers that had just been called from the house of Anton Marron. He might have told us more but Holmes insisted he did not, knowing that the whole episode was to be kept secret.

A quantity of electrical equipment had been recovered from the house in the 16th arrondissement. It had been sealed in a large crate that travelled with us to Calais and was now stowed in the little boat that was taking us to England. It was destined for the Marconi company in Chelmsford, where they discovered it was a transmitter for very low frequency radio waves. The tall mast at Marron's house was not just a support for weather instruments, it was for transmitting radio at a frequency far below any previously in use, and so not watched for by the allied side.

Terrance had returned to his regiment at Le Touquet and the men of the Deuxieme Bureau had returned to their duties. Captain Yates was below, the seasickness having taken him again. In our walks in the Tuileries Garden and along the Seine, I learned more about Herbert and his friend Peter, who had died with one of his platoons when a German artillery shell exploded in their dugout. Herbert could have taken discharge from the army when he was crippled, but he stayed as he felt so ashamed of his behaviour. This despite having served over twenty spells in the front line. Finally, he had agreed that he should seek his discharge, as no longer physically fit for war service, when we got home.

Above the cliffs, King Henry's keep stood, firm and redoubtable, at the heart of Dover Castle, the key to England. Holmes had been silent, puffing occasionally on a modern short-stemmed pipe.

A question occurred to me. "How did Marron manage to provide good forecasts of the weather to the French authorities?"

Holmes took a couple of puffs. "Maybe he did know a little meteorology. But if you predict the weather tomorrow will be the same as it is today, more than half of your predictions will be correct."

We watched a seaplane take off from inside the

harbour and turn over St Margaret's Bay as it began its patrol.

"We did some good, didn't we, John?"

I was astounded at the question. "Good? My dear friend, we have done great work this week. Who knows how long Marron's network of spies might have continued their infamous work if you had not ended it? I have seen the messages of thanks you have been sent: General Haig, General Joffre, Marshal Pétain, they all wrote to congratulate you."

"And to urge me to keep the story secret. They don't want the world to know how the Germans had them in their sights for so long. This will be another of our adventures that you will have to consign to your archives until this war is long over. No, I meant before these times. We did some good in the last century, in the days of the old Queen?"

I was even more astounded. I had noticed over the past week that Holmes had changed; he had become more mellow and more relaxed, even using my first name. We change with age. Could it be that he was now showing some doubt about his towering achievements?

"You really need to ask – Sherlock?" I used his name for the first time in a private conversation with him. "You have ended the evil careers of terrible men. Professor Moriarty and his gang – Colonel Moran and the rest – would top the list but there have been dozens. Murderers, thieves and blackmailers who would have continued their lives of crime if you had not stopped them. And then there are all those who were not career criminals but had caused harm, or were about to, until you stopped them. You have returned countless items of stolen property, saved innumerable lives and brought freedom to people who were wrongly accused of the crimes of others."

"Yes. Yet now we see whole countries being stolen and killings on a scale the world has never seen before. It makes our efforts look small."

I could see how his work, however magnificent, was on a miniature scale against the horror of the Great War. I composed my reply before delivering it: "No act that does good, however small, is made pointless by any act of evil, however great."

He looked at me and smiled. "As ever, my old friend, you provide me with your honest good sense. I just want this war to end."

"Your work this week will have helped it come to an end. If all goes as hoped, it will be over before the leaves turn this autumn."

"Let us hope so," he said.

THE ADVENTURE OF THE ABSENT SPY

A reflection and a summons

Late April 1916 found me back at Challis House, the auxiliary hospital where I work as a volunteer, reflecting on my recent adventure with Sherlock Holmes. We had returned from France less than a week earlier and already the events seemed as if a dream.

But evidence of their reality was present in just how exhausted the adventure had left me. We all learn about old age for ourselves as it creeps over us. Holmes and I had a few days in Paris, after the adventure ended, before travelling back to England, but that had not been enough time for recovery. Once, we might have completed an exhausting adventure one night and be ready for the next early the following morning. Now I found that helping with writing a few letters and changing some dressings left me in need of an hour's recovery in a deckchair on the scrubby lawn that lay in front of Challis House. I prefer not to think of myself as an old man but the aches and stiffness that had still not faded told a different story.

Part of the reason for finding it hard to accept that these events had really occurred is that I was unable to discuss them with anyone. When patients and colleagues at Challis House asked where I had been during my absence, I told them a vague story of having to visit a sick relation in the country. We had been sworn to secrecy until such time as the War Department agreed to their release, which I was assured would be at least a hundred years from now. Over the past few days, I had completed my written account of events and had delivered it to the security of the bank vault off The Strand, in central London, to join so many other records of adventures that could not yet, perhaps not ever, be published. I had called the tale 'The Detective at War,' thinking that it would be the only example of my great friend using his extraordinary gifts in the service of his country at this time of dire need. I did not know, as I sealed the story under this title into a metal box, that a further adventure was about to start.

I lay back in my deck chair and let thoughts revolve in my head until I suddenly found it was getting dark and chilly.

The next day was Good Friday and the Hospital Supervisor had arranged a delivery of hot cross buns for the men of Challis House. These helped create a jolly mood, further brightened when I received a visit from a former patient: Private Bruce had received machine gun wounds to his legs early in 1915. He was one of the first men I encountered in my role as hospital volunteer, and we struck up a rapport. He was recovered from his wounds and considering what to do next.

The increasing problems of food supply had led me to build a hen house in the grounds. I had managed to scrounge materials and caring for the birds gave the more mobile men something useful to do. The flock had a case of the gapes and Bruce had recommended dosing them with drops of whisky. He had gone into the main house to return the bottle when he called out to me: "Doctor Watson, telephone call for you."

It was Holmes. Because we had been sworn to secrecy about our adventure, and an operator could be listening in to a call at any number of stages in the connection, he had to speak in a coded style. He did not even give his name (not that he had to): "Doctor! It's your old companion here. You remember the patient we had to treat together earlier this month? One of his relations has been in touch with me. It seems they have urgent need to discuss the case with us."

"My word Ho... My word, my old friend. Do you think they might have another case for us to investigate? I mean, another case to treat?"

"I could not say, although I might hope. It might be they simply want to learn more about the symptoms or causes of the illness we were able to cure. We shall discover on Monday, when we have been requested to attend an office in Kingsway at ten o'clock. It might be best to pack for a few days away as the case might require a period of treatment."

The aches and stiffnesses were gone immediately. It seemed certain that the army needed our help again and another adventure, another chance to serve our country, was at hand.

A rebuke

I had to contain my excitement over the Easter weekend. When I told the Hospital Supervisor I needed to go to London on Monday, and might have to be away for a few days, he said he hoped I would be back soon, as he appreciated the work of all his volunteers, but he did not ask the reason for my absence. He is a busy man.

I also kept myself busy over Saturday and Sunday, helping with the men, treating the chickens and doing my usual evening readings of published adventures with Sherlock Holmes. After a reading of the Adventure of Black Peter a Sergeant asked me when I had last seen Holmes. I replied that we had been on a walk together a couple of weeks previously. After reciting the story of Silver Blaze, a Gunner asked whether I was likely to see Holmes again soon. I remained enigmatic, saying I hoped to be able to meet him in town before long. I could give no 'bark in the night' that we were between adventures of potentially national importance.

On Easter Monday I was up early and had time to walk from Euston Station to Kingsway, where I met my old friend at a Lyons tea shop. Like me, he looked excited at the prospect of a new adventure. "Well, well, Watson, it seems there is life in the old dogs yet! Who would have thought, when we took rooms together thirty-six years ago, that we would still be a partnership in our dotage, and still of some small service to our country?"

We walked together to a forbidding building of white

stone, wrought iron balcony fronts, net curtains and imposing entrance. It was a bright morning, warm for the season, but the room we were ushered into was dark and chilly. We passed the time talking of past cases and clients. Holmes was still in touch with some of them and gave me their news. I was astonished to learn that Mr and Mrs McCarthy (Mr James McCarthy and Miss Alice Turner when we met them in connection with the Boscombe Valley mystery) were grandparents. Captain Jack Crocker, formerly of the Adelaide-Southampton line, was now a Captain in the Royal Australian Navy and married to Mary, nee Fraser, formerly of the Abbey Grange in Kent and now of South Australia.

It is just as well that always have so much to talk about, as I suddenly realized we had been waiting for two hours and had not even been offered refreshment. I returned to the anteroom and the young woman who had greeted us when we arrived. She apologised for the delay, explaining, "Major Wilkes is meant to be seeing you, gentlemen, but he seems to have been held up. I'll call Lieutenant Hamer-Jenks and see if he is available."

Fifteen minutes later we were ushered upstairs to a dark-panelled office with dark furniture, a dark floor but a very pale young man who introduced himself as Hamer-Jenks. He was in civilian clothes but wore them with a military fastidiousness, moustache and bearing. He was of medium height but his slender build somehow made him look taller. The effect, in such a dark room, was of a ghost haunting his former territory.

He gestured us to sit in the high-backed chairs which faced his bare desk. "The first thing that Major Wilkes would want me to impress on both of you is that you must never, under any circumstances, discuss with anyone your visit here or any contact you have with this organization."

Holmes responded, "That is a safe request, given that we do not know the name of this organization. The sign at your door refers to Falcon Limited, a firm of 'shippers and exporters'. But I assume that is not your name or your business."

The Lieutenant gave a shrewd and unpleasant look. The smell of furniture polish in the room was overpowering and was starting to give me a headache. "No, that is not who we are, Mr Holmes. We go by different names. I think, though, that Major Wilkes would be prepared to tell you our business. It is intelligence, Mr Holmes. Secret intelligence. That is our profession and as professionals, we are extremely concerned when amateurs invade our operational domain and, to be blunt, risk queering our pitch."

I gave an audible sigh. So that was what this meeting was about. The classic accusation of 'amateurs' muddying the waters for 'professionals'. How many times had I heard this complaint? Even Inspectors Gregson and Lestrade, who came to rely so often on Holmes's skill, sometimes showed disdain when he took enormous pains to examine minutely some crime scene that they had assessed with no more than a cursory glance. In past days I might have felt my blood rise and jumped to defend the reputation of my illustrious friend from such an unworthy slur. As it was, I simply felt weary at hearing this silly comment, and disappointment that our summons to London did not herald a new adventure, simply an old reproach.

Holmes sat in silence, so Hamer-Jenks continued.

"You know what I'm talking about? Major Wilkes explained it all to me, and I can tell you he was none too impressed. Starting your adventure in Folkestone, of all places, right under the nose of... well, never mind who. Then galivanting off to France, using your reputation to get agreements for your actions from various army personnel, co-opting men at a rest camp to roam around France as your agents and, to cap it all, getting involved in a shoot-out on the streets of Paris, as if it were the Wild West!"

Holmes remained silent for a moment, then said, "I do know of the events to which you refer. We have been requested to speak to no one about them, so you will understand if we stick to that agreement."

Hamer-Jenks gave a snort and went on, "Well, that's something I suppose. I half expected to read the full story in The Strand Magazine. Major Wilkes pointed out that you can hardly be trusted to maintain military standards of secrecy when details of criminal cases, personal emergencies and family secrets are recorded and published for all the world to read by the doctor here."

At this point I was about to lose my cool and started up with a "Now, look here..." But Holmes waved me down and gave a private smile. I don't think anyone else could have stopped me from making quite a scene for this impertinent young officer, certainly not with barely a word and a subtle gesture. But this was Holmes. He kept his calm magnificently as he spoke. "Lieutenant Hamer-Jenks, I can assure you that no report of any of my adventures has been made known, either by Doctor Watson or myself, to anyone not involved until either all criminal trials were completed and events were already in the public domain, or until we had express permission from the families and individual citizens involved, other than in cases when all parties had expired and had no descendants from whom we could seek consent. Have you ever heard of an instance when publication of our work caused embarrassment or inconvenience to a client? My career, such as it was, would have been over very quickly if clients could not rely on our absolute discretion for as long as it was wanted or needed. I will only go so far to break our steadfast rules as to inform you that Doctor Watson has compiled a great number of records of cases which cannot yet be revealed, and perhaps never will be. This archive resides in the basement of one of this city's most reputable banks, with clear instructions about the circumstances which must be fully met, in each case, before it can be revealed. In the cases of any recent trip abroad we may have made, and any further commission on behalf of His Majesty's forces during the current war, such circumstances will include the unconditional approval of the War Office."

The Lieutenant had the good grace to appear slightly abashed as he muttered, "Well, that's good, because I know the Major was concerned…"

I had to say my piece, although I endeavoured to match the calm and friendly manner Holmes had used, as if he were congratulating a favourite nephew on winning a school race. "I would like to add that the 'various army personnel' who co-operated with our investigation included a Colonel, a General and a Lieutenant Colonel. I hope you do not imagine such officers can be easily tricked into working with Mr Holmes, or so awestruck by two old gentlemen of modest reputation as to exercise poor judgement. Indeed, it was at the request of the Colonel that we undertook the investigation and the trip overseas. I understand the problem was offered to official channels at first, but they decided the problem was beneath them. Finally, Mr Holmes has made his living as a detective so that would disqualify him from the status of amateur. Even if it did not, you are part of a citizen army. I don't know if you yourself are a regular soldier or a wartime volunteer, but most of your colleagues in arms are volunteers or conscripts – in other words, amateurs. The majority of the men who stand between us and the German army are amateurs and I thank God for them."

I fear I had over-done it. The pale Lieutenant moved to defend himself. "I have no doubt of the ability of the officers and men fighting in France! But none of the people you encountered are specialists in intelligence. They should have properly explained the problem to us, then we would have addressed it. They have no understanding of the delicately balanced networks and activities we need to co-ordinate, and nor, with the greatest respect, do you. I know you both did fine work in the last century, recovering stolen jewels or finding missing people. How does that qualify you to meddle in the finely tuned operations of the secret operations behind a twentieth century mechanised war? You are detectives who investigate crimes, not secret agents who disrupt an enemy power. When Major Wilkes gets here, he will, he will…" The steam seemed to have run out.

Holmes gently interrupted, "What exactly has happened to Major Wilkes? I do look forward to meeting him."

The Lieutenant appeared to deflate a little. "He did not arrive for work. Most unusual, he is normally here early. I sent someone over to his flat in case he has fallen ill." He walked over to the door, wrenched it open and called, "Is McGillian back yet?"

A voice in the anteroom answered, "Yes sir, he's back but he wasn't sure if you were to be disturbed."

"Send him in."

The young man who entered would have been a prime candidate for The Red-Headed League, if that society was real. His hair was cut short because it was clear that it would form into bright curls if it were allowed to grow to any length at all. His naturally ruddy complexion was highlighted by his obvious anxiety at being summoned to report to the officer. His apprehension was shown to be legitimate by the way the Hamer-Jenks spoke to him.

"Well man? Where's the Major? Is he ill?"

"No sir. I mean, I don't know sir." The messenger swallowed nervously.

"You don't know? Did you find him or not?"

"No sir. He's not at his flat sir."

"Are you sure? Did you wait long enough for him to get to the door? It might have taken him a while if he's sick."

"I searched the flat, sir. He's not there."

"How did you get in? You didn't have a key?"

"No, sir. The door was not closed properly. I knocked

and went in and looked around sir, there was nobody at home sir." There was a pause while we all stared at the scared young redhead, then he continued, "I spoke to a neighbour sir. He came running in when he heard me in the flat. He said he was going to call the police, sir, but he'd been unsure whether that would be the right thing to do. He was going to call the police this afternoon if the Major had not returned."

"The police? Why on Earth did he think of calling the police?"

"It's just that, sir... Well, he said, sir... He thinks the Major might have been abducted, sir."

There was silence as the impact of that last sentence seemed to reverberate between the dark walls. Then Holmes spoke. "So, Lieutenant Hamer-Jenks. Do you think you might have need of a detective who finds missing people?"

The investigation begins
Holmes was never actually commissioned to take the case of the absent spy. He simply took charge of the situation. The Lieutenant seemed taken aback by the news that his superior might have been kidnapped and was worried about whether he should report the news to the head of his organization (whom he referred to as 'the Captain') immediately or wait until there was more information. Holmes let him worry while he established that McGillian had locked Major Wilkes's flat, having obtained a spare key from the neighbour. Holmes sent McGillian ahead of us to find a cab (they were hard to find in those days, even in Kingsway) and then steered the bewildered Hamer-Jenks to the street. In very little time we were dropped at quiet avenue in Bayswater,

where McGillian led us up three flights of stairs to a bright, airy flat.

"Keep them occupied, please," Holmes whispered to me. I knew he would want to examine the flat minutely and would not want to be disturbed while he did so.

To this day, I don't know how to refer to the other two men. Hamer-Jenks used his officer rank but I don't know if he was still in the military or was now a civil servant. I don't know if McGillian had ever worn military uniform. The organization which employed them is generally known as the Secret Intelligence Service but has other names as well, and I am not sure if it is a military or civilian outfit. They watched with open mouths as Holmes briskly went through the drawers of a bureau and the pockets of coats hanging by the door.

"I say, should you be doing that?" asked Hamer-Jenks.

I cut in before Holmes could answer. "McGillian, could you take us to meet the neighbour? Lieutenant, could you come with us? I think someone of your rank would set his mind at rest that the matter is being taken seriously." I do not like to be manipulative but Holmes needed to work uninterrupted. The young man with the bright red hair took us out to the stairwell and knocked on the door of the opposite flat. The door had one of those tiny lenses set in it, and I saw it darken as the occupant watched us for a moment. Then the door creaked open to reveal a shrunken, crusty old man with an air of disappointment in his expression. An aroma of stale cigarette smoke and kippers blew over us. He recognised McGillian and solemnly waved us in.

The flat was a mirror image of Wilkes's in terms of

layout and the complete opposite in terms of appearance. Where Wilkes kept his flat bright, clean, tidy and fresh, Mr Newland (McGillian performed the introductions) had his home painted in dark colours with dark curtains not properly opened to admit the spring sunshine. There was clutter everywhere: old newspapers, clothes, boxes and bags. I saw spiders' webs in most corners and a potted plant on the windowsill, long dead.

"Thank you for admitting us, Mr Newland. Please tell us everything you saw and heard."

"I was just doing my washing up" (this seemed unlikely) "and I heard someone climb the stairs and ring Wilkes's bell. The door opened and they talked, quiet like at first." He reached behind him for a stained and chipped tea mug and took a gulp. I was glad he had not offered us refreshments. "Well, then I hears Wilkes, talking more loud now. 'No, no, you can't' he shouts. The other bloke talks some more, in normal voice so I can't hear, then Wilkes again, he says 'This cannot be happening! This can't be real!' So I go to my door – I have one of those peep-holes in it, you probably saw. So I see them. Wilkes, he was white as a sheet, looked terrified. I couldn't see the other one's face, not then, but they went into the flat for a while. Then I heard the door open again and saw them come out. Wilkes looked a mess, like he'd just been told he was dying or something like that. The other man was much younger, probably no more than twenty, he had his arm around Wilkes's arm and was guiding him, firmly, to the stairs. I didn't like the look of him. Fierce, he looked, like he was on a dangerous mission. He had a bony face with a scar on it, just here," Newland indicated a line down his left cheek. "Didn't like the look of him at all. I heard one thing he said: 'You have to do this for your enemy,' he said. Foreign, he sounded, like a German. Not English, that's for sure, and very serious, very grim. Then they set off to the stairs and didn't even close the door to the flat properly. Most unlike Major Wilkes, that."

"What happened next?" I asked.

"I went to my window and saw them come out the main door onto the street. The young man with the scar frog-marched poor Major Wilkes up the road towards Paddington. I was getting into a right state over whether I should call the police. Then young McGillian here comes along, says he works with the Major and now here you are."

"Well thank you, Mr Newland. We will leave you in peace for now. We may have some more questions for you, once I have reported back to the leader of this investigation, Mr Holmes."

Newland gave a short laugh. "Holmes! Like the detective! A good name for someone investigating a kidnapping!"

It was a relief to leave the dark and malodourous flat for the lighter and fresher one opposite. Holmes was on the floor, examining the carpet. "Ah, gentlemen, perfect timing: McGillian, I wonder if you might lend me some support?" Holmes always presents an air of energy and alertness, so that it is easy for me to forget that he has aged as well and that the attacks of rheumatism can leave him stiff and sore. The young man helped him back onto his feet and then into an armchair.

"Thank you, McGillian. I must say, the Major is a man of excellent habits. He has a carpet brush that is a roller built into an attachment at the end of a pole. You simply push this device up and down your carpet, the brush rotates and flicks dirt into a pan concealed in the attachment." For a moment I wondered if old age was starting to have any other effects on my friend, as he had never shown interest in or admiration for any cleaning tool before. "It leaves the carpet beautifully brushed! Footprints are left with remarkable clarity."

That gave me relief – the appeal of the device was something that only Holmes would value. "What did the footprints tell you?"

"The Major had walked to and from this chair I now occupy many times since the carpet was last brushed. He seems to have a favourite pair of brogues, judging by the wear to the tread. He has had only one recent visitor, who wore army boots. He sat in the chair opposite."

"This must be the young man with the scar," said Hamer-Jenks who, I noticed, was starting to look hot and agitated. We related to Holmes all we had learned from the neighbour in the opposite flat. "A duelling scar, in all likelihood," continued the Lieutenant. "These Huns love their fencing and having a scar on the face is a badge of honour in their savage land. What else can you tell me about the visitor?"

Holmes shrugged. "Not much, I'm afraid. As I say, he wore boots – British army boots, or similar. About five feet and eight inches tall, very slim, long fingers for his height, nervous disposition, left-handed, smokes State Express cigarettes and probably has a cold."

"Oh, really sir!" said Hamer-Jenks. "I know all about your reputation and how you love to show off your supposed skills. It is possible you may have been able to see footprints in this carpet but the rest of it is obviously just guesswork."

"As you will, Lieutenant," replied Holmes calmly. "I believe this flat is not Major Wilkes's main residence?"

"Isn't it?" asked Hamer-Jenks, who by now had beads of sweat on his face.

"That's right, sir," said McGillian. "He has a house in the country, an old family property."

"Oh, yes, I remember," stammered Hamer-Jenks. "Surrey somewhere? Or was it Sussex?"

"Suffolk," said Holmes. "I found correspondence forwarded from an address in Lowestoft."

"Yes, that's right, Mr Holmes," answered the young redhead. "He talked to me once about fishing in the sea there."

"What else can you tell me about him? Not married? No family?"

The Lieutenant shook his head. "We do not encourage conversation about matters outside work. Best to keep things in their compartments."

"Ah, well sir, I have a few pieces of very basic information." It seemed as if McGillian almost wanted to apologize for the crime of learning a little about his colleague.

"Please go ahead, McGillian," said Holmes in his most friendly and easy manner. "He comes from Suffolk?"

"Not really, sir, he was born in London and his family moved to South Africa when he was young. Had his formative years there, then came back to England to study at Oxford. That was... '96 I think. Yes, he mentioned last week that it's going to be twenty years this autumn since he came to England."

"And the house?"

"He inherited the house in Lowestoft from a cousin who went down with the Titanic."

"He did not return to South Africa after his studies?"

"No sir, his parents had died and he said he had no one left there. He does not have many people here either. There were two younger brothers but one went missing at Ypres and the other fell at Gallipoli. There are University friends he sometimes talks about, and he sings tenor in a local church choir."

"No affairs of the heart that you know about?"

"No. He once said something about being unlucky in love. I got the impression he had been put off that kind of thing, sir."

"And now I have a couple of questions for Mr Newland." Holmes rose from the chair, perhaps with less spring than once, left the flat and knocked on the door opposite. "Mr Newland, I am sorry to trouble you a second time. No, there is no need for me to trespass on your hospitality, this will take only a minute. First, how long, in your estimation, was the interval between the Major and his visitor entering the flat and their subsequent departure?"

"Well, it was quite a while, I suppose. About half an hour? Maybe a bit longer."

"Thank you. And secondly, are you aware that the Major has a safe hidden in his flat?"

"A safe? No, there isn't one in my flat and I didn't know there was one in his. I've not ever been in his place. We weren't friendly like that, just neighbourly, like."

"Very good. Finally, I know the visitor was a man in his twenties and had a scarred face. What else can you tell me about his appearance?" Apart from the facts that the mystery man wore 'just normal clothes', looked 'just ordinary' and had 'darkish hair', Holmes was not able to extract more. But Hamer-Jenks asked, "Would you say he was fat or thin?"

The wizened old man rubbed his chin. "Thin. Yes, now you say it, he was a very thin young fellow."

We set off down the stairs, Holmes deep in thought. The younger men reached the street well before we got there. By now the Lieutenant was starting to look quite unwell. He was sweating freely, his face was red and I noticed tremors in his hands and voice.

"This is a disaster! A nightmare! I'll have to tell C. I'll have to report to the Admiralty, Room 40 will be frantic! If the Huns have got Wilkes, he's a brave man but, goodness knows, if they find out what he knows about, about how far we have got with... And to think the Germans can abduct an officer of the service in the middle of London, in broad daylight..."

Holmes put a hand on his shoulder. "Calm yourself, Lieutenant. We do not know for sure that there has been an abduction."

Hamer-Jenks started at Holmes for a moment. "He's

gone though? You agree that he's not coming back?"

"Yes, I would say he has gone. He has emptied his safe and did not bother to secure the door to his flat. It does appear that he is not expecting to return soon."

"You can't be suggesting he went willingly? Even if the abductor had a gun, I would expect Major Wilkes to die rather than go over to the enemy. Unless... yes, unless he is being blackmailed somehow. Perhaps they have kidnapped someone else and threatened harm to them if he did not co-operate. McGillian, can you think of anyone known to the Major who, if their life were in danger, would drive him to any extreme? Ah! I know, it could be the brother who went missing at Ypres. The Germans might have him as a prisoner. Dear me, if that is the case he's probably already telling them what he knows. Perhaps he already told them, if they took the hostage a while ago. He might have been passing information to them for months..." To his credit, Hamer-Jenks took control of himself and changed his style of speaking to a calm and firm manner. "There is no time to lose. McGillian, we must go to Whitehall immediately. You go to the Admiralty and book me a meeting with Mr Ewing for..." He checked his watch. "At three. That will give me time to brief C and instruct Special Branch to put out a watch for them. We have a photograph of Wilkes on the files, we must get that printed. He is with a young German who carries a fencing scar and is very thin, not surprising as we hear they are all starving in Germany now, because of our blockade. Mr Holmes, Doctor Watson, thank you for accompanying us today, you have helped confirm that Major Wilkes is gone. You may return to your homes." The rare sight of an empty cab appeared at the corner of the road and Hamer-Jenks waved it down.

"Thank you, Lieutenant but we will not be going home just yet. Watson, how does a trip to the coast appeal to you? The Suffolk air at this time of year will be most invigorating."

"Now, now, just a minute," said Hamer-Jenks. "I've given you the message that Major Wilkes wanted delivered. This is a matter for professionals. Wilkes has information that would be of immense value to the enemy. We may have to assume that he has given it to them, in which case urgent steps have to be taken. We also need to start a watch for them, we need people monitoring all possible escape routes to Germany. This requires the full power of the state, as well as men who are trained in modern methods and understand the absolute requirement for security. You are to forget everything that has happened here and return to your normal lives."

He and McGillian climbed into the cab, the driver flicked the reins and a moment later Holmes and I were alone on the pavement outside the block of flats.

"Yes, Holmes," I said. "A visit to the Suffolk coast would be very welcome."

The war comes to us

Holmes was silent as we walked to Paddington Station and as we rode the Metropolitan Railway east. I knew better than to interrupt him while he thought. At Liverpool Street Station we had a late lunch at the cafeteria, where I then rested while Holmes went off to send a telegram. While I waited I watched the people come and go. There were all sorts: traders, ladies up from the country to spend the Bank Holiday in town, and men and women in all variety of military uniforms.

When Holmes returned he had our tickets and said he had telephoned ahead to reserve hotel rooms for us in Lowestoft, as it would be late in the afternoon by the time we arrived. So we placed ourselves in the hands of the Great Eastern Railway. As we steamed through East London, Holmes looked out of the window at streets he had known so well in earlier times.

At last he came out of his reverie and was disposed to talk. "So, Watson, once again the game is afoot."

"But what is this game? Kidnapping? Treason? Do you have any idea what has happened to make Major Wilkes abandon his work?"

"Many ideas. Some seem more likely than others."

"And we are going to Suffolk to follow the most likely?"

"I am not sure that we are following the most likely trail. But I think we are following the trail than can most readily be determined as true or false. If we are chasing a wild goose, it will at least allow me to cross one set of possibilities off the list I have conceived."

We steamed through Chelmsford and I briefly thought of the work that was going on at the Marconi factory there. "Holmes, I must ask... You could see that the prints of the boots on the carpet looked like the tread of an army boot. You were able to estimate the height of this mysterious young man from the length of his stride. But how do you know he is slim, long-fingered, nervous, left-handed, an afficionado of State Express (a horrible brand of cigarette, by the way) and probably has a cold?"

At the mention of cigarettes, Holmes took out his pipe and set it smoking. "The seat opposite me, where the young man sat, had a soft, plump cushion. A slim person had most recently sat in it. In fact, if we had not been told that the visitor was a man, I would have thought the visitor most likely a woman or a man not yet full grown." He took a few more puffs on his pipe. "He probably required some courage to do whatever he was doing with Major Wilkes. A calm man would have sat steadily. But did you see the tassels on the antimacassars on that armchair? Long, golden tassels. But the ones on the left arm were twisted, frayed, and knotted. Completely ruined, I would say. The knots were made casually, by a nervous man twisting and turning them. I tried to replicate the result on the right-hand side while you were with Mr Newland. It would require longer fingers than mine to get the result that was on the left. So, nervous, long-fingered and left-handed."

"Perhaps he had something else in his right hand. Perhaps he held a gun."

"Perhaps."

"And the cigarettes? I looked and did not see ash anywhere, not even an ash tray."

"No. No one has smoked tobacco in that flat in the past few days. But the tassels, I am sorry to say, carried an unpleasant aroma that must have been transferred to them by someone who had recently used that brand."

"The cold?"

"Again, not the most pleasant of clues. Tissue paper, Watson. In the wastepaper basket. Recently used. None that was dried. I concluded that it was the visitor who had found need of them."

We had to change trains at Ipswich, where there was a long delay while we waited for a military train to pass through. I trust that, once the war is over, England can at last build a railway system where the trains run on time for the convenience of the travelling public. Beyond Ipswich, we were in proper countryside: a gently undulating land with the crops already showing the bounty of the earth and rural stations with quaint names.

Finally, we steamed into Lowestoft. I felt quite stiff after the journey. A porter told us it was no more than a ten-minute walk to our hotel on The Esplanade but it took us fifteen. We dropped our bags, made a reservation for dinner then asked for a carriage to take us to Major Wilkes's house. When it arrived, it was pulled by a donkey. This would have been preposterous once, but now it was no surprise, as most horses have been commandeered for work abroad. The house was a fine villa set in its own grounds in the Kirkley area of the town. If Holmes had expected to find the Major there, with a warm welcome and a simple explanation for the mystery of his disappearance, he was quickly disappointed. Not only was there no one at home, close inspection of the drive and the doors gave him no sign that anyone had entered the house for days. But the garden was being worked: a large pile of shrubs looked as if they had only recently been dug up from beds that now presented neat ridges of soil. The house had clean windows that gave views inside, showing the furniture covered in dust sheets.

We returned to the donkey and carriage, which

Holmes had asked to wait for us. The driver, a man called Mayhew, spoke in a broad Suffolk accent which is hard to describe, harder to capture in writing and almost impossible to understand until you get used to it. "Tha's bin emp'y a wharl new," he said, which I interpreted to mean that the house had been empty for a while now.

"But someone is looking after it," said Holmes. "It looks as if a gardener and housekeeper are employed. Someone has been forwarding the mail."

"Ah, reckon so."

"Do you know who has been looking after the house?"

"Sorry, gov. Reckon I can ask about tho'." He drove us back to our hotel. Holmes gave him a generous tip with the promise of more if he could supply anyone who had been looking after the house.

"Well, well, Watson, an exhausting day for two elderly gentlemen such as ourselves. I believe we have earned ourselves a good dinner and a refreshing night's sleep."

We had a good dinner of local sea bass. But the refreshing night's sleep was not to be. I got to sleep readily enough. A terrific crash blasted me from my slumbers in the early hours of the morning. I sat up, entirely bewildered at first. The whole room seemed to be shaking. There was a flash of light, which penetrated the curtains enough to show me that my room was full of dust from the collapsing ceiling. The flash was immediately followed by another terrifying crash and the shaking became more intense. I could not even frame my thoughts enough to wonder where I was or what was happening. Then my door burst open and in rushed Holmes, wearing a dressing gown and a thick layer of dust. "Come, Watson, to the cellar."

We staggered down the stairs, alongside other guests and staff. There were more bangs and crashes, some near, some far. In between, I was able to discern the whistle of incoming projectiles and I finally worked out what was happening: the town was being shelled from the sea.

We all crowded into the cellar, coughing and stumbling, staff and guests mixed together. That distinction did not matter now. A young maid was crying and a lad was wailing, "I'm going to die, I don't want to die!" I spotted the old man who had served us at the bar the previous evening and asked if there was any brandy in the cellar. He quickly produced a couple of bottles and I went around the packed underground rooms dosing those who needed it – including myself. My ears were ringing from the noise of the explosions.

The whistles and crashes stopped after a few minutes. The lad was still in a bad way but the young maid had pulled herself together, saying, "I don't know why I'm making such a fuss. My Derek's over in France, he's had this for months now."

We now know that Lowestoft and Great Yarmouth had both been shelled that night by the Imperial German Navy. At the same time, Zeppelins dropped bombs on several towns, including Norwich, Lincoln, Harwich and Ipswich. The German ships were driven off by the Royal Navy and the Zeppelins returned to base. Cowering in the hotel cellar, we did not know the attack was over. But at about half past four o'clock, perhaps twenty minutes after I had been woken and ten minutes after the last crash of an exploding shell, some of us went upstairs and outside. In the light of the very early morning, the sea looked tranquil but smoke was rising from several places in the town. I went upstairs and dressed as fast as I could, then went out to see what I could do to help.

I could not do much. At each damaged house there were people already sifting through the ruins, seeking their valuables once all the people had been accounted for. The police and fire brigade were in action and army & navy men had been mobilised as well. Streams of people were packing up and leaving the town to stay with friends and family further inland. I spotted a man whose baggage showed him to be a local doctor, so I introduced myself and he welcomed my assistance in patching up some minor wounds. In all, two hundred houses were seriously damaged and four people died.

By the time the sun was up properly, it became clear that there was little more I could do to help. I was also aware of a tiredness that seemed to run through me, right down into my bones. It was a tiredness I had not felt before. I could diagnose age and activity as causes, combined with the shock of the night's events and the horror that a modern European navy would consider it reasonable to open fire on a town's civilian population. The Royal Navy has a presence in Lowestoft, certainly, but only a few minesweepers and small coastal patrol boats. No longer could the war be seen as a distant event.

I made it back to the hotel, which had sufficiently recovered to lay on breakfast. The building was not damaged apart from some broken windows and collapsed ceilings in my room and one other. There was an extraordinary air of cheerfulness. Like the maid earlier in the night, most people seemed to think the raid had brought them closer to friends and relatives serving abroad.

The staff told me that Holmes had already broken his fast and left to visit the Post Office. He returned as I finished my meal.

"Any news?" I asked.

"Something. Possibly nothing." Holmes seemed downcast. Our lack of success at the house yesterday was a partial cause and I am sure he shared my horror with the events of the night.

"Wotcher, guvnor!" said a cheery voice. It was Mayhew, our carriage driver from yesterday. His broad accent was even harder to understand now that I had to listen through the ringing in my ears. "Good to see you gents both a'right. Bit o' a barney last night, ay? I got summat for ye. I's in The Plough & Sail las' night, before Fritz kicked off, and I met ol' Jimmy Dix. He's being doin' the garden at that ol' house and his missus lookin' out for post an' that. Got their address, they says they'll be glad to see yeh." He handed us a scrap of paper.

"Very good, thank you," said Holmes. "Can you drive us there?"

"Not likely! Cart caught one in the night! Just an 'ole now where I left it. Lucky old Whisky was in the meadow with the other donkeys and mules, tho' they's all scared witless by the shellin'. Bloody Huns. They think blowin' my old cart to kingdom come's goin' ta win 'em the war?"

He gave us the address and directions, so we set off on foot. The house was north of the River Waveney, part of a row of fishermen's cottages. It transpired that Mr Dix was a retired fisherman. He was not a young man (there were few young men anywhere except in the forces) and years of being out on the North Sea had given him a red and salty look. He and his wife subsisted by doing odd jobs – a bit of gardening here, a bit of housekeeping there – although there is not a large middle class in this part of the country to provide such work. He and his wife also had broad Suffolk accents which meant we had to ask them to repeat themselves more often than felt polite.

They had not seen Major Wilkes since the start of the war.

"I pop in now an' then, check all's well, forward his letters and that," said Mrs Dix.

"An' I been keeping the garden aright up to now," added Mr Dix. "But lately I decided 'as a waste, all that lan' just for a few bushes. So I dug 'em up and put spuds in. Can't imagine he's to mind that. Country needs the food, see."

"He wrote me sayin' his work's keepin' him down London," said Mrs Dix. "Not seen hide nor hair on 'im since summer of '14."

"Not even when we 'ad to move 'is boat," added Mr Dix.

"His boat?" asked Holmes. "He has a boat. Can you tell me about that?"

"Yeah, well, he used ter like ter do a bit o' fishin'. Herring mainly o' course, bass, some cod. Kept the old

105

tub down in the harbour. But in 1914, navy say's they're all to clear out, harbour just for navy and the fishing fleet. Have to keep the fishing fleet, country needs fish, especially time o' war. I wan'ed to get back on board me self but just could nah be much use to a crew now."

"What happened to Major Wilkes's boat?"

"Me an' some o' the booies moved the boats which their owners couldn't for one thing or another. Moved 'em upriver. Out o' the way, like. Moored up at Oulton."

"Is it still there?"

"Reckon so. None likely to steal an old tub like that. You can go see if you like. Head on up to Oulton, ask at Broad House for Roger Carley, he's the old booey that keeps an eye on the boats moored up there."

So we continued to follow our trail of old Suffolk characters. We took a train to Oulton Broad and walked to Broad House. Carley was another weather-beaten, cheerful, active fellow who turned out to be a general handyman for the area and, thankfully, with a less strong accent than most locals. Holmes asked him if he knew the boat that belonged to Major Wilkes.

"Ah, yep, Peggotty's Pride, fifteen-foot, nice sturdy little thing. Nice motor on 'er too. Funny you should ask about that one. Gone!"

"When did she go?"

"Ooh, now, she were there yesterday mornin', I always likes to look 'em over, first thing. But last night, about seven it were, I noticed she were gone."

"Do boats often get stolen?" This was the only question I asked.

Carley chuckled at the idea. "Stolen? This in't yer London! People don't steal boats. Can't hide 'em, for one thing. Besides, old Peggotty's Pride's in't worth an' ol' shillin' if yer ask me."

"Nevertheless, do you know if anyone saw who took the boat, or what time they left?"

The old boy shrugged. "No one's said nuffin', not to me anyhow. Boats still come an' go, not so much as before, mind. Bit o' a surprise she's not back though. Long time to be out on a little thing like that. I hope she ain't got caught up with them Germans las' night."

"Mr Carley, do you think a boat like Peggotty's Pride could go far out to sea? Across to Holland, for example?"

He chuckled again. "Ooh, I dunno, I wouldn't advise it! Get across to Holland on a thing like that? Even if there's none o' them Germans buggering about firing off their shells."

"But it could be done? The weather yesterday was fine enough."

"Oh yep, not saying it couldn't be done. Just don't reckon it's a clever thing to try."

Holmes took down a description of the boat, gave Carley a tip, and we sat on a bench looking at the expanse of Oulton Broad. Once again, I maintained my silence until Holmes broke it.

"Are you still ready to travel, Watson?"

"Of course, although I could do with a proper night's rest before we move again. I find weariness harder to shake off than I once did. Could we stay another night, to get some strength back?"

"I will follow my doctor's orders, old friend," he said with a smile.

"You think they came here and took the boat without visiting the house?"

"It is safe to assume they were in a hurry."

"They might not have come here at all. Someone else could have taken the boat." I was a little irritated that Carley had found my suggestion of theft amusing.

"They could have but it would be a coincidence for the Major and his boat to vanish on the same day."

"Someone must have seen them?" Holmes agreed that it would be good to get confirmation that Wilkes and the man with him had been seen. We walked to the station at Oulton Broad South, where travellers from London would have alighted, and asked the staff there. They had seen many men coming and going so could not confirm that they had seen the pair we described.

We returned to Lowestoft, stopped for a quick lunch at the station and walked to the harbour. Holmes wanted to ask the Harbourmaster if the departure of Peggotty's Pride had been recorded yesterday, but everyone was too busy repairing the damage that last night's shelling had caused. We did not want to interfere, and it was clear that the boat had gone somewhere, so we returned to the hotel. There was still a great deal of clearing up going on but they said they could get rooms ready for us and would be able to provide a meal that evening.

While we waited, we rested in the hotel lounge.

"You think they have gone to Holland?"

Holmes was thoughtful for a while. "It seems unlikely that they came to Lowestoft and collected the boat merely to sail it to another destination on the English coast." Holmes took a few puffs on his pipe. "If it is an abduction by Germany or a defection to that country, they will have sailed for Belgium. But if they want to avoid the war, a neutral country would be their destination."

"You think we should follow them?"

"Yes, I do. It seems this Major Wilkes has information that would be of great value to our country's enemies. If we can find out what has happened to him, and whether his information is safe or at risk, we will have done our country a service."

"Then there is no question. Of course we must go. But go where, exactly?"

Holmes smiled. "We cannot go to Belgium. Tomorrow we sail for the Kingdom of the Netherlands."

Back across the sea

The telephone is a modern marvel. Before it was invented, advance travel arrangements would have to be made by telegram, which was costly and slow, or letter, which was cheaper but even slower. The alternative was to trust to luck and hope that seats on a train or ship, or rooms at an hotel, would be available when you arrived. After our conversation in the hotel lounge, Holmes rang a travel agent in Ipswich and explained our needs. In less than an hour the agent had called back with all the details of our journey. So, after another good dinner and an undisturbed night, we took trains to Ipswich, then Colchester and finally Harwich. I felt much refreshed after a good sleep and the ringing in my ears had almost completely subsided.

At Harwich I was delighted (and, I must confess, slightly alarmed) to discover that we were sailing on the *SS Brussels* under Captain Charles Fryatt. Perhaps, by the time this memoir is eventually published, readers will have forgotten that, back in March 1915, the *Brussels* had been threatened by a German submarine and ordered to stop. At that time, the Germans gave passengers and crew time to move into lifeboats before sinking a ship. Rather than obey this command, Captain Fryatt had turned his ship towards the 'U-boat' (as they are called) and would have rammed it, if the enemy vessel had not performed a 'crash-dive' (gone deep very quickly) to avoid the collision. He had previously managed to out-run a 'U-boat' in another ship of his line. It was an honour to meet such a brave and celebrated man, although it did make me aware that we were taking a risk in travelling across what we all now call the North Sea. Even ships sailing to a neutral country are considered targets by our amoral enemy.

Holmes had decided it was best if we travelled incognito, as far as possible. At the passenger terminal, an official had looked at our papers and asked the purpose of our visit. Holmes told him it was a private matter but the official did not like that, saying, "No travel is private at this time of national emergency." So we said that we were friends of a man interned by the Dutch government. We were travelling to visit him. The story seemed acceptable to the official and, I suppose, two elderly gentlemen did not seem likely to pose a threat to anyone's security.

I should perhaps explain here that members of the armed forces, from either side, were interned if they were discovered on Dutch soil. In other words, they were kept as prisoners for the duration of hostilities. It was a condition of the country's neutrality and was understood and accepted by both sides.

We embarked onto the ship and met Captain Fryatt briefly as he shook hands with some of the passengers. We did not introduce ourselves. There followed extensive lifeboat drills and we were issued with strange jackets stuffed with kapok. These, we were told, would help keep us afloat if we found ourselves in the sea. This was a longer crossing than those we had recently made from Folkestone to Boulogne or Calais to Dover, and less well patrolled by the Royal Navy.

Once we had established ourselves in a private corner of the ship's passenger lounge, I asked Holmes what plan he had in mind, once we arrived in Holland.

"We will endeavour to discover if Peggotty's Pride landed anywhere in Holland. If she did, we will seek to track down Major Wilkes and the scarred young man with the foreign accent. If we can learn the full story, we can report it back to friend Lieutenant Hamer-Jenks. At least they will then know whether their secrets are safe."

"If we can find no trace of the boat?"

"If they did not land in Holland, there seem to be only three reasonable explanations."

"One being that they sank in the North Sea."

"Yes. Mr Carley said he thought a trip across the sea in such a small craft carried that risk."

"A second being that they sailed to Belgium."

"Indeed. If Major Wilkes was being delivered to the Central Powers, presumably under compulsion, Belgium would be their obvious destination. In which case, we would have to inform Hamer-Jenks that his worst fears seem realized and his former colleague is in the hands of the enemy."

"What is the third possibility?"

"Not much better than the second, Watson. We know the Imperial German Navy was off the coast of Lowestoft on the night after Peggotty's Pride set sail."

"You mean a planned rendezvous?"

"Precisely. The removal of Major Wilkes from London to Lowestoft could have been planned for the night when German warships were going to be in the area. Peggotty's Pride need only to have sailed a few miles out to sea and its passengers picked up by larger ships. They would have been easy enough to find once they opened fire and the shells would have passed far above a small boat."

There were no sightings of other ships and our voyage was uneventful. Nevertheless, I was glad to see land again. We moored at the Hook of Holland, at the mouth of the New Waterway shipping canal that links Rotterdam to the sea. As we walked down the gangway I looked up at the bridge. Captain Fryatt was watching his passengers disembark. I waved to him and he saluted in return. A brave man to continue with an especially dangerous task now that he has angered the Germans.

By now it was late in the day. I was wondering how

long it would take for the Dutch authorities to admit us to their country, and how long after that before we found an hotel with space and food for us, as it had not been possible to reserve one from England. However, when we presented our papers to the official at the immigration desk, he just said, "Ah, yes, Holmes, Watson. Welcome in Holland. Over there, your driver is waiting." He pointed to a burly, beefy-looking man of around forty years, with flat black hair and ruddy cheeks rising out of a full beard. He moved quickly over to us, took our bags from our hands before I knew he was doing it and whispered, "Great honour gentlemen. Name's Brunt. Would you come with me?"

I was immediately on my guard. The man looked like a ruffian who had been put in smart clothes and hastily groomed. Holmes shared my hesitation but managed it well, shaking the man's hand and saying, "Good evening Mr Brunt. Thank you for your invitation but I am sure you will understand that, before we accompany you, we would rather know something about who you are, what organization you represent and where you intend taking us."

He stared at us for a moment. I was still on my guard and looked about to see if we were being surreptitiously surrounded by other shady characters. There were people milling around but no one seemed to be paying any attention to our party of three. Brunt smiled. It looked strange on him. "Of course. You don't know me from Adam. Though I like to think I am better dressed!" The smile became a great beaming, toothy grin before he continued, "I don't want us to be noticed standing here." He glanced around. "Look," he pulled a revolver from his pocket, which gave me another spike of alarm before he slapped it in my hand and continued, "there, now you are armed and I am not. My car is parked over there," he indicated a warehouse with a row of cars parked alongside it. "Tell you what," he reached into his other pocket and pulled out a set of keys, which he handed to Holmes. "Now you have the car keys. Let's go over there and sit in the car, I'll sit in the back and we can talk without being noticed."

It did seem safe enough and almost unreasonable to refuse, but I remained on my guard. As we walked to the car, a Vauxhall D-type with a canvas roof, I made a quick inspection of the revolver, a Webley mark VI. Both British makes. If he was only pretending to be British he had made a thorough job of it. The gun was in good condition but not loaded.

Once we were in the car, I pointed out to Brunt that he had not taken such a great risk in handing me an unloaded revolver.

"No, well, they don't like us carrying loaded firearms," he answered.

"Who doesn't?" I asked.

"The Dutch. They don't like us carrying unloaded firearms, come to that, but I feel strange without one."

"And could I further ask, Mr Brunt," said Holmes, "who you mean by 'us' exactly?"

"Before I answer you, I must have your word that you will reveal nothing about your visit to Holland – nothing you see or hear, nothing about me or anyone else you meet – without government approval." We both gave our word. "Very well. I work for a unit called MI1c. Our man in Harwich clocked your names and wired me a telegram. I could not believe it when I decoded it. But I came out here, had a word with a friend on the immigration desk and here we are. Now, gentlemen, I have to ask: what brings you to Holland?"

Holmes and I exchanged a look and my friend answered. "Mr Brunt, you have asked us to promise that we will say nothing about what occurs here. You will understand, then, if I tell you we made a similar promise to people in England."

"Oh! You've been sent here by London, have you? A bit extreme of them not to tell us. Did they really think we would not notice a famous detective and his biographer coming into our territory?" He made a disparaging noise. "Who sent you? No, you can't tell me, of course. Probably old man Wilkes, was it? No, he'd never bring in outsiders. But you're here on their authority? I can't understand why they did not tell us to assist you; we're not that secretive with each other." His gaze flicked from Holmes to me and back again. "Well, sometimes we are. Unless... they didn't send you, did they?"

"We are here in a private capacity."

Brunt grinned. "I'll bet they warned you off! You went to Wilkes with something on your mind, he told you to keep out of it. Him or his lackey Hamer-Jenks. That's London for you. That's why they didn't tell us you were coming. I don't suppose they even know you are here."

"Will you tell them?"

Brunt thought for a moment. "Sorry, yes, I think I have to. But there's nothing they can do. You've broken no laws in coming here. In the meantime, well, you don't know me but I know who you are. Therefore, I understand that you cannot trust me, while I can trust both of you. Is there anything I can do for you?"

I answered first. "Right now, an hotel with comfortable rooms and decent food."

The nest of spies

I felt that, since Brunt knew the names of Wilkes and Hamer-Jenks, he could at least be trusted to take us to somewhere to stay. He did not seem aware that Wilkes had vanished but it seemed that the London and Rotterdam offices did not share everything with each other.

I was surprised that it took over an hour to drive from the Hook of Holland ferry port to the centre of Rotterdam. During the journey, Brunt told us what it was like living in the city, along with occasional repeated requests that we keep it all secret. He turned out to be a talkative man, so we let him talk.

"You gents will know better than most that ports are grim places at the best of times. The world's flotsam washes up in places like this. Now, with the war, well! At first it was Belgian refugees. Thousands of them, poor devils, fleeing the war and the occupation of their country. The tales they had to tell! Well, you know many of them, we've not been shy in letting their horror stories be known. They've mostly gone all over now but a big slice of them started off here, very squalid conditions at first. See that warehouse, just across the river there? We had four hundred Belgians living in there at the end of 1914. Had a great effect on Dutch feelings too, the country might be neutral but lots of the people are most unimpressed with Hun actions on their neighbours to the south. They're a decent people, the Dutch, although their language hurts almost as much to speak as it does to listen to. I've picked up enough of it to get by and had a sore throat ever since. Anyway, as I say, they felt a great sympathy for the Belgians, so next on the move were Germans, or anyone with German links, based in Holland. They had to get back to Germany fast or be lynched."

"Then there have been armed combatants. After the fall of Antwerp, the 1st Naval Brigade retreated here; well, they had nowhere else to go. We couldn't pick them up off the coast. They are the biggest British group to be interned. The Dutch intend to keep them locked up until the end of the war. Then quite a few Germans found themselves on the wrong side of the border and were rounded up too. There are thousands of Belgian soldiers interned too, you can't blame them, their country was overrun. Once the German army reached the sea, well, those to the south of them could still fight, they are still fighting, in the trenches alongside our boys. But if they were north of the Germans their only choices were stand and die a pointless death, surrender to the Germans or cross over and hand themselves in to the Dutch. Well, what would you do?"

"What about deserters?" asked Holmes.

"Yes, lots of Germans crossed over at first. Didn't fancy dying for their Kaiser. They were able to surrender and be interned with their fellows, who might take a dim view of them but at least they get food and a roof over their heads. Or they could declare themselves deserters, in which case they are not considered soldiers here and are left alone if they behave themselves, but they have to look after themselves too."

"You said 'at first'," I asked. "Don't they come over anymore?"

"Not so much, not since Fritz built his electric fence. They were losing rather too many deserters for their liking. Also, they felt people were crossing in and out of Holland too easily, carrying information about what's going on in Germany and Belgium and the word was getting over to us. Which it was! But then they built their fence. It's got 4,000 volts in it, running the length of the Dutch-Belgian border, from the North Sea to Germany, and they've got other barriers and precautions running north from there along the Dutch-German border. People and messages still get across but it's not so easy now. Electrocution is a nasty way to die."

"What about now?" I asked. "What is Rotterdam like these days?"

Brunt thought for a minute. "Anxious. It's an anxious place. Rotterdam was often called Germany's largest port and it's true. Most of their imports and exports moved via the Rhine and here. Now, well, we have the port blockaded, of course. As a neutral country they're allowed to trade, can't interfere with that and wouldn't want to. But we have to make sure no one's getting anything to Germany. So the port has become quiet, businesses run down, lots of people with not enough to do." As we drove towards the city centre, the economic depression was easy to see. Many buildings looked abandoned and there were weeds growing in what once would have been busy depots. But at least there were no signs of war.

Brunt continued. "They're also worried about being invaded."

This surprised me. "Invaded? With the Central Powers fighting on fronts to the east, west and south, they would open another one here?"

"They might. The Dutch army is no pushover and the country would not take occupation lightly but it would give Germany many advantages if they held Holland. But it's not just a German invasion the Dutch are worried about. They think we might land here to use their country as a base to attack Germany in the north."

This surprised me even more. "But... But they... We entered this war because Germany violated Belgium's neutrality. If we violated Dutch neutrality, we – well, we..." Words failed me.

"I know," said Brunt. "Of course we would never invade. But I wouldn't want them to be too sure."

"Why ever not?"

Brunt gave his strange smile again, showing a great rack of teeth. "Germany keeps a number of divisions just across their border with Holland, ready to step in to aid their Dutch neighbours should the wicked British ever invade. If they are there, they can't be at the front. You could say that it's my job to keep the idea of a British invasion of Holland on the cards, so as to keep those German soldiers where they can do no harm."

My mind was reeling at the labyrinthine complexity of this intrigue, so it was just as well that we arrived at the hotel at that moment. It was called the Grand Hotel Coomans and it certainly was grand, especially after the general shabbiness of the city. The carpets looked new, the paint fresh and the furniture bore no sign of the supposed hardness of the times. We refused Brunt's offer of dinner as we were both worn out by the journey so he said he would meet us after breakfast in the morning. Before he left he gave a final word of warning: "You've promised to keep everything to yourselves and of course I respect that. But you must be careful here, even between yourselves. If Rotterdam is a colony of spies, this is their nest. Everyone here is on the lookout for who comes and goes. Everyone is listening for the tiniest bit of idle gossip. I've booked you in as Mr Simon Harrison and Mr James Weston. Please use those names, even when speaking privately to each other. Always assume someone is listening to you. I would very much prefer that no one else in Rotterdam knew who was gracing it with their distinguished presence." He briefly raised his hat, flashed his grin and left.

We were both tired but needed a light dinner, so we found a table in the hotel restaurant. I was puzzled that both Holmes and Brunt were so insistent on the need for our trip to be a secret, so, over the meal, Holmes explained the need for anonymity to me. "I do not wish to attract any attention to our trip, Watson." He explained, "There is the general need for secrecy about our mission. Furthermore, I do not wish to cause any embarrassment to the government of Holland. Maintaining neutrality while caught between the hostile powers in such a war is a difficult position for them. Although we are visiting as private citizens, with no attachment to any civil or military arm of the British state, we are looking for someone who seems to hold an important position in the British intelligence service."

He paused for a moment before adding, "Such as it is."

"But Holmes, I recall that you did a major service for the Dutch royal family. Could we use that connection?"

"That was nearly thirty years ago! Queen Wilhelmina was a child at the time. I doubt she knows anything about the problem her father faced back then, and with which I had the honour to be of some assistance. Besides, no, I cannot ask any favour of her which could be seen as aiding the Allied cause."

"Why do you think this fellow Brunt is also so determined to keep our presence here a secret? Booking us in under false names; it feels dishonest."

Holmes smiled. "Dear old Watson, even in a time of war you want to keep to your principles. Admirable. For Brunt, I expect it is just the habit of secrecy. But, as I have explained, I agree with him. It is best that our presence here remains unknown and we remain unrecognised."

"Good Lord! Can it be? Excuse me gentlemen, but do I have the honour of addressing the great Sherlock Holmes?" The speaker was a man of medium height but massive frame – perhaps once muscular, now something else but still an imposing figure. He looked about seventy years of age, with a head of bushy white hair and mutton chop sideburns. His bright blue eyes and jovial manner would have been appealing but his accent was unmistakably German. He continued with barely a pause for breath. "And, can my wildest dreams be fulfilled? Dear sir, can you be Doctor Watson? You have aged, well, have not we all? But your features, especially yours, Mr Holmes, are still unmistakable from the pictures which accompanied the famous stories of your adventures. Gentlemen, it is my privilege to welcome such distinguished visitors to my adopted country. May I introduce myself?" He did not pause long enough to allow us to give or deny permission. "My name is Count Frederick von Altmark, formerly of Leipzig, now citizen of Rotterdam." His English was perfect and he continued his stream of constant speech. "Now, gentlemen, I know what you are thinking! That I am a German, an enemy because your country and my former country are at war. Such a tragedy, a disaster. If only it could have been avoided. The English and the Germans are the same people; we are not natural enemies. It is because that is so that I live here now, we are in a neutral country. I am retired, a gentleman of some means, an old man but I hope to live long enough to see peace once again between your country and the land of my birth. Please, let us shake hands."

Holmes shook his hand, so I followed his example. Neither of us had yet spoken a word.

"So, Mr Holmes and Doctor Watson! A dream has come true in meeting you. May I ask what brings you to Holland? Perhaps like me you prefer to live in a land that is free from war. Or – now, this is a possibility – could it be a criminal case that brings you here? Are you on the heels of a thief or murderer?"

"Count von Altmark, I thank you for your welcome. Doctor Watson and I have long since retired from detective work. We are here on a private visit. We hope to visit some of the British servicemen who have been interned by the Dutch authorities. We would wish to learn what we can do for them, within the limits that the government of Holland may set, to make their confinement easier."

"A noble aim, dear Mr Holmes. However, it seems to me that the interned warriors, of both sides, are not suffering greatly. The have food and shelter and are free from the horrors of this terrible war. They are not even confined to their camps. If they give their parole, they are allowed to leave the internment camps and go where they please. Now, you must allow me to assist you. This city, my goodness, it is filled with the most terrible people: spies, agents, villains, the worst. If you were still looking for criminals to arrest, you would never run out. They like to spread the most terrible rumours and lies. If you stay in Rotterdam, you will hear dreadful things about me, for example, I have no doubt. Me, a harmless bachelor, retired from a career in public service, moderately successful, although I always regret never to have made any crowning achievement. I have no claim to any fame, yet the people here spread their falsehoods about everyone. They are forever putting people on the wrong track, partly to disguise their dirty dealings and partly just for mischief. I can help you. I know the city and I know the people. I know who you can trust and who to avoid. Come, I see you have finished your meals – let us move to a private bar they have here and we can continue our conversation over some interesting Dutch liqueurs."

It had not been a conversation, more of a monologue from this strange man. I was relieved when Holmes declined his offer. "Count, thank you for your offer and your information. But Doctor Watson and I have just arrived after a long journey and..."

"Of course, of course, you need to rest. I fully understand. Have a good night, my dear friends, if you do not think it too much of a liberty to call you friends when we have only just met. I live nearby and often come to this hotel in the evening to have a drink and engage in conversation. Although many of the people here are shady characters, they are excellent as drinking companions."

The large man continued to speak as Holmes continued to make excuses. Finally, we were able to leave him and retire.

Comfortable rooms had been found for Mr Harrison and Mr Weston and I had a good night apart from a short period awake with heartburn – nothing unusual for a man of my age.

In the morning, over breakfast, I asked Holmes what he thought of our new acquaintances, the grinning Mr Brunt and the loquacious Count von Altmark. Holmes took a sip of a milky drink we had been offered and made a face expressive of displeasure. I was not sure if his displeasure was caused by the two men or his drink. "I have made no definite conclusion. Both seem keen to know us and assist us. Brunt knew we were coming and knows the names of people we met in London. The Count made no attempt to hide his national origin. I shall watch and listen to them both. In the meantime, I see no reason not to accept assistance from any quarter if it can be taken without jeopardising our mission."

I took a sip from my glass of the milky drink and almost gagged. It was milk that had been allowed to go sour and I found it quite disgusting. It seems that the Dutch actually enjoy this beverage.

Brunt arrived as promised and suggested we go for a walk, because that made it harder to be overheard. The area around the hotel had no public park but there were some pleasant tree-lined boulevards. The streets were not busy but I could not help noticing how very tall everyone was.

"They say about the Dutch that the short ones all drowned," grinned Brunt. I must have looked bemused, as he continued, "Just my little joke, doctor. No, it's that vile sour milk they drink in gallons. Have you tried it? Makes them the tallest people on the planet. Even their beds have to be made longer than ours. On the subject of which, I hope you are satisfied with my choice of hotel, gentlemen?"

"Very comfortable, thank you, Mr Brunt," said Holmes. "I must say, the hotel appears to be doing well at the moment."

Once again, that toothy grin which looked so incongruous on such a burly man. "Oh yes. It's an ill wind – the Coomans is always busy with people on business. All sorts of business. Now, I have been in touch with London and told them you are here. Their attitude seems to be that, as you've come, we may as well see if we can help each other."

"Did they tell you what they need help with?"

"Some of it – the wireless operators and cypher lads have had a busy night on both sides of the sea. I know you are looking for something…" He looked at each of us closely. "Or should I say someone? A man who has knowledge which would be of value to the Germans if they got hold of it. I don't know who it is and I don't know if it's a German spy or a British deserter. They did say that if you find who are looking for, you are to let them know as quickly as you can. I can pass on any message you have for them. They seem very anxious to know what has become of – whoever it is. Sorry if all that sounds secretive and mysterious but that is how we are."

Holmes thought for a minute. "In that case I will follow your example and not disclose our ultimate target. But I think I will tell you what we are seeking which may lead us there. It's a boat. A fifteen-foot motorboat called Peggotty's Pride that we think may have sailed to somewhere on the continent on Monday. Could such a vessel have landed in Holland and, if so, could we find it?"

Brunt looked at Holmes for a while, with no trace of his smile. Without it, he looked angry and threatening but I do not think he meant to. "A small boat to sail here from England. But people do, or did before the war. Plenty of places to moor up."

"The boat is not especially valuable and could have been abandoned at the end of the journey."

"In that case, you've got the whole coast to choose from. Sandy beaches all the way for hundreds of miles. Sail over, jump off if you don't mind getting your feet wet, wade to the shore and, if you don't care about the boat, let it go."

"Would it be found?"

"If the tides and winds drove it onshore, yes. Otherwise it would drift. Generally northwards. It could still be in the middle of the sea. Unless it hit a mine."

"Is there a way, though, to find out if this boat has been seen anywhere on the Dutch coast?"

The incongruous smile returned. "Oh yes, I should

think so. I told you yesterday how we keep alive this idea of a British invasion? The Dutch have a coast watch, keeping a look out for our invasion fleet. The one that will never come. Leave it with me. Will it be convenient for me to join you for dinner tonight? Good, I will see you at seven." He was gone in a moment, leaving us on the street.

I was glad to have a restful day. We had travelled far over the previous three and I was still doubtful whether we were on the right track. I trusted Holmes's judgement, of course, but he was not certain we were getting any closer to Major Wilkes and the scarred man. We could but wait to see if any sign of the missing boat was found. Meanwhile, the hotel lounge was comfortable, even the coffee was tolerable and they had English newspapers which were only a day old.

But our rest was soon disturbed.

"Gentlemen! I hoped I would find you here. You are feeling rested now? Good, it is a comfortable hotel." It was Count von Altmark. He sat down at our table. "I am sorry to intrude upon you once more, but I am concerned about you. May I speak plainly and confidentially? Good. On my way here for a morning coffee I saw you taking a walk with Johnny Brunt."

"He met us yesterday," said Holmes.

"Did he indeed? I suppose it is no surprise, not much happens in Rotterdam without him getting to hear of it. A charming man, good company."

"You know him as well?" I asked.

"We are a small community of foreigners adrift in

this city. Yes, we all know each other. I have had some pleasant evenings in other bars across the city with Johnny, a most entertaining fellow. But – and I dislike speaking ill of any man, but my respect for you forces my hand – you cannot believe anything he says."

"No?"

"Really not. A fantasist and a liar. He pretends to be an English gentleman but he grew up in a rough part of Chicago. Before the war he made his living as a con man using the name Grover Ponti. He duped all sorts of people in America. His career peaked when he managed to embezzle thousands from the First National Bank of Brooklyn. The bank hushed it up to avoid scandal but they knew who had robbed them. He had to get out of America after that so he came to Europe, called himself Johnny Brunt, acquired an English accent and carried on, swindling and cheating. Then, since the war started, he has branched out. He seeks and sells secrets and information to anyone who will pay. A most entertaining but most dangerous man."

Holmes sipped his coffee and signalled to the waiter for more. "That is most interesting, Count. He did claim a connection with British Intelligence."

"Ah, yes, that is a line he uses. For all I know, he does work for them, or he may have done. He would take work from anyone and just as quickly betray them to anyone else who paid better. By all means, enjoy his company. But do not trust him."

He left us and I waited for Holmes to speak. He smoked a pipe and drank more coffee. "We have made some interesting acquaintances in our short time in this country."

"Holmes, if you want to know what I think," Holmes gave a nod so I continued, "I think it's a damned impertinence for a German to tell us his tales about Brunt. Brunt knew we were on that boat from Harwich. He knew the names Wilkes and Hamer-Jenks. He hasn't been told that Wilkes is missing but he knows we are looking for someone with valuable information. I would not expect London to tell him more than that. How could he know all he does unless he is a genuine British agent?"

"How indeed," agreed Holmes.

We were not expecting Brunt until our dinner engagement but he bounded into the hotel lounge just after three o'clock. "Gentlemen!" he said, struggling to control his excitement and keep his voice to a whisper. "She is found! I would rather not talk here; can we resume our walk?"

I understood his desire to get away from other ears, but the day had clouded over and a steady drizzle was falling. Luckily, Brunt's report was made before the damp had fully seeped through my clothing. Anyway, his news made me forget about the chill damp weather.

"Peggotty's Pride arrived early on Tuesday. She's beached at a place called – oh, I really can't do some of these Dutch names." He showed us a notepad with the name of the beach, which was written 'Strand Wassenaarseslag'. "Two men reported to the police station a little way inland and registered themselves as non-combatants." He looked at our expressions – pleased and relieved. "I assume that the object of your search is one or both of these men?"

"A reasonable assumption in the circumstances," admitted Holmes. "So can you tell us where these two men are now?"

The toothy smile faded. "Ah, sorry Mr Holmes, that's where it gets complicated."

"Perhaps if you were to explain the complications?"

Brunt lit a cigarette. "Well, gents, as I've said before, the Dutch have to play a very tricky game, being neutral. They know there are British spies in their country. Plus Belgian spies and French spies, although the French service tend to focus on Spain and Switzerland as their neutrals, while we take the lead on Holland and the Nordic countries. There's a fair horde of Germans operating here too."

It seemed obvious as soon as he said it but it had not occurred to me that anyone we passed in the street could be a German agent. "Do you know who they are?"

The smile returned. "Of course! Most of them anyway. But, as I say, the Dutch know what's going on and they're a pragmatic people. So long as we keep to the rules, it's live and let live."

"What are the rules?"

"Mainly, of course, to obey Dutch law. In particular, no violence against the other camp, not even the threat of violence, or you can expect several years locked up. There's a few Huns here whose throats could do with slitting but we just can't."

"Would Count von Altmark be among that number?" asked Holmes.

Brunt stopped in his tracks. "Most certainly. I would

place him at the top of the list. How is it that you know that infamous name?"

"He recognised us in the hotel last night and introduced himself."

Brunt began walking again, slowly, before saying, "That is regrettable. He is a cunning and dangerous man. I would rather he knew nothing of your presence here. You didn't tell him anything, did you?"

"I confess I fabricated a tale of wishing to aid British internees. What can you tell us about him?"

Brunt walked a few more paces before asking, "Your old foe; Professor Moriarty. How did you describe him? The Napoleon of crime, that was it. I would describe the Count von Altmark as the Napoleon of the German secret service in Holland. He sits at the heart of a dark web of agents and informers, collecting information, dispensing lies, creating fear and confusion. If there was one man I would wish to remove, one man whose activities here I would wish to end, it would be Count von Altmark. I did not know he frequents the Coomans Hotel or I never would have taken you there. Oh, if only we had sorted out some disguises for you! You are famous, among much else Mr Holmes, for being able to transform your appearance. Still, the damage is done and we must limit it. I suggest we move you to a different hotel."

"Thank you, Mr Brunt. I am hopeful that our pursuit of Peggotty's Pride might lead us to leave Rotterdam entirely. I must ask how you have been able to learn of the boat's arrival?"

Brunt gave his grin with a small 'ha' of amusement. "Well, we're not completely idle here, you know. The first rule the Dutch give us is to keep within their laws, as I said. The second is to tell the Dutch service everything we learn about the Germans."

"And do you?"

"Yes, why not? We decided early on to be their friends and tell them all we know. Well, maybe not all, but..."

"And do they expect the Germans to tell them everything they learn about the Allied side?" I had to ask.

"Of course, but they are not happy about that, and they show it. It's all part of our plan of keeping cosy with the Dutch while trying to freeze Herr Boche out. It's helped us build a good way of working with our friends in Dutch intelligence. That's how I was able to meet you at the dockside and how I heard about the discovery of Peggotty's Pride. But your travellers from England reported to the police. They're a different kettle of fish. We have some good contacts, but not in a village like Wassenaar. Once the two fellows surrendered themselves as non-combatants, technically they became illegal aliens. They will need to keep the police informed of their movements but the police have no reason to tell the Dutch secret service, let alone the British secret service, who they are or where they have gone."

We walked on for a few minutes, Holmes deep in thought, Brunt watching him closely and my mind reeling at the thought of all these friendly and enemy agents mingling in a neutral country, all trying to play tricks on each other, tricks which could cost or save the lives of thousands of people. Finally Holmes spoke.

"It is a relief to know we were right to follow our quarry to Holland. It may not be their final destination; it could just be on the route they are taking." We walked on a few more paces. "Mr Brunt, can you take us to meet these police officers at... at the Dutch town you mentioned?"

He thought for a moment. "It's probably about half an hour's drive. Petrol's jolly hard to get hold of, we're supposed to be very careful." He looked at us, then at his watch. "Oh, what the hell. I don't know when the police change shift but if we set off now we should get there before five so it will probably be the same lot on duty."

"Mr Brunt," said Holmes, "You have our gratitude. We are ready to go."

Closing in

Minutes later we were on the road north. Brunt pointed out a building not far from the hotel, which he said was his office and that we could always locate him by asking for him there. Once we were out of Rotterdam, driving through the flat and neatly ordered villages and countryside of Holland, I felt I was in a country at peace for the first time in almost two years. The air seemed to smell sweeter and, despite signs of economic hardship, you could not fail to notice the sense of calm and safety that has been absent from England since this war began. I very much hope that future readers of this account, if there ever are any, will not know what it is to awake every morning and remember that your country is embroiled in a terrible war, with hope and fear balanced for control of your mind every time you buy a newspaper or when someone says, 'Have you heard the news?'

In a little under an hour we arrived at the police station in the neatly ordered town of Wassenaar. At first, Brunt felt he should not accompany us inside, as the presence of a British agent might prejudice the police against our little party, and he said he was not willing to pretend to be anything other than what he was. But Holmes and I know no Dutch and it seemed unlikely that any Dutch policemen in a small town would have good English, so Holmes persuaded him to come inside with us to translate.

We entered the building and strode up to the desk. Holmes gave a warm smile to the officer on duty, who looked up with a bored expression. "Good afternoon. My name is Sherlock Holmes. I am an English detective. These are my friends and colleagues Doctor Watson and Mr Brunt. Do you happen to speak English?"

The look of boredom was replaced with a look of astonishment. "Holmes? Watson?" He spoke some Dutch, which made Brunt laugh and they exchanged a few sentences in that strange language.

Brunt translated, "This is Officer Brouwhuis. He says he only joined the police because he loved the stories of Holmes and Watson when he was a boy." The Dutchman came from around his desk and shook our hands, beaming, while chattering away in his native tongue. Brunt continued with his interpretation: "He's explaining which are his favourite stories, says he knows each one, Hound of the Baskervilles is his favourite, he's delighted to welcome you to his country, he can't believe it's really you, he always thinks of you as young, active men but says of course you will be old by now. He says he took his wife to London on their honeymoon ten years ago and he made her walk around all sorts of places associated with your adventures. He has a picture of them both outside 221B Baker Street. He's asking if you will come to his house for dinner and meet his wife and daughters. He says one of them is called Irene."

"Mr Brunt, please thank Officer Brouwhuis for us and explain that we are here on a case. We understand he cannot give the names and destinations of the two men who surrendered themselves here on Monday, but that I have a proposal which I hope he will find acceptable."

Brunt translated, Brouwhuis became serious and indicated that he was ready to hear what Holmes proposed. "You know the names they have given, and the addresses where they have said they will be residing?"

Brunt translated the question and the Dutchman nodded.

"Can the officer at least tell us the name of a major town, close to where they intend to stay?"

They exchanged some Dutch and Brunt gave us the conversation in English. "He's made a lot of apologies about not being able to give us all the details but he's not supposed to. Helping you on a case is a dream for him and he would very much like to tell you everything. He feels he can tell you the town they said they were heading for. It's Breda. That's south of Rotterdam."

Holmes smiled and clapped the police officer on the shoulder. "Tell him I understand that he cannot tell us more. In fact, I respect him for keeping to his rules. Indeed, tell him that we ask him to keep our presence in his country to himself." Once Brunt had translated this,

Holmes asked, "Do either of you know of an hotel in Breda? I believe Watson and I need to find a local base of operations." They didn't, but after some discussion and reference to a telephone directory they were able to suggest the Hotel Mastbosch.

Holmes sat on a bench and wrote a letter. He handed it to the police officer and, via Brunt, asked him to post it to the address given by the two men who arrived from England. He also agreed to write and sign a further note, which read 'To Officer Raymond Brouwhuis, with my thanks for your valuable assistance – Sherlock Holmes, April 1916'.

Having politely refused the invitation to dinner, citing the need to keep our visit private, we returned to Rotterdam. "The letter will not arrive until tomorrow morning at the earliest. We can spend one more night here and decamp to Breda in the morning."

"What did your letter say?"

"It is an invitation to meet us. I have said we will be available at the Hotel Mastbosch every evening at six o'clock for one week, if Major Wilkes would do us the honour of paying a visit."

"Do you think he will come?" I realized it was a foolish question as I asked it.

"I believe so. I told him what I know, or at least suspect, about the reasons for his journey. I have given him certain assurances and communicated the desires of his colleagues to know his intentions. Yes, I think there is every reason for optimism that our quest will end at Breda."

I was glad to get an early night before resuming our travels. Unfortunately, I made the mistake of having a coffee after dinner. Dutch coffee is rather strong and I think that it contributed to a bout of indigestion that kept me awake for much of the night.

In the morning we left the Grand Hotel Coomans and Holmes gave the Hotel Mastbosch as our forwarding address. Brunt was good enough to drive us to Breda and left us at the hotel. "So sorry, gents, would love to stay with you but there are plots to plot and schemes to scheme!" The broad toothy grin was on show. "Now, sorry to remind you, sure you don't need it, but we want to keep your presence here secret."

The Hotel Mastbosch is a striking building. I suppose you would call it High Victorian Gothic, built with red brick, white stone, tall windows and a looming central tower. It sits between the town centre and a vast forest, once the hunting ground of princes and poachers and, it occurred to me, now the hunting ground of two elderly English travellers. I was still not sure what we were hunting: a traitor or a prisoner?

Inside, the hotel was comfortable and we were made welcome but Holmes seemed alive with energy. First, he wanted to inspect all the sitting and dining rooms available for public hire. Having settled on the main dining room, he got the staff busy erecting screens to hide one corner of the room from the rest. I knew he was concerned for our secrecy but he made the staff get more screens out of the hotel cellar and erect a bizarre labyrinth leading to and concealing our corner. The staff were bemused by the eccentric old

Englishman arranging his little maze but generous tips smoothed any annoyance.

All this effort struck me as over-elaborate, especially since the dining room had windows all the way around it. Sitting at our table by the arrangement of screens, we were well hidden from the rest of the restaurant but on full display to anyone passing the hotel on the street. Holmes then destroyed any hope of our presence in Breda remaining a secret by telling the staff that any visitors requiring Mr Holmes and Doctor Watson should be directed to our corner. I asked Holmes why he had given our real names.

"If Major Wilkes comes, he will need to ask for me."

"You should have given him false names to ask for. We could have checked in under those names and no one else would know we were here."

"A good idea, Watson. But it is too late now."

"And why erect all these screens when we are sitting in the window, on display like mannequins in an Oxford Street store? Can I ask them to draw the blinds?"

"No, do not trouble yourself, Watson. We have said we will be available to Major Wilkes at six o'clock in the evenings. If he has not arrived by seven we can retire for the night, and it still will not be dark enough to warrant closed blinds."

I didn't know whether to be exasperated, amused or worried by this strange mix of secrecy and openness. I had to assume that Holmes had taken the precautions he felt were necessary and did not think it necessary to take more.

It was only early afternoon, yet I found myself

weary, so I suggested we take a rest before establishing ourselves in our place. Holmes agreed that I should take a rest as he might need me fully alert that evening. He, however, wanted to stretch his legs and see something of the town.

We met at our specially created rendezvous at six o'clock. Holmes had instructed the hotel to wire a telephone set to our table, presumably in case Major Wilkes telephoned for us, but we had no visitors that evening. Instead, we enjoyed a good dinner and a restful night's sleep. The next day we walked in the forest and were again established in our corner at six o'clock in hope of a visit. This time we were not disappointed. Two men, one old and solemn, the other young and scarred, appeared at the space between the screens.

"Good evening, Mr Holmes, Doctor Watson. My name is Percy Wilkes and this is my son. Thank you for your invitation. It arrived this morning and, I have to say, relieved me greatly."

The family saga

Holmes invited the two men to join us at our table. Once they had settled, Holmes asked the younger man, "You are Mr Gerald Farmer, I believe?"

"That is correct," said the young man. "How do you know my name?"

"We can come to that," said Holmes. "But first I would wish to know your story, Major Wilkes. Your colleagues are most concerned about your whereabouts."

"Yes," replied the older man. "I have been worried

about what my colleagues must be thinking. I know I need to tell them what has become of me but I could not think what to say or where to start."

"Please start at the beginning, Major Wilkes," said Holmes.

"Oh, you can't call me Major anymore. I've deserted my post. Abandoned my country. But I had to come here, I had to help young Gerald for the sake of Annemie."

"Your Annemie?"

"Well, yes, that's – why do you say that?"

"Your son was overheard. Or rather misheard. Your neighbour, Mr Newland, thought you had said 'You have to do this for your enemy'. I think, Mr Farmer, you said 'You have to do this for your Annemie'?"

"My mother. My birth mother," said the young man. He spoke with an accent I recognised as that of the South African Cape.

"The only person I ever loved," said Wilkes, "and I disgraced her. I didn't know, I never understood until last Monday."

He became somewhat emotional, so the younger man gave his story first. "I was brought up by a Doctor and Mrs Farmer in Cape Town. Better parents I couldn't hope for. I always knew I was adopted. They told me my mother was dead. They did not know about my father but we all assumed he must have died as well. The fact that I was adopted was unimportant. We were a happy family and I had an idyllic childhood. My father, that is, Doctor Farmer, died four years ago while I was still at school, at the South African College. I was still there when I turned eighteen last June. Well, all my chums were joining up. There were a few months of training, then we were kept in reserve for the campaign in German East Africa. Then, just a few weeks ago, we were told to prepare to sail. My lot were to be part of the South African Overseas Expeditionary Force, to fight in France."

"We were given two days of leave to see our families before we sailed. I went to see my mother, that is, Mrs Farmer. I thought I was bringing bad news about sailing to France but she had worse news. Cancer. Incurable, of course. We knew those two days would be our last together. She came into our sitting room with a small dusty package. She said it was my mother's papers. She had never opened them and she wanted me to have them before I 'went off to war,' as she put it." He stopped to light a cigarette.

"Is that a State Express?" I asked. He looked at me with some surprise.

"No, I bought some of those in London. Horrible, threw them away. This is some Dutch brand. They are not much better. Anyway, for the first time in my life I could read my birth mother's papers. All your letters are here, father, as you know," said the younger man to the older as he took from his inside pocket a long, fat envelope. "You wrote to her for months after you left for England, your letters becoming increasingly desperate. But the church organization that took her in did not let her reply. Their view was that she had been abandoned and it was best not to contact you. The Dutch Reformed Church, I suppose they meant well, but they are very strict." I noticed the long fingers of his left hand had started to play with the tassel on a cushion on his seat.

"If I had only known! Known about you, Gerald," said Wilkes. "I would have abandoned university and gone back to South Africa right away. We would have got married. We had talked about marriage after I graduated. But my letters got no reply so I assumed Annemie had changed her mind. I abandoned all ideas of returning to Africa and decided I would never marry."

"You mentioned the Dutch Reformed Church," said Holmes, "and her name is Dutch. So she was a Boer. I almost fear to ask this, but what became of her?"

"I think you must have guessed," said Mr Farmer. "When the Boer War started, the British concentrated Boers in camps. At first, they said it was to provide refuge for families displaced by the war. But soon, all civilians were interned in the camps to prevent them from helping or resupplying the Boer fighters. Tens of thousands of women and children were rounded up and imprisoned."

I had heard of this scandal. "Not a glorious episode in our history," I said.

Farmer continued. "Then you know. Conditions were terrible, disease was rife and rations were poor. Thousands died. My mother was one of them."

While his father cried softly, Farmer continued. "There was a Scottish doctor working at the camp. He arranged for me to be adopted by a doctor he knew in Cape Town. That was Doctor Farmer, my adopted father. As I have said, I had a good life with them. Until my adopted mother gave me the papers of my birth mother, I had no idea she was a Boer. I had assumed I was British South African, like everyone else I knew. I was proud to join their army and wear their uniform."

"Your mother's papers caused you to change your mind," said Holmes.

"Of course they did. I read them again and again on the long voyage to Southampton. I was wearing the uniform of the army that had forced my mother into a terrible camp where she had died. The sea journey was terrible, I was very ill all the way. I could not eat and lost so much weight that they put me in a hospital when I arrived, where I picked up a terrible cold. Coming from South Africa, I don't seem to have much ability to fight off your northern illnesses and I was in a weak state already. Once I had enough strength I simply left the hospital and came to London. I now knew the name of my real father and it was not hard to find him. I explained my story and my situation. I was a deserter. I could not stay in England and I would not be safe in South Africa either, even if there was any way to get there, even if there was still anyone there waiting for me. My father here decided that the only course of action was to help me reach a neutral country – the country of my mother's ancestors. We came to a town near here as my mother's papers included a line where she said she thought her family came from this area. We have not yet found anyone who could be my relation but it has only been a couple of days. Either way, we will sit out the war and then decide where to go and what to do."

"Luckily I have money," said Wilkes. He had recovered enough to speak. "I was stunned when Gerald came to my flat in London. I did not even know he existed. I knew I had to get him away from this awful war. I had two younger brothers you know, both dead now, killed. Gerald is my only living relative and the son of the only person I loved. You will condemn me for deserting my post and my country. I have no regret."

There was silence for a time before Holmes said, "Your former colleagues are most anxious to know what has become of you. I understand you have information which would be of great use to the enemy."

"Yes, and I have been worried about that. I may have abandoned my country but I wish it no harm. I have been thinking, since I decided to leave on Monday, that I need to tell them that their secrets are safe. But what was I to say?"

"Perhaps you may leave that with me. If I can assure them that you have no intention of releasing any confidential material, I think it might save a great deal of anxiety and avoid actions based on the worst assumptions of what may have become of you. However, perhaps you could indulge my curiosity. What are these precious secrets you hold?"

"Really, Holmes, we can't ask that!" I was indignant. Holmes waved me down.

"My friend the good doctor is right, I should not ask, but I cannot resist. Could you just tell me what your precious information is about?"

Wilkes looked at Holmes for a moment. "As you have agreed to help me out, I think I can tell you, so long as you never let it be known."

Holmes repeated our well-practised script about wartime confidentiality.

"In that case, and without going into detail, the German government and its armed forces use several codes for their confidential messages. We have had some success in breaking some of these codes – in other words, we can decrypt them and read the messages. Other codes are harder to break and some have resisted all our attempts. If the Germans knew how well we were doing against each of their coding systems, why, they would simply stop using the ones we can break and switch to using only the strong ones. We don't want that."

"Thank you. I think I have heard enough." From behind one of the screens emerged Count von Altmark, pointing a gun at us. "Mr Holmes, I told you I had never had a crowning achievement to my career. Now, finally, I have and what an historic achievement is it. I have outsmarted the great Mr Sherlock Holmes and I shall bring to my country a British spy who will give them valuable information about how far the British have penetrated our codes."

"I don't know who you are," said Wilkes, "but I can assure you I will not be going anywhere with you. You had better fire your gun and be done with it."

"I thought you might say that," said the Count. He turned his weapon slightly so that it pointed directly into the scarred face of Mr Farmer. "But I, in turn, assure you that I will shoot your son right now unless you agree that both of you will come with me. There is a crossing point I use near Nijmegen. We will be in Germany in time for a late dinner. I promise you that you will be perfectly safe there provided you co-operate. You must understand that a German victory in this war is certain. By helping to bring it about sooner, you will save thousands of lives. Mr Holmes, Doctor Watson, you will have to come with us for the journey so you cannot raise the alarm. You need not cross into Germany though; I will release you at the crossing."

"You will have to shoot me before I take one step under your direction," I exclaimed.

"There will be no need for that," said Holmes, who was infuriatingly calm.

"Indeed there will not!" It was Brunt, who had suddenly appeared from somewhere in the labyrinth of screens and immediately had his revolver against the Count's temple. "Lower your weapon, Count." He seemed to have adopted an American accent.

"Mr Brunt!" I said, "What a relief! You have arrived at the perfect moment. But why are you speaking with that accent?"

The Count lowered his weapon and looked at me furiously. "That is his accent. I told you, he is from Chicago." He turned to look at Brunt, which meant the grinning man's weapon was pointed right into his eyes. "You have no business here, Brunt. You're not an official agent of the German government. You're just a pirate. Clear off, you ruffian, you cad."

Brunt's grin got even wider. "'N' informed me as well as you that Sherlock Holmes was sailing to Holland. I have as much right to this chase as you do. Drop your gun and sit down with the others, Count."

The Count did not move. "I know you never keep rounds in that weapon, Brunt."

"You're looking at the cylinder, Count. What do you see?" He pulled the hammer back with his thumb. The Count must have been able to see rounds in the cylinder as let his gun drop to the floor and came to sit with us.

"Brunt, what is going on? What is 'N'? Who are you, and whose side are you on?" I asked.

"I am sorry Doctor Watson, Mr Holmes. I have rather misled you. Since you ask, 'N' is *Nachrichten-Abteilung im Admiraltstab* – German naval intelligence. They decoded the message from Harwich to say you were on your way and invited me to investigate your visit. It seems they asked the Count to do the same. Maybe they asked others. They sometimes like to make us compete. I got to you first. I really did want to help you find what you were looking for."

"Only because he thought there might be money in it," said the Count. "I told you, this man cannot be trusted. To answer the last of your questions, Doctor Watson, he is on his own side. Johnny, I was here first, this is my victory."

"I know you were here first. I saw you enter the hotel. I was hiding among the trees across the road. I even watched you creep across the dining room and take up your position among the screens before I left my place and crept in after you, hiding behind the screen across from yours. Like you, I have heard everything. But really, Count, attempting to kidnap Sherlock Holmes? Attempting to smuggle into Germany people you had illegally taken prisoner? The Dutch would give you ten years for that."

"You're the one threatening us with a loaded weapon, Johnny," said the Count. "And I assume you plan to do the same?"

"Not at all. Kidnapping, secret border crossings, people travelling at gunpoint? So unnecessary, so elaborate, so foolish. No, I simply require Major Wilkes to tell me which German codes and cyphers the British can read and which they cannot. Then I can leave you all in peace while I run along to sell the information. The only intention I share with the Count's plan is, I am afraid, the promise to kill your son right now if you do not tell me what I need to know."

"I am sure we can bring this matter to a conclusion without the need to discharge any firearms," said Holmes, with another infuriating smile. "If you could answer one question of mine, Mr Brunt, then I can promise that you will be on your way very soon. It appears that German naval intelligence knew that Watson and I were on a boat from Harwich but did not know why. Is that correct?"

"Since you ask, that's correct. You see..." said Brunt, but before he could continue, the Count shouted, "Be quiet you fool!"

Holmes smiled. "I believe I have all I need." He leant over to the telephone set. "I think now, Captain van Eik." There was a shout, a stampede of boots and suddenly our little enclave was filled with Dutch policemen. Brunt was disarmed and he and the Count were in handcuffs before I had grasped what was going on. Last to enter the area was a distinguished looking man, tall even by Dutch standards, dressed in what was clearly the uniform of a senior police officer. "Gentlemen, allow me to introduce Captain van Eik of the Breda police. I made his acquaintance on the afternoon we arrived in this town and explained that two foreign agents were likely to commit serious crimes under Dutch law, in his domain, very soon."

The Captain spoke excellent English as he shook hands with me, Major Wilkes and Mr Farmer. "Welcome to Breda gentlemen. I hope you are not too shaken by this episode?" Wilkes and Farmer were staring at him in utter astonishment, with their mouths hanging open. I realized I must have been looking as stunned as they were, and closed my mouth abruptly.

The Captain continued, "Count von Altmark, Mr Johnny Brunt, you are under arrest."

Brunt simply looked crestfallen but the Count was livid. "I will have you for this, Holmes! And you Brunt, you fool, you have wrecked everything. And you, you grinning Dutchman, you will learn what happens when the people of a tiny nation dare to interfere with Germany! We will come for you all one of these days, you remember this, you say you are neutral but we know what you do. One day, you will pay for opposing us!" He was still raving as they led him away in handcuffs.

The town with three names

The police left, taking their captives with them. I felt I was in a race, far, far behind the leaders. It was a familiar sensation. I had so many questions that I did not know where to start. I think Wilkes and Farmer were just as bewildered as I was. However, it was Holmes who asked the first question.

"Mr Farmer. If you don't mind my asking, how did you get your scar?"

The young man seemed to jump out of a reverie. "Oh, that? Yes, I have been told it makes me look quite sinister. I fell off a horse when I was fifteen. My fault entirely. I have a question for you, Mr Holmes. How did you know my name?"

"I used my contacts to see if any South African soldiers, recently arrived in England, were absent without leave. There were not many, as you would expect. Yours was the only name I was given. Now, one matter remains: how are we to get our news to London as quickly as possible? Watson, I think we must return to Rotterdam and see if we can locate a genuine British agent."

"There is a quicker way," said Wilkes. "I almost used it myself but, on top of my worries about what to say, I thought I might be at risk of arrest if I entered Belgian territory."

This idea surprised me. "Why, yes, if you entered occupied Belgium the Germans would certainly arrest you. Why did you think you could contact London from there?"

"Not occupied Belgium, Doctor Watson. As well as the thin slice of the country at its eastern end, around Ypres, that is in Allied control, there are some fragments of Belgium surrounded by Dutch territory that remain free. The town is called Baer-le-Duc, or Baarle-Hertog to the local Flemish, although the Dutch call their part of the town Baarle-Nassau."

This sounded very complicated and so it proved to be. The Treaty of Maastricht, in 1843, settled the border between Belgium and the Netherlands. But disputes could only be resolved by breaking the land in and around this town that seems to have three different names into many little parcels of Belgium surrounded by Holland. Some of the pieces of Belgium are no bigger than a single field while others contain little pieces of

Dutch territory entirely within them. The border runs through streets and buildings. Many houses straddle the two countries.

These fragments of Belgian territory are surrounded by Dutch territory, meaning the German army could not occupy them. They remain free and the Allies have a wireless transmission station there. Wilkes explained it was only about a half an hour's drive from where we sat.

A short time later I was driving southeast out of Breda, with Holmes reading the map beside me. We had left the father and son to return to their home. We still did not know where that was, but they had given Holmes a means to contact them in case it ever became necessary. Once again, I found the sense of driving through the countryside of a nation at peace, especially as the evening drew on, deeply affecting. I was able to assess how far I had been able to catch up with events. Holmes had set a trap. That was why he gave a forwarding address in Rotterdam and used our real names in Breda. That was why we had all the fuss with the screens, to allow two hiding places. The telephone, I had learned, was wired on a closed circuit to another in the hotel manager's office, where Captain van Eik was listening. I decided to start with him.

"It was good of Captain van Eik to let us borrow Brunt's car."

"Brunt won't be needing it for many years. Both he and the Count will be unable to play their games and trade secrets from prison."

"So it is double congratulations, Holmes. Not only

have you solved the mystery of the absent spy, you have also removed two German agents from business."

"Without wishing to flatter myself, there is a third element. I have learned that the Germans can decipher the code used at Harwich but were not able to understand any later messages about this matter."

"So we have learned the very information about the Germans that they were hoping to learn about our side?"

"A little of it, perhaps."

We drove on a little further before my next question. "If the message from Harwich was meant for British agents in Holland, and intercepted by the Germans, why did no British agents attempt to contact us? Why have we encountered only German agents?"

"Maybe the British did try. As Brunt said, he got to us first. Maybe they have more pressing matters and a shortage of men. Or perhaps they are searching Rotterdam as we speak."

This did not fill me with confidence. We drove through a small village called Chaam where children ran out of their houses to watch the car go past. As we left the village, another question occurred to me.

"I can see why you suspected the Count. What set you on the trail of Brunt? He seemed a decent chap."

"It was the Count who made me increase my doubts about Brunt. I think the only time either of them told us a word of truth was when each was talking about the other. I had noticed the way Brunt watched us as he spoke, trying to read from our faces when he was on the right track and when he had wandered off. He had picked up some knowledge of the British Secret Service, which may not have been hard for a practised confidence trickster in a city like Rotterdam. Of course, I knew of the theft from the First National Bank of Brooklyn by Grover Ponti, who then vanished. Brunt fitted the description and was the right age. When Count von Altmark mentioned that crime, the pieces came together. I was not entirely sure if Brunt was Ponti, which was why I led him into the same trap as the Count.

My thoughts turned to the father and son we had just left.

"You put Wilkes and Farmer in danger, arranging for them to be confronted by our enemies. Was there no way to trap the Count and Brunt without risking one of them being shot?"

"I did not think our adversaries would take the risk of exposing themselves unless there was much to be gained. I had to let them hear what Wilkes' great secret was. There was an element of risk but we had armed Dutch officials standing by."

"I don't know about those two, Holmes – Wilkes and Farmer, I mean. Their story is very sad but they are deserters. They have broken the law."

"They have broken no Dutch law, so far as we know. Even if they had, we are here in no official capacity. I share your concerns but I, who have never been to war, am in less of a position to judge them than you, who have faced enemy fire. Do you condemn their actions?"

I had some sympathy for Farmer. Who would want to wear the uniform of an army that had interned his mother and allowed her to die of their neglect? But

Wilkes? I can see why he wanted to help his son. But this war is demanding sacrifices from so many, why should Wilkes be excused?

By eight o'clock we had arrived at the Allied wireless station in Baarle-Hertog. At first, we could not make ourselves understood to the Belgian soldiers manning the station, but they roused a liaison officer who was supposed to be off duty. This turned out to be Lieutenant Lindsay, from New Zealand originally, but here as he had a Belgian mother (and an Ulsterman father). He explained that the station did not allow visitors. But once Holmes had introduced himself and said a little of our mission, he showed his practical and friendly antipodean style by waving his hand to show all rules were cancelled. He was only too happy to help us. He told us that the Germans were less than two miles away, in the main body of Belgium, and that they kept a field glass on the building all the time. I shuddered to think of them, so close, watching me.

Holmes wrote a message to Lieutenant Hamer-Jenks: 'We have located your goods and I can give you my personal assurance that all is intact. You have nothing to worry about.' I thought that cryptic enough but Lindsay put it into code before transmitting it.

"That should bring some sighs of relief in London," said Holmes. "We can tell them the rest of our news when we return there. Lieutenant Lindsay, you have my thanks. Watson, I believe we should return the car we have borrowed. If we leave now, waving to the German observers on the hill as we go, we should be back at the Hotel Mastbosch in time for dinner."

THE PICKVALE HALL MYSTERY

Death of a teacher

"My word – it says here that my geography teacher has been killed."

I looked up from my lunch and across a couple of trestle tables to where Wensome, a Corporal of the Royal Leicestershire Regiment, was reading a newspaper. I had been avoiding the news lately as I found it disturbing to read of endless battles, sinkings and executions. Even when the news was presented as something to celebrate, I had my doubts. Had Jutland really been a victory, despite all those losses? The French were holding on at Verdun, but at what terrible cost? We were all waiting for the start of our 'big push', which was meant to end the war by the autumn but it had still not begun. Meanwhile the slaughter continued. I left my bread and jam and walked round to where Wensome was still staring at his copy of The Times.

"Sorry to hear that, old man," I said. "Where did it

happen? Ypres? France? Palestine?"

He looked up at me. "No, Doctor Watson, he wasn't killed in action. No offense, but he would have been almost as old as you. Well, perhaps not. Fifty, anyway. It seems he's been murdered, back in Leicestershire, near my old school. Nothing to do with the war. More in the line of your famous friend Mr Holmes."

I sat down beside him and watched his young face, which bore scars but no longer the bandages which had covered much of it until recently. "I suppose that's worse. We've come to expect death from fighting but it must be hard for you to lose someone in that way."

He turned the page of his newspaper. "Doesn't bother me. I hated him, hated all the teachers, Pickvale Hall was an awful school, got me nowhere and I hated every minute of my time there." He continued reading and I returned to my lunch, reflecting on how the war seemed to have turned so many young men into hard, heartless creatures. I am sure that, before the war, he would have been dreadfully saddened at the murder of an old teacher, even one whom he did not like.

It was June 1916 and I was at Challis House, the auxiliary hospital in the northwest of London where I had established myself 'for the duration' and tried to make myself useful by helping the staff and the patients, all wounded men, with whatever little services I could provide. I had also made modest contributions to the war effort in recent months through two trips abroad. These had been adventures with my friend Sherlock Holmes. Despite our advancing years and everything that goes with that – the aches and pains, the slowing of speed and the even greater slowing of recovery from any exertion – we had been able to end the activities of several spies and secret agents, solve the mystery (and consequent anxieties in Whitehall) about a British agent who went missing and, upon our return to England, Holmes had been able to give an insight to the authorities about the extent of German success in decrypting the cyphers used for our wireless communications. Holmes later returned to Holland to be a witness in the trials of the agents he had helped the Dutch police to capture while I had returned to my life at Challis House, recovering from our adventures and writing my accounts of them. I have to keep my notes, drafts and final fair copies locked in a cabinet as they cannot be made public for many years; perhaps not ever.

The same may be true of the adventure which, although I did not know it then, had already begun.

It was later that day, Tuesday the 13th, when I received a telephone call from Holmes. As was usual, he did not give his name on the telephone as operators often listen in to calls, either seeking gossip or just to alleviate the boredom of their profession. He asked if I had heard of the murder of a schoolteacher in Leicestershire.

"Yes, one of our patients saw it in today's paper. He had been a pupil at the school and knew the murdered man."

"Excellent," said Holmes, which struck me as a response which would have been wholly inappropriate coming from anyone else in the circumstances. "They are advertising for the post of science teacher at the school and I want you to apply."

"Steady on! I can't work as a science teacher. I... and do you mean they are seeking a replacement for the murdered man so quickly?"

"No, the first victim taught geography and art."

"So why are they seeking a science master? Just a moment, did you say the 'first victim'?"

"Yes, there has been another killing. A Mr Bushey, the French teacher. I heard about it only an hour ago in Scotland Yard."

"Scotland Yard? What were you doing there? I thought you were in The Hague, at the trials of Count von Altmark and Johnny Brunt?"

"Completed. Ten years each, and Brunt will probably be extradited to the United States after he has completed his sentence."

It seemed that every answer Holmes gave to one of my questions generated yet more questions. It led to a telephone conversation of almost an hour. I have never spoken on the telephone for such a long period of time and I doubt that many people have. I shudder to think what the call cost Holmes but he did not seem concerned, even though we were interrupted several times by operators asking if we wanted the call to continue.

In summary, Holmes had stayed in Holland for the sentences to be handed down and then returned to London, where he had been asked to give briefings on anything useful revealed by the trials, both to the Admiralty and to Scotland Yard. It was while he was there that news reached the police in London of a second murder of a teacher at Pickvale Hall, a preparatory school in the north of the county of Leicestershire. Before the war, it would have been routine to dispatch an Inspector from London or another major metropolis to assist the local constabulary in such a matter, as they would have no experience of such crimes or of the modern methods of detection usually required to solve them and bring a conviction. But now the police are very short of men, as so many have exchanged their blue uniforms for a khaki one.

Having heard about the murders, Holmes offered to help but he was told that the local police had arrested a suspect for the first murder and claimed they knew who was responsible for the second; this suspect was being hunted but no description had been issued. The official police said they considered the matter closed. The second suspect would be apprehended in due course. There was no need and no manpower for Scotland Yard to get involved but they offered no objection when Holmes offered to look into the matter.

He went on to explain to me that Pickvale Hall had been without a science master for over a year, ever since the holder of that post had joined the army. He could not explain why they had only advertised the vacant position a fortnight earlier – before either murder. He wanted me to apply for this post as a means of gaining entry to the school where two of the staff had been killed in the past three days.

"But, look here, old friend," I said, careful to avoid using names, "it was one thing to help our country with those two matters that took us overseas recently. That was doing our bit. This is not the same at all. We've retired from all that. We don't have to go roaming around the land anymore, chasing clues and crooks. We're old men. Besides, you have been told that the local police have it all in hand. We should leave such matters for the official force. We should leave it to younger men."

"Doctor, I understand and I would not want either of us to exert ourselves once more if I was certain that these matters are closed and there is no danger remaining. But I am not convinced. If I am right, there is still a danger to the people at that school. The police are short of men; by helping them, are we not helping the national effort just as much as we did in recent weeks?"

I was not convinced. It even crossed my mind that Holmes wanted to investigate the murders for his own purposes. Perhaps the adventures in France and Holland had re-awakened his urge to work on criminal mysteries. Perhaps chemical research and beekeeping no longer had sufficient appeal. Besides, my work at Challis House, while not essential, was of use to the men there. We had recently admitted a number of British and Canadian men who had suffered greatly from gas attacks, as well as conventional weapons. I helped them in many small ways and knew I would be missed if I went off to Leicestershire on a wild goose chase.

As usual, Holmes had anticipated my thoughts. "My friend, you hesitate, and I understand why. I know you do valuable work where you are and you are reluctant to abandon your post. Most commendable. You also suspect that my motive is more one of vanity than a desire to seek justice for criminals and safety for future victims?"

I felt a little abashed, but he had described my thinking perfectly. I said nothing so he continued, "Doctor, I quite understand. You may even be correct; I have given some thought to my motives. Perhaps if a second person were to confirm my analysis that the danger is not passed? Meet me in London, first thing tomorrow, and let us see if we can have my anxieties about the situation confirmed, so that we may proceed with clear consciences."

"Tomorrow? So soon?"

"If I am right, there is little time to waste. Suppose there were another victim? Suppose there is an attack in progress as we speak?"

"Yes, yes, very well, I will come to London tomorrow. When and where shall we meet?"

"Under the clock at Waterloo Station. Bring things enough for a few days away, you can always return to your hospital immediately if you are not convinced that we are needed. How early can you arrive? Shall we say eight o'clock?"

It meant an early start but I agreed. Finally, Holmes asked me to find out whatever I could about Pickvale Hall school from the alumnus who was currently at Challis House. I replaced the telephone earpiece on the stand and went to find Wensome but he was not keen to discuss his former place of education.

"It's supposed to be a preparatory school but I don't know what it prepared us for. Being cold and living off poor food, I suppose. Even the army does better."

"What were the staff like? You said you did not like your teachers."

"Perhaps that was unfair, they were not all bad. Mr Turner, who taught us English, he was a kind and generous soul. I also liked Mr Yarding. He managed to get me to understand some maths, which is a jolly fine achievement, I have to say. Then old man Wheatfield, he never managed to teach me any German, which might actually have been useful as things have turned out, but I had some happy times in his woodworking shop."

"But you did not admire the remaining masters?"

"A lot of old fools and nasty, some of them. I was interested in drama but Mr Clearly, who taught that and history, supposedly, just shouted at us all through the rehearsals and would give you the cane if you forgot a line. I soon gave that up. He didn't know anything about history either. We joked he was given the job of teaching it to help him learn the subject. And, sorry to speak ill of the dead but Mr Dolman, the geography master who's died, well, we called him Dullman behind his back. Nothing to him. He barely bothered to teach us, just sat at the front while we were supposed to teach ourselves by reading the schoolbooks. I don't know if he was lazy or stupid or just had no interest in engaging with us. Perhaps he was all of those things. He only seemed to come to life when he had an excuse to take his cane to one of us. Mr Lighterman, the science teacher, was a strange cove too, although at least he wasn't actually cruel like Clearly and Dolman."

"Any others?"

"I've tried my best to forget them all. Let me see… yes, there was Mr Bushey, he was supposed to teach us French and was in charge of games. I learned more

French in my first leave behind the lines than I did from him in two years. He was like Clearly, always shouting at us. I was lucky, I was quite good at sports and games but he bullied anyone who was not and you could tell he enjoyed doing it. He was another one who was very quick to get out his cane. I can think of some boys who probably still have scars from his beatings."

"Wensome, I am sorry to have to tell you this, but it seems Mr Bushey has been killed as well."

"What? Another one? Also at the school?"

"I do not have any details. You have not said anything about the headmaster."

"Ah, the Reverend Daniel Smythe MA. That's how he always introduced himself to grownups. He gave me the creeping feeling. Some of the stories that went round about him! But I don't know. He taught us religion and I've never liked it since. He was like someone out of a Dickens novel, a man who preaches goodness and holiness but is nothing of the kind. Sorry doctor, I'm getting upset just thinking about him and his awful school. I'll wish you a good night."

We shook hands and he limped away.

A reunion

Waterloo Station the following morning was a hive of activity. Commuters were coming in from across the Southwest and flooding through the station towards their jobs in the City or the West End. Between the tides of bowler hats were streams of khaki caps as troops were led to trains that would take them to the channel ports for embarkation to France. Also, an ambulance train had just arrived, carrying wounded men back from the front. I noticed that these heroes were guided (or carried) out to the side entrance, onto York Road, mixed with men and women handling milk churns, sacks of flour and other produce being brought into the metropolis.

I was watching the crowds when Holmes took my arm and guided me in the same direction as the wounded, out to York Road and from there it was a short walk to St Thomas's Hospital. We were barely able to speak above the noise of all the people in the station, it was little quieter on the road among the walking wounded, ambulances, trucks, carts and crowds. It was even louder when we reached the hospital. The wounded men were being processed by exhausted doctors and nurses. Holmes led me past this scene of suffering and confusion further into the hospital, past a grand statue of Queen Victoria, and finally to a ward towards the southern end of the establishment where elderly men were receiving care for ailments that come with age rather than from fighting. At the far end of the ward lay a very old, very large man who seemed to be asleep, wearing a gas mask.

"It provides air enriched with additional oxygen," said Holmes, as he positioned screens around the man's bed. "They have developed this system for men who have suffered poison gas but it works for people with chronic respiratory disease." He rocked the large man's arm gently and said, "Hello. It's Sherlock. Are you awake? I need you."

The recognition came with a jolt. Mycroft Holmes, the brother of my great friend, lay before us. He was older than we were and had always carried a large, corpulent frame. His hair was lank and thin, and his skin had a touch of grey, but when he opened his eyes, they became clear and sharp on seeing us standing over him. He pulled the mask away to speak.

"Sherlock! And dear Doctor Watson. It is so good to see you." He gasped as he spoke but he held on to my hand after we had shaken. "I told them. I warned them. I could see it coming. Sherlock will confirm what I say. I keep thinking that we could have prevented it." He had to pause to catch his breath so his brother continued for him. "You will remember, Watson, that twenty years ago I told you that Mycroft was an essential component of the British government. Indeed, I think I said (just before we were able to help with the matter of the Bruce-Partington plans) that you would be right in a sense if you said that occasionally he *was* the British government."

"I remember. It is good to see you again, Mycroft. How are you?"

"Not well, alas. Age and a sedentary life have left their mark but worse is the tragedy that has swept over our beloved land. War! More terrible even than I imagined."

"You foresaw the war?" There had been predictions of a European war for years and many popular adventure stories had been published, before it began, based on an imagined future conflict.

"I could see it was possible, nay, likely. The great powers with alliances and divisions between them, tensions rising and, worst of all, the lack of restraint on the leaders of powerful nations. A despotic Tsar in Russia, an aging Emperor in Austria-Hungary, a paranoid Kaiser in Germany and no one to hold them in check.

Decent people were not allowed to question the autocrats. The outcome was inevitable. I warned them."

"Who did you warn?"

"Our government! Politicians. Diplomats. Lords. Generals." He gasped for more breath. "If only I had been better able to explain the signs as I read them."

Holmes continued for him. "They did not like what they were being told so, instead of acting upon his warnings, Mycroft was given his retirement, after so many years of distinguished service."

"Some listened, some could also see the signs. But many more refused to accept the prediction. It was too terrible. They preferred to turn a blind eye. Insisted the world would not go mad. I believe the war could have been prevented if we had accepted that it was a real risk. Even if war was inevitable, we could have been better prepared. Now, it is too late and there is nothing we can do."

"Mycroft, we can still be of service. Have you heard about the Pickvale Hall murders in Leicestershire?"

"I do not read the newspapers anymore, little brother. The news is dire and my eyes are not fit for the strain of reading."

Holmes summarised what he knew. "A teacher at Pickvale Hall prep school was killed last Sunday night. The police have arrested a local girl. She was in custody when a second teacher was found dead early yesterday. The police have not released the girl. They say they know who committed the second crime but they are not giving any details, only that a suspect is being sought."

Mycroft gazed into his brother's face for a moment. "Presumably there is great security at the school now? The remaining staff are under official protection?"

"I believe not," said the younger Holmes. "The police consider the matter solved, once the arrest of the mysterious suspect is achieved."

Mycroft sat up in his bed. It was a struggle for him but I was able to assist. "Most unlikely!" he gasped. "Possible but not probable. The likelihood is that there is danger still. Can you not go and protect them yourself? You have managed jaunts to France and Holland, is Leicestershire too far to go to perhaps save a life?"

"The good doctor has suggested we should leave the pursuit of ordinary criminals to younger men."

Mycroft turned to me. "Doctor Watson, the younger men are away fighting the Central Powers!" He lay back down. "I have seen it in government departments, universities, schools and now hospitals. The best are run as faithful societies where people work together and seek the best from each other. The worst are spiteful places, full of petty jealousies, where people guard their own interests. I don't know about this school but if it is of the type that accepts poisonous people, who nurse their bitterness and grievances, with a weak leader who tries and fails to rule through power rather than inspiration, then you have the recipe for failure and the potential to hatch evil."

We left him to rest, returned to Waterloo station and found a refreshment room. Holmes was thoughtful.

"Your brother is not well."

"No. I visit him most days. His body is failing but his mind remains as sharp as ever. Watson, people are in danger at this school. The official force does not see that. They are under strength because of the war. Are we not doing our bit for the national effort by preventing a possible crime?"

I thought for a moment.

"Very well, Holmes, I will do as you direct. Of course I will."

It was clear he had been waiting for this moment. "Thank you. Now, you need to make a telephone call to the school – here is the number – and say you can travel to the school today to attend an interview tomorrow."

"Today? An interview tomorrow?"

"We have no time to lose. Besides, tomorrow is the interview day. See the advertisement for the position here."

He pulled out a page from a copy of The Times, dated a couple of weeks before, and showed me the advertisement:

> PUBLIC APPOINTMENTS. PICKVALE HALL
> PREPARATORY SCHOOL LEICESTER.
> Applications are invited for the POST of
> SCIENCE MASTER. Salary £180 per annum
> without a house. Applicants must be
> graduates of a British University or hold
> equivalent qualifications and ideally will
> have experience of teaching boys.
> Knowledge of Latin an advantage.
> Interviews will be held at the school on
> 15th June and duties will commence in

September 1916. Appointments for interview may be made with the undersigned. Candidates will be required to present three recent testimonials. Canvassing, directly or indirectly, will be looked upon with disfavour. Mrs M. HOOD, Secretary.

I read the notice carefully. "But I don't have experience of teaching boys and I don't have any testimonials."

"Never mind. Here is what I want you to do. Telephone the school and ask for an interview tomorrow. Say you have only just been shown the advertisement by a friend who thought you might be interested. Say you are a retired doctor, so you have ability in both science and Latin. Say that, although you have never taught boys, you have experience of treating them and needing to use your authority in a medical context."

"But…"

"I know that is something of an exaggeration but it is not an untruth. Explain that you wish to come out of retirement during the war to help the nation. Don't mention that you are already providing immense worth at Challis House or they will be puzzled that you wish to leave. Say that you have always thought you would be a good teacher but never took that road. Now you have the opportunity to address that regret while helping to keep a vital task (the education of the next generation) proceeding during this national emergency."

"But Holmes…"

"I'm sorry Watson, but there is little time. Tell them

you will be able to provide ample testimonials if they should wish to pursue your application for the post."

"I could say I can provide a testimonial from the famous detective Sherlock Holmes."

"Please do not. I do not want anyone at Pickvale Hall to know I am interested in events there until I decide the time is right. If there is a murderer at large I do not want him or her alarmed. Do not let them know that you are associated with me."

I looked over the advertisement again. "£180 per year does not seem to be a generous salary for a schoolmaster."

"It is not. Say you are willing to work for that sum but no less. Now, I need to make haste with my preparations and so do you. Make the telephone call and travel to Pickvale Hall tonight. I will see you there in due course."

Holmes departed towards the platforms of the Bakerloo Railway with great energy for a man of our age. In contrast, I felt somewhat worn. It had been an early start followed by a great activity and now I faced making a telephone call under false pretences followed by a journey across the land to continue with the performance.

I tried to recall the energy I had felt in my younger years whenever a new adventure with Holmes began. How many times had Holmes asked me to slip my service revolver into my pocket before we set out to confront a villain? I recalled dressing in dark clothes and mask to break into a house in Hampstead. I recalled making an intensive study of Chinese pottery and taking a strange name to call upon a man described to us as the most dangerous in Europe. I had undertaken these risks with a sense of excitement. Now I was to tell a few half-truths to some provincial schoolmasters. Why did I feel such anxiety at the prospect? Perhaps that, too, comes with age.

From the refreshment room, I could see more soldiers embarking onto trains that would take them to the continent. This allowed me to pull myself together, for I was planning to undertake risks trivial compared to those brave lads. I found the public telephone and called Pickvale Hall. On reflection, I think I was expecting some element of interrogation about my potential skills as a science master, my reasons for seeking the post and why I was applying at the last minute. But Mrs Hood, the school secretary, did not seem interested in any of these matters. I hurried through a speech I had prepared about who I was and why I was calling.

"Right." That was all she said when I finished. I was rather taken aback.

"Ah… may I take it, then, that I can attend an interview tomorrow?"

"You said that is what you want." She had a slow style of speech, as if every word was an effort.

"Yes. I do. Very much." Silence from the other end of the line. "Well then. At what time would the headmaster be available to see me?"

There was an audible sigh and I heard some pages being turned. "Half past nine?"

"Thank you, half past nine will be agreeable. I was thinking it would be best to travel up from London today. Can you suggest a nearby inn at which I could overnight?"

"You can stay in the school. The boys are on a holiday. That's why we are seeing people now."

"Yes. Well, thank you, Mrs Hood. I will travel to the school today and look forward to meeting you either tonight or tomorrow morning."

"Very well. Goodbye." She hung up. I was bemused. She spoke as if we were enemies of long standing but we had no contact before this morning. I remembered Mycroft's words about people who nurse their bitterness and grievances. Perhaps Mrs Hood saw me as an enemy because she sees everyone as an enemy.

After a few minutes I realized I did not know how to get to the school. I was so put off by the manner of the call that I forgot to ask. I rang again and this time a man answered. "Hello, it's John Watson here. I rang a few minutes ago."

"Oh yes, Doctor Watson. Mrs Hood just told me about you. She's in with the headmaster right now. Do you need to speak to her again?"

"No, I don't need to trouble Mrs Hood again, we have made our arrangements. I just wanted to know how to get to you. I'm in London now and have been invited to come today and spend tonight in your school."

"That's right. There's you and one other gentleman staying over tonight to see Reverend Smythe in the morning. He's the headmaster. My name is Evans, me and the wife are the only staff left besides teachers and Mrs Hood. The others have all gone for war work. But the missus will get a bed up for you and we'll welcome you as well we can." The contrast between Mr Evans and Mrs Hood could not be more extreme. We agreed that the best course was for me to take the train that left St Pancras at twenty-five minutes past two o'clock. I would have to change trains at Derby. Mr Evans would meet me at Melbourne station and get me to Pickvale Hall in time for a late supper.

To Leicestershire

I made my way to the Midland Grand Hotel at St Pancras and treated myself to a good lunch and a period of rest before taking the train. It was as well that I did so as the journey was long and uncomfortable. The day was cloudy and breezy but dry. Melbourne Station was outside the town, at a small village called King's Newton. The sky was overcast when I arrived, the breeze was gentle but chilly and there was no one about. What was I doing here? After a few minutes a very old growler pulled into the station yard, pulled by a very old horse and driven by a very old man.

"Doctor Watson? George Evans. Sorry I'm a few minutes late, got held up on the road and poor old Kitty here," he indicated the horse, "she's not as young as she was. We used to have four horses up at the Hall but army took the other three. Didn't want old Kitty. But she still does us proud." He climbed down and made to help me up but I felt a little awkward at being assisted by someone who appeared to be even older than me. I took my seat and Evans threw a blanket over my knees. "No point in getting a chill, you'll know that as a medical man." He flicked the rein and Kitty started to climb the rise out of the station yard towards the road.

"Still got plenty o' light to see us back, that's just 'cos

they had us put the clocks forward an hour back in May. Daft idea. City thinking, if you ask me. There's just longer days in the summer than in the winter, always has been, and fiddling about with clocks don't change that. If you want more daylight in the summer, get up earlier, like country folk do!"

Evans continued his monologue. "The wife's made a bed up for you in one of the dorms. You'll have the room to yourself; our dorms are quite small. The other gentleman also has a room to himself. The rooms do get chilly so we put eiderdowns out for both of you. Now, you've missed dinner but there's a cold collation ready for you in the staff room. The staff that live out will all have gone home but we've a few live in, you'll meet them like as not."

"Will I meet the Reverend Smythe tonight?"

"No, no, the headmaster lives in the village."

"Mrs Hood perhaps?"

"No, not her neither, Mona has a flat above the grocers."

"I found her a little taciturn. Is she usually a woman of few words?"

"Ah now, don't make anything of that. She's pretty sparing with words with most of us. She is friendly enough with Miss Harting, that's the English teacher. My wife says she's had a few chats with her too, but not often. With the rest of us, Mona, Mrs Hood that is, keeps mum. She's finding the war hard, husband's a regular soldier, see, and he was never around even before this war kicked off. Some as get lonely talks a lot and some as lives on their own gets used to life that way. The way I see it, people have worse faults than being a bit quiet. I don't mind 'em like that."

This assessment seemed consistent with the preference Mr Evans was displaying for being the person doing the talking in an encounter.

"Who might I be able to meet tonight?"

"We've got Mr Clearly and Mr Yarding living in the school. You might meet them. Mr Yarding, that's our maths master, he usually sits in the staff room of an evening. I keeps the room warm, see? Mr Clearly might be there or he might be holding court in the Pickvale Arms, that's the pub in the village. Very popular in the Arms is Mr Clearly. Teaches history and puts on the school plays. Oh, and you'll probably meet Mr Crossman too. He's the other gentleman staying over to meet the headmaster in the morning."

I thought Holmes would want me to ask about the recent murders. "I understand there may be posts available for both me and Mr Crossman."

Evans looked round. "What do you mean?"

"Only that I heard somewhere that one or two teachers have, um, died recently?"

Evans was silent for a few moments, the first silence since we had met. Finally he spoke. "We have lost a couple of the masters, yes. The headmaster asked me not to talk about that. All very sad."

Further conversation was delayed by three soldiers stepping out from the roadside and signalling to Mr Evans to stop the carriage.

"You lot again?" he asked the soldiers. He turned to

me and said, "This is why I were a bit late meeting you, Doctor Watson. These lads here stopped me on the way out." He turned back to them. "Now lads, I was talking to you not twenty minutes ago, remember? I told you then I was on my way to the station to collect a gentleman for Pickvale Hall and here he is."

One of the soldiers moved towards me, apologised for the halt and asked me a few questions about who I was, where I was going and on what business. It seemed very perfunctory and we were quickly waved on.

"Are you lads going to tell me what you're looking for this time? What's going on, eh?"

The soldiers told him it was nothing to worry about and we should move on. Once we were moving again, Evans gave a small chuckle and said, "As if we can't guess. They've lost another one from Donington."

"What's Donington? What have they lost?"

"Donington Hall." He indicated north with his whip. "It's being used for German officers. Prisoners of war. The army's had them there since 1914. It's a fine old place, beautiful grounds. There's over a hundred of them there, living a life of luxury. The stories you hear! Silver service in the dining room, tablecloths, choices from the menu, wine, the lot. Of course, it's ordinary German soldiers who do the work and wait on them. They live in huts in the grounds. But the wire fence gives them all a huge amount of space to relax in. They have sports tournaments, they put on plays, it sounds like a terrific life. The local Post Office has had to take on extra staff because of all the parcels sent from Germany. Lot of folk around here very unhappy about it. I suppose we want Germans to surrender, don't we?

Easier than having to kill them all off. But it makes us all sick to think of them with their feet up, in our country, smoking cigars after a fine dinner. You know what the food we get in the shops is like. Surprising really that any of them want to escape."

"Ah, so that is what you think has happened? A German prisoner has escaped, which is why the army is blocking the roads?"

"That's my guess. Two got out last year and the story is that one of them made it all the way back to Germany, though the official news doesn't say so. When they got out of Donington Hall it was reported in the Daily Sketch and there was news later of one of them being caught at Millwall. That's in London. The other, we think, got home. Since then there's been rumours of Germans cutting through the wire and even digging a tunnel but you won't read anything about that in the papers. If another one's out they'll keep quiet about that too. 'Bad for morale' is probably the excuse being given in an army office somewhere. Truth is, they don't like news getting out that shows a German being smarter than our boys. But why else would soldiers be out at night stopping us and old Kitty?"

We were driving alongside a brick wall that snaked along besides us, in an out, like a wave. "See that?" asked Evans. "Runs right round the school grounds. Built when the hall and everything were, over a hundred years ago. They say it's crinkle crankle like that to make it stronger. Looks to me like the builder had had a few too many. But here we are." We turned into a wide break in the wavy wall, between two imposing brick pillars and onto a gravel drive.

"Might as well close up," said Evans. He climbed down, closed and fastened two huge iron gates and returned to the driver's seat.

"Is it really necessary to lock the gates at night?" I asked.

"Headmaster's orders. He says it's a good habit to lock the gates at night, even when the boys are away, as now."

We set off down the drive. Immediately on the left was a church, which I later found out was St Philip's, and before me was Pickvale Hall. Brick was clearly the favoured building material as the building was made from red and black bricks forming some form of pattern. The central block stood at the end of the drive: three stories tall with the top floor consisting of a series of triangular gables in front of a tiled roof. One each side, a single-story wing curved out from the central block like arms reaching out to snare the visitor. The arrangement reminded me of Roylott House in Stoke Moran, Surrey, location of the Adventure of the Speckled Band. The windows looked small for the scale of the building. It had become a gloomy evening and clouds were gathering in a way that suggested heavy rain. The impression Pickvale Hall gave in the circumstances was most forbidding.

"Looks like rain," said Evans. "I'd better get the buckets out before it starts. Sorry, Doctor Watson, but I have to see to Kitty as well. Would you mind? Just go in the main entrance there, follow the corridor, the staff room's at the back of the building on the left. Give me your bags and your coat, I'll take them up."

I climbed down and followed Evans's directions. The

main building was larger than I had thought as it extended back a considerable way. I passed a magnificent staircase halfway down the passage. One small window at each end provided the only illumination for the entire corridor but I found my way to the staff room.

My first impression was a warm and bright room after the cold, dark passageway. There was a small fire in the grate, an extravagance for June. But next I noticed the shabby, ill-assorted armchairs scattered around, the paint peeling off the walls and window frames, the threadbare, dusty carpet and a general smell of damp and decay which the fire had not been able to drive off. There was one person in the room, a young man who came to me as I stood in the doorway taking in the scene. He was of medium height, slim, a head of pale brown hair that looked as if it needed a lot of work to keep it neat and a smiling, boyish face. I noticed he walked with a limp.

"Good evening! You must be Doctor Watson, how do you do?" We shook hands as he continued, "My name is Simon Yarding. I teach our boys mathematics. Before you ask, I was born with a club foot and the surgeons made something of a mess of their attempts to correct it."

"I'm sorry to hear that, Mr Yarding."

He waved it away. "Can't be helped. I've had it all my life and got used to it. But now... Of course, the military won't touch me. Can't do my bit. But never mind that, come and sit down over here, there's food and drink waiting for you." He led me over to a table where a meal lay under an upturned bowl. All I can say is that it was fortunate that I felt ravenously hungry or consuming the offering would have required considerable willpower. As I ate, I asked Yarding about the school and it was immediately clear he was torn between a desire to be honest and a need to encourage a candidate for a post on the teaching staff.

"We… we have our problems, doctor. The building needs some repairs but it's very hard at this time. Shortage of materials, shortage of men, shortage of mon… What I mean to say is, we have to run a tight ship at the moment."

"Do you have enough boys enrolled to meet the school's financial needs?" I asked between mouthfuls.

He looked down. "Filling the roll has been a problem. So many boys' fathers have joined up, pay in the army and navy is secure but not generous and times are hard for families. Furthermore, I regret to say, we have had to break the worst news to five pupils since the war began. All but one were withdrawn from the school very soon afterwards. I am sure their widowed mothers wanted their sons near them as well as needing to manage their pensions carefully. Doctor Watson, you've come all this way to see about getting a job. I don't want to put you off but I have to be honest. I am not sure the school will survive."

"Really? You think it is as bad as that?"

"I do. We lost some good teachers who volunteered to do their bit. Quite right, I'd have gone with them but I could not. Now these recent events. I cannot help thinking how many of our boys will return after this holiday, let alone after the summer break. We need 100 boys to cover our costs. Ten years ago, there were 130.

In the last half we had just 76. It's just as well that we have fewer staff, we could not pay them all."

"Who are the teachers who left to fight?"

"Mr Turner, the English teacher. I liked him and so did the boys. Very popular. Inspiring. He's in the Royal Hampshire Regiment now, we stay in touch, exchange letters once a week. Mr Lighterman, the Science teacher, the one who has left the post you are now seeking. He's serving with the Royal Warwickshire Fusiliers. Rather a strange fellow but a good teacher, he always wanted what was best for the boys. I tried writing once or twice but got no reply. We lost staff as well. Matron went first, as you might expect, joined the Voluntary Aid Detachment in August 1914. The gardener is in the Royal Navy, the bursar went to manage an armaments factory and took the two girls we had as general maids. I understand they are manufacturing shells and bullets now. We had a general handyman as well, he's in the Royal Artillery. It is only now he is gone that we see how much he did to keep this old place intact."

I finished the plate of cold leftovers. I no longer felt hungry but rather nauseous instead. I decided to find out if Yarding had been told, as Evans was, to avoid the subject of the recent deaths among the staff. "Tell me, Mr Yarding..."

"Please just call me Yarding." This modern familiarity is something I will have to get accustomed to.

"Very well, Yarding, I was sad to hear that two of your colleagues have died recently."

He looked at the floor for a moment, whether through sadness or the need to think, I could not tell.

"Yes. They say lightning does not strike twice in the same place. But it has struck twice here."

"Can you tell me what happened?"

"I'm not supposed to. The headmaster has said it is bad for the school to discuss these events and told us that it is *sub judice* and so we should not discuss them for legal reasons."

"Yarding, two of your colleagues here have been (if I have heard it correctly) murdered?"

He paused again. "Yes. But these two events are not connected with each other and have nothing to do with the school."

"How do you know that?"

He looked about. "Dolman – that's Mr Dolman, the geography teacher – was found dead in the woods last Monday morning, the day before yesterday. The police have arrested a girl from the village. It seems that he and she used to, ah, meet by appointment somewhere out of sight."

"Do I take it that this was, hum, a commercial arrangement?"

Another long pause. "I cannot speak ill of the dead."

"I understand. And the second death?"

"Reg Bushey, our French master. Found only yesterday outside the ruins of the old church. It can't be the girl from the village as she's still being held by the police. But we're assured it's nothing to do with the school either."

"What are you being told? Who is suspected of the

second crime?"

He looked down again for a moment and I felt he was screwing up his courage. "Very well, doctor, but all I know is…"

At that moment the door burst open and in strode a large, grinning man of about forty years. His dark hair was parted in the centre and smoothed down over his almost spherical head. A cavalry moustache completed the impression of a man determined to present a bold, confident appearance. He also had the flushed, ruddy cheeks of a man who liked to drink.

"What ho!" he cried. "Who do we have here then? Yarding, you old woman, not boring our guest are you? No one will want to join our crew if they find they'll have you as a shipmate!"

Yarding stood up, his face set. "You've been drinking again, Clearly. That does not excuse your behaviour but it does explain it. I wonder if you would ever speak like that to a man who was not crippled. Doctor Watson, I wish you a good night."

The new arrival was followed into the room by an ancient man, far older even than me. He was stooped, frail and his head was surrounded by a cloud of fluffy white hair. His skin had a strange greyish quality with a liberal scattering of liver spots. In a quavering, reedy voice he introduced himself as David Crossman, then collapsed into an armchair by the fire and seemed to fall asleep immediately.

The younger man introduced himself as Mr Matthew Clearly, history master and producer of school theatre. He took the seat that Yarding had vacated. "Don't worry about poor Yarding, I'm just teasing him, it's all for fun.

Goodness knows, we all need a bit of fun in these dark days! Young fellow can't take a joke."

I felt anger rising at the rudeness of this vulgar man and his use of the standard bully's excuse of 'just a joke' to justify his malice. It was entirely consistent with what Wensome had told me back at Challis House, that Clearly liked to use his cane on boys. Besides all that, I was sure Yarding was about to tell me something vital before he was interrupted.

He learnt forward and continued in a whisper, "If the job's between you and the old man asleep in the armchair over there, I don't think you've got much to worry about. It seems he arrived here a couple of hours ago and, on hearing one of his potential colleagues was in the pub, he decided to come and take a drink himself. I can barely understand what he says and I thought I would have to carry the old fool back here. He can hardly walk!"

He chuckled at his dismissal of the old man and my disgust rose further. However, I decided to stay calm to see what I could learn from the oaf who sat before me. I could smell the drink on him but forced a smile.

"Mr Yarding and I were discussing the recent tragedies here."

"You mean the murders! My word, isn't it extraordinary!" He beamed with delight. "Quite a tale I will have to tell during the long dark winter evenings. Not that I shall ever see a winter evening again once this blasted war is over."

"Whatever do you mean?"

"You have to know, old man, that I'm only here to do

my bit. I can't serve in the forces; you wouldn't know it but my eyesight is terrible, so I'm doing what I can for the next generation. The boys here will have to fill the shoes of those who fall. I am fanatical about helping to shape young minds and start young people on the right road. But I don't need to work here."

"No?"

"Not at all. Had some success in business over the years and invested in land. I have 3,000 acres in Canada and just under 2,000 in Southern Rhodesia. I have cattle, crops, fruit and, I have good reason to believe, a quantity of gold under my land. Not safe to visit my estates just now. But once it's all over, I will spend every summer in Canada. Once the leaves turn, I'll board ship and spend the southern hemisphere summer in Africa, before returning to Canada once the snows there clear. Eternal summer, just think of it!" He clapped me on the shoulder. I confess to feeling some envy that such a life awaited so odious a person. But I was here with a purpose.

"I was talking with Mr Yarding about the tragic deaths you have suffered here. He seemed to think they are unconnected and solved, although..."

Clearly interrupted. "Yes, tragic of course. But I'm afraid Dolman brought it on himself. If he insists on going off into the woods with that tart Elsie, or whatever she's called, he's asking for it. I think Bushey was just unlucky though. Wrong place, wrong time. I have to say, they are both a loss to the school. I was just saying how ardent I am about shaping the boys. Dolman and Bushey understood what that means. We have to teach them stuff, of course – history and maths and

English, all the main school subjects. But that's just stuff they have to learn. Most of it will probably never be any use to them. I want to develop the boys into men, and that means you have to be tough with them sometimes. No point in mollycoddling boys, does them no good. They need to learn discipline and they need to be tough. Need to put the fear of God into them! That's what I believe. Dolman and Bushey shared my view. Yarding and his type – huh! Can't see beyond just teaching the boys stuff. We had other teachers like him, Lighterman and Turner. They've gone off to play at being soldiers. No loss to teaching. We've still got Wheatfield, Wet Field I call him. Another softy. He teaches Kraut, why would we want any young English lad learning the language of our enemy?"

He was slurring his words and looked to be becoming drowsy with drink. I decided to turn the conversation away from Clearly's views on education and back to the crimes I was here to investigate. "Mr Yarding seemed to think the police know who killed Mr Bushey."

Clearly's gaze swung up from the floor and he fixed me with bloodshot eyes and his smirking smile beneath the wide moustache. "Did he say that? Well, we've all heard the rumours."

"I have not."

For the second time, I was frustrated on the verge of making a discovery, for at that moment an elderly woman strode into the room. Despite her age, she carried herself with confidence. I quickly formed the impression that here was a woman of ability. "Good evening, Mr Clearly. Been out entertaining at the

Pickvale Arms again? You must be Doctor Watson. Good evening sir, I'm Sarah Evans, my husband drove you from the station. I have your bed all ready for you, may I show you the way now? I need to lock up and get to bed myself." She went over to the chair that accommodated the ancient Mr Crossman. He must have been asleep as she shook his arm. "Come along Mr Crossman, you too."

It was getting late and I was tired. I followed Mrs Evans back into the long corridor with Crossman wheezing along behind us. When we got to the main staircase I wondered if Crossman would be able to climb, but he managed perfectly well. Mrs Evans was explaining, "The dormitories here are rather small, so I've been able to give you each your own room. I'll be in the kitchen from eight tomorrow morning, so if you want breakfast, please come down to the main dining hall between then and half past. The necessary is at the end of each corridor and there's a bath beside one of them but there will be no hot water."

When we reached the top floor I saw that Mr Evans had put out the buckets he mentioned, and just in time. It had started to rain and the first drops were coming through the roof and landing with precision in a variety of metal receptacles placed in well-known spots. I was shown to my room, a draughty dormitory of six beds, one of them made up for me. There was no fire. I went to sleep as the sound of water hitting the buckets changed from a ping to a splash as they slowly filled.

The next morning
I made my way downstairs and found the dining hall, a long, low, wood-panelled room with French windows looking out onto a crumbling terrace and an overgrown

lawn. Several long tables with benches would have accommodated the boys during term time. At the far end was the only table which ran the width of the room. It was furnished with chairs and was clearly the staff table. The chair in the centre, facing the room, looked more like a throne.

Sitting together at one of the tables for pupils were two women who could not have presented more of a contrast. Readers of my stories have written to me suggesting I should not assess women so much by their appearance, and I daresay that is right for the twentieth century, but in the case of these two, I could not help but form first impressions. The first was a young lady who had the grace of Miss Violet Smith (who introduced Holmes and me to the Adventure of the Solitary Cyclist), the chestnut hair of Miss Violet Hunter (former governess at The Copper Beeches) and the face and figure of Miss Hatty Doran (otherwise Mrs Moulton, the vanishing bride of the Noble Bachelor). She was plainly dressed and wore a black ribbon around her arm, a sign of bereavement, but gave me a charming smile as she introduced herself as Miss Harting, formerly a school secretary and now teacher of English.

Her companion looked at me with contempt. This expression was not mollified by her natural appearance; nature had not been kind to her. She had a broad, ruddy face, fuzzy hair and a squat nose. As I move into senior years, I have come to believe that young people have the looks they are born with but as one gets older, one acquires the appearance that is deserved. Goodness, faith and virtue can shine from the most rugged features. Cruelty, greed and indolence will soon make their mark on a face of classical beauty as it ages. The lady introduced to me as Mrs Mona Hood appeared to have combined an unfortunate lot at birth with a decision to punish the world for her misfortunes.

"We're having a private conversation, Doctor Watson," said this unhappy person. "You can sit over there," she pointed to the staff table, "and Mrs Evans will be out shortly. The Reverend Smythe will see you at ten. Mr Crossman is seeing him first."

I took my seat and, as promised, Mrs Evans appeared, explained what she had on offer and took my order. While I waited I could not help but overhear the conversation between the two ladies.

"Why not come into Derby with me today, Mona?"

"What for? I've no money. Just because you're a teacher now, Anna, don't forget that I'm paid no more than you were when you were a secretary."

"I'm not paid much more! The headmaster pays me half what he pays the men, you know that, you see the accounts."

"What do you want to go to Derby for anyway? What's there?"

"Just a chance to get away from here, after all that has happened. We're not needed here today. Come on, there's a bus from outside the Pickvale Arms in half an hour. We'll have a nice tea, my treat."

"Well... I do like the idea of a break from this place. I hate it more than ever. A useless, crumbling building full of useless, crumbling men." She shot a glance in my direction. "Even if there was no war, no one with any ambition would stay in a hole like this."

"Well, why do you stay, Mona? You're always saying you don't feel appreciated here. You complain about the pay. You say we're not doing enough for the war effort. Why not get a job that does?"

The door opened and a man peered into the room. He was younger than me, perhaps fifty, his height emphasised by being strikingly slender. His grey hair was cut very short and his pale face carried an expression of great sadness.

Mrs Hood stared at the new arrival for a moment then stood up and said to Miss Harting, "I think I will come to Derby with you, Anna. There's suddenly a strange smell of sausage in the room. I'll go and get ready." She left as Mrs Evans brought in my breakfast.

"Here you are, Doctor Watson, ham and eggs. Only one egg I'm afraid because we're a little short, like everyone these days. I'm sorry the ham is cut in such a mess too, only I can't find my best knife. But I've given you two slices of bread, fresh from the baker in the village, that will set you up for the day."

Miss Harting came over to me.

"I suppose you could not help hearing Mona, doctor. Don't judge her too harshly. She's not had a happy life. Her husband was a regular solider before the war and of course is caught up in it now, somewhere out east. We've never even seen him here."

"I think the war has brought you loss as well, Miss Harting," I said, nodding at her armband.

"My fiancé, Edward. Salonika, last November."

"I am so very sorry."

She smiled and left. The man whose entry seemed to have caused Mrs Hood to leave had been standing near the door. He opened it for Miss Harting then came and sat opposite me. "You must be one of our visitors. Welcome to Pickvale Hall. I do hope you decide to join us here."

"Doctor John Watson. I have not yet been offered the opportunity to join you."

"Eric Wheatfield." We shook hands. "No, but I think we are in no position to refuse anyone who would be willing."

"I have not made up my mind." After all I had heard from the other members of staff, I decided to move straight to the heart of what seemed to me to be the school's problem. "Would you say this school has, ah, a good team spirit? What I mean to say is, do you think everyone here wants to work together to do the right thing? Do all the staff want to, to use a poor analogy, march to the beat of the same drum?"

I felt I had been very inarticulate. Wheatfield looked at me mournfully for a moment, then gave a weak smile. "Do you mean, are we a happy school?" I indicated that was what I was asking. He continued, "Who has a right to be happy in these days? Did you know that four former pupils of this little school have been killed in this war? Who can say how many more, once happy young faces within these walls, will find a monstrous end on a battlefield before it's all over?"

"The sacrifice is immense, for sure," I commented, but I wanted to follow up on an idea that had started to form in my mind. "But among your colleagues, here, now. Would you say you all rub along well enough? Do you all, shall we say, have the same idea about how to do the best for your young charges?"

Mrs Evans brought us a fresh pot of tea and some toast for Wheatfield. He poured us both a cup and stirred his while he said, "If you are thinking of joining us, Doctor Watson, you should know that we do not all see eye to eye on that. Good debate about education policy is to be welcomed, but..." He looked up at me. "Just a minute! Doctor Watson! Are you by any chance the Doctor Watson who wrote the biographies of the detective, Sherlock Holmes?"

I had prepared a way to address that question. I smiled and said, "A lot of people ask me that. But you were talking about differences in approach among the teachers?"

"Oh yes. Well, I suppose it comes down to this. Do you believe a boy is best turned into a man through encouragement and kindness or through criticism and..."

"Cruelty?" I offered.

"A strong word, doctor. But yes, if you like. I have no problem with caning boys who do bad things. I gave six of the best to a lad just the other week because I found him bullying one of the little ones. I can't stand that. But some of my colleagues will dish out a beating to a boy for making an honest mistake in his work. Do we have to motivate them to try harder with a threat of the cane? I don't believe it works."

"So why do you think some of your colleagues do it?"

He sat up straight and looked me fiercely. "Very well,

doctor. I believe some of the masters enjoy it. I'm not just talking about caning. They shout at the boys, make fun of them for any little thing, they put them down and humiliate them. They say it's all done for the boys' best interests, that it will toughen them up and make them stronger men. I've seen boys in tears after being humiliated and some of the injuries... But I've said too much. Come and join us, Doctor Watson, and help us make the move away from these barbaric methods that should have ended in the time of Dickens."

I decided it was time to direct the conversation away from ideas about teaching and towards a better understanding of the school. "I am sorry ask, Mr Wheatfield, it's likely I have the wrong end of the stick, but does Mrs Hood hold some kind of grudge against you?"

Mr Wheatfield sat back in his seat and managed to look even sadder. "I teach woodwork and German here. Woodwork is not seen as important by most of the other staff and German..." He shook his head. "I believe we need to understand our enemy. Not just their language, their way of thinking. Mrs Hood does not agree. Besides, she has always been friendly with those of my colleagues who favour the more, shall we say, the harsher approach to teaching." He reached across the table and grasped my arm. "Two of the worst are no longer with us. I'm not saying that's a good thing, it's tragic. But we need to look to the future. With new blood we could rebuild this school. Make it a kinder, happier place."

The door burst open and Mr Clearly bounded into the room. "What ho! My word, Watson, you had your supper last night with Yarding and now breakfast with

Wheatfield! So sorry about that, don't let them put you off!" He grinned as if this was all a tremendous joke. "Where did you bunk off to yesterday afternoon, Wheaty? The window in my room needs fixing and, as we don't have a handyman to hand any more, I thought we could finally put your woodworking skills to some use. But no one could find you. Not the first time. Where do you slope off to old man? Pop home to the wife in that little cottage of yours?"

"I was called away on private business." Wheatfield put down the remains of his toast and drained his teacup. "If you will both excuse me, my reason for coming to the school today is to do some reorganization of the woodwork shed." He left and Clearly picked up the last piece of toast.

I did not want any more of Clearly's company and I felt I had much to report to Holmes. But how was I to contact him? I had no idea where he was. He had said he would meet me here. I decided I would call his house in Sussex and leave a message with his housekeeper, then try some of the London hotels I knew he favoured to see if I could trace him.

"I am sorry to leave you so immediately, Mr Clearly, but I am seeing the headmaster at ten o'clock and I wish to make a telephone call before then. Is there a telephone in the school?"

"Yes, there's one, it's in the school office, where Mrs Hood usually sits, with an extension to Smythe's office. He doesn't like it used for personal calls. Tell you what, there's time for you to come into the village and call from the Post Office. I'm going there anyway and it's a pleasant enough stroll. Give you a chance to see something of the place that you're thinking of moving to."

I could think of no excuse and I did want to leave messages for Holmes so I agreed. We went to the staff room so Clearly could collect his coat from the wardrobe there. "Where's yours, old man?"

I said mine was still upstairs in the dormitory but the day looked fine enough for a walk without a coat.

"Nonsense, old man, let's see what we can lend you. Reg – that's Mr Bushey – had a lovely new ulster coat, deep maroon in colour, he was so proud of it." He rummaged through the wardrobe. "Not here. I suppose he had it with him. Not to worry, here's Peter's jacket." He pulled out a long, drab coat that had belonged to Peter Dolman, the first victim. I was not eager to wear the apparel of either dead man so I insisted I would be warm enough in my day jacket.

"You're probably right. Off we go then!" We set off down the gravel drive to the brick pillars. The iron gates were standing wide open. The day was bright but cool. "Hope you will be warm enough. Let's pick up the pace to make sure. Wretched English weather, good to know I won't have to put up with it after the war. I told you of my plan to spend the northern summers in Canada and the southern summers in Africa?"

"You did. When were you in those countries to acquire your estates there?"

"Let me see… I went to Canada as a young man, must have been in '95. Had success in the banking field in Montreal. Decided to try Africa in 1904. Made some useful investments in mining and railways. Came to England in '09, meant to be just a visit but I met Smythe and he invited me to try teaching for a while. I found I enjoyed it, I think I am good at it and it's important work. I had planned to have stopped by now but the war came so here I am, suffering the English climate. Hopefully not for much longer."

"I am sure we all hope that the war will end soon."

"Yes, yes. Just over here." He indicated a stile which we crossed. "It's across this meadow then the path takes you right into the village. Now look over there." He pointed to our left, where a grey flint tower rose above the trees and bushes. "You can see the tower of the old church, built around 1680 but when the Owensthorne family built that splendid edifice that is now my place of employment, they wanted the village church within their walls. So they built the new St Philip's, the old one was left to rot. The village has to walk to Pickvale Hall to attend church, rather than the Owensthornes having to walk to the village."

"It was outside the old church that your friend was found?"

"Poor old Reg, yes. I wasn't in the pub that night, he must have been walking back after a late one. It's a longer route to go past the old church but easier in the dark. I suppose he…"

But at that moment a voice shouted from behind us. "Watson! Clearly! Get down! There's a gunman on the tower!" I turned round, bewildered. The voice was unmistakable. Holmes was here and had shouted a warning at us. There was no one at the stile leading back to the school but I heard footsteps along the road, hidden by the hedge, running towards the ruined church. Holmes's voice rang out again. "Watson! Get him on the ground! Do as I say!"

My moment of hesitation was over. I shoved Clearly and fell on top of him as a shot rang out. "Stay down," I said to Clearly. He looked utterly terrified. I jumped up but my knee gave way and I collapsed into the grass. I hauled myself to my feet, staggered back across the meadow and stile, then turned right along the road. I had lost my breath and it is some years since I was fit enough to run. I stumbled down the road until I came to the entrance to the yard of the old church. There was no sign of anyone. I had to stop to catch my breath, then continued to make my unsteady way, along the path to the ruin. The flint walls were largely intact but there was no roof and nothing in the windows, which gaped like the eyes of the dead on the derelict graveyard. I found the gap in the walls where the door had been and entered just as a man emerged from the entrance to the tower. It was the ancient Mr Crossman. But no, it was Holmes. I collapsed onto a stone seat, panting as my old friend approached me.

"Are you all right, Watson?" He was breathless as well and sat down on the bench beside me.

"Holmes!" It was all I had the strength to say. We sat there together for several minutes while we recovered from our exertions. "You have not lost your talent for disguise."

He shook his head. "At our age, making the appearance of further aging is not so great a challenge. I went to see a friend at the Lyric after I left you at Waterloo. He gave me this ridiculous wig and some makeup. A bit of grey stage paint with some brown spots, some petroleum jelly around the eyes. I am sorry

I did not reveal myself to you at the school but I did not want to surprise you while others were around."

My breathlessness turned into a coughing fit that took further minutes to subside. I lit a cigarette to ease my breathing and wiped my eyes. "Who took the shot?"

Holmes shook his head again. "Gone by the time I got here. I am not as fast as I once was. Whoever it was had time to descend the tower and, I presume, flee into those bushes before I was able to see him. There is a rifle, abandoned at the top of the tower." He paused to take some more breaths. "I left it *in situ* so the official police can examine it there. Not much I could make of it, it's a very old weapon. No other evidence presented itself."

We paused to recover further. "Holmes, I have learned some interesting facts about the people at this school."

This time he nodded. "Yes, I listened to your interrogation of Mr Clearly last night. You did well."

"And I have heard more today. This school is split into two factions."

"I know but we cannot discuss it now. We must get Clearly safely back into the school and your meeting with the headmaster is due to start before long. As soon as you are done, meet me in the Pickvale Arms."

We hurried as best we could back to the meadow where Clearly was still flat on the ground and very frightened. We got him up and ferried him back to the staff room, one of us on each side of him. He was too dazed to notice that the ancient man he had so recently derided as barely able to walk was suddenly able to support him in locomotion. Once he was settled in an armchair, I found my way to the headmaster's office, a grand room above the main entrance. It had an ornate desk with a huge chair behind it and, in front of it, two pale settees. A large fireplace with an oak surround held a roaring blaze and above it a mantlepiece carried an array of sporting trophies. Around the walls, pictures of hunting alternated with packed bookcases and occasional sporting memorabilia: a canvas bag of golf clubs, a hockey stick, an oar painted with long-faded names and crests and an ancient tennis racquet mounted on a plaque. There was a powerful smell of old dust and cheap cigars. The Reverend Daniel Smythe was younger than me though not by much. He was neither tall nor short, but I noticed he had thick heels on his boots in an attempt to create an impression of the former. A circle of grey hair ran right around his face and he had a habit of rubbing his beard. His moustache was stained the particular orange caused by tobacco smoke.

I decided I had better start by telling him the news that someone had taken a pot shot at one of his staff. He listened with a frown as I related what had just happened.

"So you heard a shot?"

"That's right, headmaster."

"What makes you think it was aimed at Mr Clearly? Was he hit? Did a bullet come whistling past?"

"No but Mr Ho... that is, Mr Crossman said he saw a gunman on top of the tower, aiming at us." I was not sure if Holmes wanted his identity revealed yet.

Smythe smiled and rubbed his beard. "I like David

Crossman. I hope he may be joining us. But, with the best will in the world, I don't think his senses are quite what they were. Nothing wrong on the inside, I am sure, but his eyes are not of the best. You probably just heard someone shooting a rabbit."

"But I thought, after what has happened to two of your teachers..?"

"Tragic, of course. But nothing to do with the school. Besides, they are in a better place."

"I understand there are differences of opinion among your staff over the best approaches to teaching?"

He looked cross. "Some people get a little immersed in their pet theories."

"Don't you, as headmaster, set the approach for your school?"

He looked more cross. "I am a leader. A leader of a community. I have to rise above petty differences. It would be wrong for me to take sides."

I decided to try to calm things down. I looked around his room and said, "A sportsman, headmaster?"

At this he smiled. "Yes, in my younger days, when I was up at St John's."

"St John's Oxford or Cambridge?" I asked.

The frown returned. "It doesn't matter. Now, I believe you applied for the post of science master?"

He asked me a little about my medical training and whether I knew any Latin. "I have been teaching the Latin myself. It's simple enough at the level expected here and the parents do expect it." When I said I had no Latin beyond medical terms, he asked whether I spoke French or knew much geography – the main subjects taught by the victims.

"I did wonder whether we still need to teach science. After all, it's all done, really. I am sure future generations will devise more efficient steam engines and bigger ships but I don't think there are any more major discoveries to be made. However, we will always need doctors. I can't imagine a woman knowing anything about science but it would be grand to find one who knew enough to teach it." He grinned at his observation and rubbed his beard.

"Because women do not command the same pay as a man?"

He did not like my tone. "That's not my concern. A man has to provide for his family. A woman only needs to work for herself until she gets married."

"Many women will struggle to find a husband now," I pointed out. "I am sure you know that your Miss Harting has lost her fiancé in battle."

"Yes, but a pretty little thing like our Anna won't have any trouble, I'm sure." He grinned and rubbed his beard again. I longed to leave. I am sure my expression showed I did not share his humour or his values.

"Just tell me, Doctor Watson, what salary would you expect?"

"Your advertisement offered a salary of £180. That would be the minimum."

He nodded and stared at some papers he had in his hand. "Indeed... Well, thank you for coming to see us. I hope you have enjoyed your visit. I think I have all I need."

We shook hands although our reciprocal animosity was clear. I collected my bag and coat and left.

The official police

I felt a surge of relief as I passed between the brick pillars and made my way to the Pickvale Arms. It was a modern building, large for the size of the village and showing signs of wear in the cracked plaster and peeling paint. On presenting myself, I was welcomed and shown to an upstairs parlour. It was a dark, dusty room with a creaky floor beneath a threadbare carpet. Inside it were Holmes, who had removed all traces of the Crossman disguise, and a short, tufty man of about forty years who was introduced to me as Inspector Underwood of the Leicestershire Police Force. He immediately began defending himself.

"Doctor Watson, I'm honoured of course. But I must ask you not to keep any record of events here. It does appear that certain errors might have been made in the course of our investigations into recent events. You must know that we have no detectives currently in Leicester; my job is managing officers on the beat. So many men are away in the military forces. I would not want anything published which could cause embarrassment. Can I have your word, doctor?"

I assured him that no record would be published unless all involved were in agreement or long dead.

"Then, with your permission, Inspector," said Holmes, "I will summarize what we know for the benefit of my colleague. Mr Peter Dolman, teacher of geography and art, was found three days ago, early on

Monday 12th June, in the woods west of the school and the village. He had been killed the evening before by violent blows to the head. You found the suspected weapon nearby, Inspector?"

"Yes, the local bobby found it very quickly," said the tufty Inspector, as if trying to salvage some credit for his organization, "a cricket bat. It had the initials 'DS' carved into it."

"And who did your constable conclude was the owner of the bat?"

"Well, he thought of Derek Sandling. He was the best cricketer in the village for years. Played for the county back in the nineties. Died about six years ago. Left a daughter, Elsie, she lives alone in a tiny cottage at the edge of the village."

"Your man went to see her."

"He did. She said she did not know if the bat was her father's. The cottage was somewhat cluttered. She did confess to, hum, living immorally. She said she used to meet Dolman on Sunday nights in the village cricket pavilion. She said she had gone there the night before and waited but he had not arrived so she went home." He looked at us both with something of a plea in his eyes. "Well, you can see the reasoning!" I noticed Holmes smirk. "The body was in the woods between the school and the pavilion! No one else would have known he would be walking that way so late at night!"

"I believe at least two of his colleagues knew of his arrangement with Miss Sandling," I said.

"Was Dolman robbed?" asked Holmes.

"No, his money and watch were on the body. The girl

could have panicked or maybe there was another reason for the attack – a lovers' quarrel, who can say?"

"Can you think of no one else with the initials DS who might have a collection of sporting equipment?"

I suddenly thought of someone. "Holmes! What about…"

But he silenced me with a wave of his hand. "So, Inspector, you transported this unfortunate young woman to Leicester Police Station and have kept her there expecting a confession. Without that, you must agree your evidence is wafer thin. You must charge her or release her. I suggest you tell her she is free to go and offer her a good meal before transporting her home. She must have been terrified these past days."

"But that leaves us without a suspect!"

Holmes frowned at him. "Better no suspect than the wrong one. Now, let us move on to the second death. Early on Tuesday, two days ago, Mr Reg Bushey, teacher of French, was found stabbed beside the ruins of the old church. He was last seen alive in this inn on Monday night. He left late and was presumably attacked on his way back to the school, where he had a cottage in the grounds. Inspector, be so good as to tell Doctor Watson who you suspect of this crime."

"Very well. But everything I am about to say must be kept secret until the authorities release it to the public. We believe the killer of Mr Bushey to be *Oberleutnant zur See* Konrad Schleger of the Imperial German Navy."

It all fitted. "I take it that this Schleger escaped from the Donington Hall Prisoner of War establishment?"

"He is thought to have made his escape on Sunday

night. He was last seen around eleven o'clock and was discovered missing on Monday morning. The army have been out searching for him ever since."

I tried to think this through. "This German escaped on Sunday night, got some distance from Donington then decided to hide somewhere during the daylight hours... The ruined church!"

The Inspector nodded. "Exactly. We explored the crypt on Tuesday and found evidence someone had been there recently. The dust was disturbed and there were food wrappers. We believe he hid there during Monday and crept out after dark. He had no English money, so when he saw a man returning home from the pub he presented an easy target. He just had to creep up from behind, make a quick blow into the neck with a long, sharp knife and it's done. Bushey was robbed which would give Schleger funds to travel. So we have issued an alert to all eastern ports for authorities to be on the lookout for him. We have the description of him and his uniform. Of course, he will have used his knife to remove all the naval insignia so it might look like an unusual but otherwise unremarkable dark blue suit. He can readily pretend to be a Belgian refugee or something. He will say he is a merchant sailor and try to get work on a ship sailing to Holland. But I am confident our boys will find him."

Sherlock Holmes had listened to this account with closed eyes and fingertips together. Now he opened his eyes and spoke. "Would he head due east? The East Anglian ports are small and the rail connections not so direct from here. In his place, I would head for a larger port; London would be an obvious destination but I believe a previous escapee from Donington was arrested at Millwall? No, London is too obvious. Hmm, perhaps your German would move in the opposite direction from the one you might expect. Now, you say Bushey's money was taken. Do you know if anything else was removed?"

"Like what, Mr Holmes?"

"Items of clothing. Was Mr Bushey wearing a hat or a coat when he was found?"

"I..." The inspector pulled out a sheaf of papers and ruffled through them. "Ah, here we are. No, just wearing normal civilian clothes... no mention of a coat or hat."

I had another flash of inspiration. "Bushey's coat is missing then!" I cried. "Clearly said his coat was gone from the wardrobe in the staff room. An ulster, new, deep maroon."

"The colour is significant," said Holmes. "Well, well, Inspector, if you were willing to take my advice, it would be this. Find out from the staff here whether Bushey had his coat and a hat when he left on Monday night. Then issue your description of *Oberleutnant zur See* Schleger again, but this time saying he is wearing... no, perhaps carrying, a stained maroon ulster coat and whatever style of hat Bushey wore. Finally, this time, issue it to your colleagues in Liverpool."

"Why Liverpool?"

"Because that is the port I expect to have been his destination. From there, he could take a job on a ship to the United States or any neutral country. I do, however, agree with your guess that he will claim to be Belgian. More likely to attract sympathy."

The Inspector rose, looking much happier. "Thank you Mr Holmes, I will do that now. If we help catch an escaped prisoner and solve one of the murders, that will be something." He made to leave the room.

"One more thing before you leave us, Inspector," said Holmes. "The knife. Was that ever found?"

"No. We assume he stole it from Donington. He used it to cut off his insignia and kill Bushey and presumably took it with him, in case he felt the need to use it again."

Holmes nodded and the Inspector left.

"This matter has been most deplorably handled," said Holmes. "I understand the police are short of resources in the present emergency, but to leap to such erroneous conclusions so quickly and then to stick with them." He shook his head.

"DS," I said, "Daniel Smythe. He has a large collection of sporting kit. There's something else. Mrs Evans at the school told me she cannot find her best knife."

"These do seem to point to the school as the source of the troubles. Before you joined us, I expressed that concern to Inspector Underwood. He has reluctantly sent men to the school to watch over the staff."

"You told him about the shot being fired from the church? You are quite sure a shot was fired from there, towards where Clearly and I were walking?"

Holmes smiled. "Let me do something I rarely do: guess. My guess is that the Reverend Smythe MA doubted the story?" I nodded. "A foolish man. One who believes and disbelieves whatever best serves his interests. He has put his colleagues at risk by insisting the school has nothing to do with the deaths. Do you know he offered me a job?"

"Congratulations, Holmes."

"I played Mr Crossman as a deaf old fool who had little to teach and no experience of teaching. But I said I would take a salary of £150 and that made Crossman the ideal candidate."

"You don't think it possible that Smythe could be responsible? The cricket bat could have been his and he could have taken the knife from the school kitchen."

"He would have had to move fast to get away from the tower before I got to it, and just as fast to be back at the school in time for your meeting. Tell me, Watson, did he seem at all out of breath when you met him?"

"He did not seem so."

"So probably not the Reverend Smythe, unless he is fitter than he looks. But I think our killer is someone from the school. Mr and Mrs Evans appear unlikely to be able to move fast enough to evade me. Do you think Mr Yarding's physical condition would prevent him from a rapid escape?"

"His limp does appear to be an impediment," I answered.

"What about the ladies?"

"Miss Harting and Mrs Hood had left to catch a bus into Derby."

"One does not like to think of a woman committing violent crimes but such events have occurred. We must get the Inspector to confirm they were on that bus when the shot was fired. We should rule Clearly out as well, if we presume that he was the target of the shot, unless there is a conspiracy and more than one person is involved."

"We should not rule that out, Holmes. That school is riven with factions and disagreements." I told him what I had learned about Clearly, Dolman and Bushey being one faction, who believed in strong discipline, while Yarding and Wheatfield believed in a more encouraging style. "If this division was strong enough to lead to murder, then, why then, we must consider Wheatfield, the German teacher."

"Watson, do you believe Wheatfield hates his colleagues enough to murder two of them and try to murder a third? Does he strike you as such a person?"

"In reality, Holmes, no. Not at all. I would say one of the least likely to do such things."

"I am sure you recall the German master at the Priory School who died trying to save a pupil."

"But what about this escaped German naval officer? Might he have been involved?"

"Possibly. He needs to be found in any event." He thought for a moment. "We have prevented a third murder. The police are keeping the school safe. Watson, I need you to tell me exactly what all the members of the school staff have told you since you arrived. Then I have some errands to run. I suggest you take a room here at this inn, as I have. You will find the rooms neither comfortable nor especially clean but they will serve. Let us meet for dinner at seven o'clock, then we shall be about our business once again."

A gathering of suspects

I related to Holmes every word I had exchanged with the school staff then took a room at the inn and had time for a rest. After dinner we set off across the meadow back to the school. Holmes had explained over our meal that he had asked all the teachers to gather in the staff room for a meeting at eight o'clock. As we entered the room I looked around at those assembled: Mr Clearly, trying to project his air of confidence though obviously still shaken by the morning's events; Miss Harting, beautiful but sad; Mrs Hood, angry at everyone and everything; Mr Yarding, anxious and pale; Mr Wheatfield, downcast and trembling; and the Reverend Smythe, rubbing his beard and looking uncomfortable (I later learned that he never visited the staff room, preferring to stay away from his staff in his study upstairs). He had also brought his odour of cheap cigars. The gathering was completed by Inspector Underwood and a Constable who was holding a rifle.

"Should I ask Mr and Mrs Evans to join us?" Underwood asked Holmes.

"I do not think that is necessary at the present time," said Holmes. "I have Mrs Evans' description of her missing item of cutlery."

"Now look here," said the headmaster. "Just what is going on? Inspector, why are you asking for direction from this man? Who is he and why is he with Doctor Watson, who only came here to be interviewed for a teaching position?"

"I am sorry for the deception, headmaster. I wore some stage effects and pretended to be David Crossman. My name is Sherlock Holmes."

There was a gasp from several of the people in the room and Eric Wheatfield said, "So you are that Doctor Watson!"

The headmaster stood up and spoke with heat. "Sherlock Holmes and Doctor Watson. So, neither of you were really interested in working here? You are the only applicants we have had and your visits here were based on a lie! By what right do you come to my school under false pretences and waste my time discussing posts you do not want?"

"Reverend Smythe," said Holmes, speaking more quietly than the headmaster but somehow with more authority, "two of your teachers have been killed and your concern is that we may have wasted some of your time? I have made an apology for the deception. I felt it was necessary to learn about your school without anyone knowing I had an interest. Please resume your seat."

The headmaster sat down, his face alternating between anger and abashment. The Inspector asked the first question. "Do any of you recognize this rifle?" He took it from the Constable and held it up.

Simon Yarding recognised it first. "Why, that looks like one of the school rifles. We have a shooting range in a barn behind the kitchen garden. It's only used on days that are too wet for sports or gardening now. We give the boys some drill and shooting practice. God knows, it looks as if they will need it."

The Inspector turned to his junior officer. "What make did you say it is, Rogers?"

"It's a Lee-Enfield rifle, sir, dating from 1895. Standard British army issue of the time, sir."

"That's right," continued Yarding. "A number of them were donated to the school a few years ago. Can I take a closer look?" He examined the weapon. "Yes, I know this one. It's the best one we've got. How did you get possession of it? We keep the rifle range locked and the key's hidden in the drawer over there." He went to a corner cabinet. "It's not here."

The Inspector took the rifle back and handed it to the Constable but did not answer. I assumed it was the firearm found on top of the tower of the ruined church.

Holmes continued, "I have reason to believe that the two murders, and an attempted third, are connected with each other and with the school."

Mr Clearly interjected. "Not the second one, surely? We all heard that Reg was set upon by an escaped German."

"That is still a plausible theory," said Holmes, "and it may be correct. But if my hypothesis that the deaths are linked to this school is correct, then I am afraid to reveal that you are all potential suspects and, if the murderer has not completed his or her undertaking, you are at risk of being future victims."

The staff exchanged horrified rules but Mrs Hood spoke up. "If it's one of us, there's no problem in saying who."

"Who do you suspect, Mrs Hood?" asked Holmes.

"We've a Jerry here. An enemy." She turned to her colleague. "Your name's not Wheatfield, is it? Your father was called von Weizsäcker. You're a German, an enemy agent. Who knows what you get up to in that woodwork hut? Probably hiding escaped prisoners in there. And I know you go to Donington Hall to visit your friends there."

"Really, Mrs Hood," said Mr Wheatfield with some dignity. "I would always have been happy to tell anyone who cared to ask what my father's original name was and why he came to England, had they enquired. My father held political opinions – opinions I do not share, I hasten to add – which made life in Germany at that time dangerous for him. He decided he wanted to raise his family in a free country and I am eternally grateful for that. I can assure everyone here that I would do nothing to harm the interests of the land that gave refuge to my parents, my siblings and me."

"What about your visits to the prisoners of war?" asked the Inspector.

"I have been asked not to discuss that. But since it has been raised in this context, I will simply say that British officials have asked me to come to the prison on occasion to assist their enquiries." He looked around at the blank faces. "They are short of interpreters. I have been invited to assist the authorities at Donington Hall," he explained. "Fluent German speakers are needed on the continent so I have assisted in interrogations of prisoners. They've all been questioned on capture, of course, but we hope some may have mellowed during their incarceration and become more co-operative, especially when speaking to a civilian who can chat with then like a native." He turned to the Inspector. "Go to the camp and ask Major Dee if you require confirmation. It's my modest bit to help England."

Mona Hood still looked at Mr Wheatfield with great distaste. "Your name's still a lie, though."

Mr Clearly gave a hoot of laughter. "A lie? You're a fine one to talk, Mona. Tell us about your husband. A regular in the army, yes? Was away fighting for the empire long before this war began. Now he's away fighting in the trenches, right? But he's never been here. Never had home leave? I have never known a letter from him to be in the school mail and I have never seen you write to him. There is no Captain Hood, is there? You have never been married, have you?"

"Is that right, Mona?" asked Miss Harting.

"Ah, so what? Lots of mature ladies take the title 'Mrs'. What would I want with a man anyway? I only made up that little story as the world seems to expect women to attach ourselves to a man, someone to control us and run our lives for us. No, thank you. Besides, who are you to complain? What about all your farms and mines in America and Africa? You love to tell everyone about the land you have bought with your business success, but then why are you living in one tiny room here in the school? Why not buy a grand house? Where are these estates? I've laid a map in front of you and asked you to point them out but you made some excuse. You don't own a square inch of land anywhere, do you?"

Mr Clearly stood up, his face crimson. "I don't have to put up with this! If you want to find a real liar, someone who sets out to deceive, why not ask our esteemed headmaster where exactly he gained his degree and by what right he uses the title of 'Reverend'?"

"You are correct, Mrs Hood," said Holmes, who then turned to Mr Clearly. "Please sit down again. I have

214

been on the telephone to Scotland Yard this afternoon and we have been able to match your description and the dates you gave to Doctor Watson for when you were in Canada and Southern Rhodesia. I believe your real name is Jonathon Leeson. Mr Leeson has nothing waiting for him in either country but large debts and, in Canada, several charges of fraud and one of common assault. The assault was against a child, whom he subjected to a beating. I do not have the details but it does appear that cruelty towards those in his power is a feature of Mr Leeson's character."

There were more sharp intakes of breath from those remaining in the room. They looked at each other with shocked, horrified faces. Clearly's glance flickered between Holmes, the Inspector and myself. "Utter balderdash," he said. "I don't know what you're talking about. I've never heard of this Leeson. You've no proof. A description given over a telephone and some apparent alignment of dates! Sir, I demand you retract these ignoble accusations!"

"A motorcycle dispatch rider is on his way from the Canadian High Commission as we speak. He carries identification photographs and a reproduction of Leeson's fingerprints. He will be in Leicester by morning. Knowing that, is there anything else you would like to say?"

Clearly gazed fiercely at Holmes, his jaw clenched and his face getting increasingly red. "All right then, Mr Holmes. I have used the name Jon Leeson. I have changed my name, nothing illegal in that. I am aware of these ridiculous charges that stupid colonial oafs have levelled against me. But I tell you this: I never took anything that I did not deserve. I earned every penny."

"Through deceit, false accounting and misrepresentation, according to the local authorities," replied Holmes.

"Rubbish! All of it!"

"And the assault on the boy? I understand he was twelve years old."

"Boys need discipline! They need to learn! Dolman and Bushey understood, it's for the best, it's in their best interests! I can't stand weak teachers who won't see what's needed!"

The Inspector nodded at the Constable, who made the formal arrest and led Clearly, or Leeson, from the room, still protesting, "I've done nothing wrong! Ignorant colonials have made false accusations against me because some investments did not pay off. I only wanted what was best for my investors."

There was a period of complete and heart-subduing silence. Finally, Simon Yarding spoke. "Headmaster? I don't wish to pry and would quite understand if you chose not to answer, but do you know what Mr Clearly, I mean Mr Leeson, meant about your degree?"

The headmaster shifted in his chair and rubbed his beard. "I utterly reject the notion that I have lied. I have always said I gained my Master of Arts at St John's. If I have been remiss in specifying which particular establishment of that name, I apologise, but no deceit was intended."

Yarding continued. "Then, if I may, which one was it? Neither the St John's at Oxford nor the one at Cambridge?"

More rubbing of beard. "I am a graduate of the St

John's private college in Lahore. A very well-respected establishment locally. I was granted the sobriquet 'Reverend' by the Church of the Modern Apostles of the Punjab." He looked around and saw disbelief on the faces of his employees. "It has since been disbanded, purely due to lack of funds, but in its day it was well known for good works and missionary duties among the natives. I studied hard to get my degree and was awarded my ecclesiastical title on merit. No disrespect to our own ancient universities but my *alma mater* represents nothing of which an *alumnus* should be ashamed."

Mona Hood was now grinning with delight. "May I ask, 'Reverend' Smythe, did you collect all those bits of sporting equipment you have in your room upstairs while studying at the St John's private college in Lahore?"

Smythe thought for a moment and muttered "Most of them. Many of them. Some."

"What about cricket, headmaster?" asked Holmes. "Do you own a cricket bat with your initials on it?"

"Yes. I played a lot of cricket out in India. The game's popular with the natives. Jolly good at it too, some of them, by Jove. I do have a cricket bat such as you describe but I can't say where it is just now. I noticed it was missing the other day. I think Evans must have taken it for oiling. You need to oil a bat regularly, you know. But why are we talking about such trivial matters? Two of my staff have been killed and you tell us, Mr Sherlock Holmes, that these tragic events are linked to my school. Well now; have you gathered us together to make a dramatic announcement of who the murderer is? Which one of us do you suspect?"

Holmes looked around the room. "At the present time I have no single suspect. However, your school is under attack. I gathered you together for your protection."

There was a knock at the door and a constable entered, breathless. "Telegram for you, sir," he panted and handed a slip of paper to the Inspector.

Underwood opened it, read it and spoke to Holmes. "They have him. Caught at Liverpool docks, just as you predicted. He's being brought back to Donington Hall overnight."

Prisoner of war

The exhaustion of the day trumped its excitement and I had a surprisingly good night of sleep at the Pickvale Arms. In the morning, Inspector Underwood and Mr Wheatfield joined us after breakfast and a police car came to collect us.

"Thank you for agreeing to come, Mr Wheatfield," said Holmes. "I have no idea if *Oberleutnant zur See* Schleger speaks any English and my German skills would not be up to the task. Also I must thank you, Inspector Underwood, for arranging for us all to interview him."

"Oh, that was no difficulty," said the tufty little man. "I've been in touch with Major Dee at Donington Hall about the escape, of course. When I said who wanted to come with me to interview the prisoner he was beyond delighted. Your name opens doors, Mr Holmes, and even the gates of a prison."

Sure enough, wide gates in the high barbed wire fences opened and we approached the hall, a mock

Gothic stately home with an imposing central tower and broad wings of grey stone. The guards recognised Inspector Underwood and Mr Wheatfield.

Once inside, we were made welcome and quickly shown to a small room where Holmes, the Inspector, Wheatfield and I sat on one side of a table. After a few minutes, Schleger was brought in by two armed guards; they sat opposite us. The German was obviously terrified and began speaking rapidly, his eyes wide and flicking between us.

"He's saying he had nothing to do with the murder," said Mr Wheatfield. "He says the man was dead when he found him." Wheatfield spoke to the German to calm him down and soon was able to relate his tale. "He says he escaped on Sunday night as there seemed to be fewer guards that day. He hid in a pile of grass cuttings before the prisoners were locked indoors. After dark, he used wire cutters he had made himself from odds and ends to cut through at a place where the lights were not strong. Once out, he simply ran, in order to put as much distance between himself and the camp before daylight. Shortly before dawn on Monday he came across the old church near the school and decided to hole up in the crypt to rest and recover. He had cut himself on the wire but had some food. He intended to move again as soon as it got dark but fell asleep and was woken late at night by a scream. It was terrifying. He lay silent for a period of time; he thinks about half an hour. Then he crept out and found the body of a man who had been stabbed in the neck. He knows that what he did next is wicked and he says he's very ashamed. He took the man's coat, to cover his uniform. He took his hat and his wallet. He also, and he is very ashamed of this, he also took the knife."

"Did he have to remove the knife from the body?" asked Holmes.

Wheatfield asked the German and gave his reply, "No, it was just lying on the grass."

"Ask him to describe the knife."

Some conversation in German and then, "He says it had a long handle but a short blade. He thinks it must be an old knife, sharpened many times."

"That fits the description of the missing school utensil," said Holmes. "Mrs Evans told me that the end of the blade broke off a couple of years ago and she had it recut. Ask him why he took the knife and where it is now."

Through Mr Wheatfield, the German told us that he took it to cut off his naval insignia and, he was ashamed to admit, in case he needed to use it in defence. He left the church immediately and aimed for Derby, using his maritime skills to aid navigation but quickly became disgusted with himself for carrying the knife. He threw it in a river. He was in Derby by daybreak and went to the station. He just said the word 'Liverpool' at the ticket office and Bushey's stolen money had been enough for a ticket. He had been exploring the docks looking for a ship going to a neutral county. Holmes's prediction of his behaviour had been perfect. The police had arrested him last night and had a precise description of the coat. He had thrown away the hat, he thought it might be conspicuous. The coat did have blood stains; he had not seen them in the dark. He kept it folded in his lap while on the train and carried it folded during the day. But he kept it because he thought he would need it at night.

"He's very sorry for having robbed the body," continued Wheatfield. "He's going on about it being the duty of a captured officer to attempt to escape, he is sure we must understand that, but he knows he went too far in taking Bushey's things. He's pleading with us to believe him. He's scared he's going to swing for murder."

Holmes gazed at the scared young German for a minute. "Cutting a man's throat produces a great deal of blood. Even if the victim falls to the ground immediately, it is not credible that the victim's clothing should escape staining. A dark maroon woollen coat is less likely to show the stain. But he was wise to conceal it in daylight." Holmes paused for thought once more. "Ask him again what he heard of the murder," said Holmes.

After conversing with the prisoner, Wheatfield said, "He can't say anything more. He was woken by a scream, which was cut short."

"I have all I need," said Holmes. "Inspector, do you have any further questions?" Underwood did not, so we left, the German still protesting his innocence. Major Dee wanted us to stay to lunch and meet the Colonel in charge, but Holmes felt it best if we discussed the case away from German prisoners, so we returned to the Pickvale Arms, where we said goodbye to Wheatfield. Holmes, the Inspector and I once again took possession of the dusty upstairs parlour.

"What do you make of the German's story, Holmes?" I asked.

"I believe him," was the simple reply.

"He was credible," said the Inspector. "I've seen

people lie and people tell the truth. Funny, because I couldn't understand his words, I was able to pay more attention to his voice and expression and what not. I think he was telling the truth. But, Mr Holmes, have you thought of this: how do we know that the teacher was translating truthfully? The German could have been speaking the truth but Wheatfield telling us something quite different!"

"My German is not fluent but I am competent enough to be able to assure you that the translations were faithful."

"Then we have a suspect. The knife came from the school, do you agree? And the cricket bat belonged to the headmaster, yes?" The tufty man rubbed his hands. "A curious character, our 'Reverend' Smythe. He tells his story in a way which he knows will lead people to believe he was a sporting man at Oxford or Cambridge, while he's nothing of the kind. He's running a failing school with all sorts of nasty stuff going on, his people taking sides against each other. Did you see the hatred on some of the faces last night? Do you know what I think? Blackmail. Dolman and Bushey had found out about Smythe. They knew he was a fraud. Who knows what else they found out? Perhaps he had his fingers in the till, that would not surprise me. Maybe something worse... you do hear horror stories coming out of some of these boys' schools. Maybe Dolman and Bushey, they were friendly I believe, maybe they found out something really nasty about him. Clearly, or whatever his real name is, he was part of their clique, he was in on it as well, that's why Smythe took a shot at him. Yes, yes, it all makes sense. Well, thank you for your help, Mr Holmes, it's so good to have someone to talk things over with. My way is clear now: I'll interview Clearly, I mean Leeson, and find out what they knew about their boss. Then I'll take what I have gathered to confront this 'Reverend' Smythe and see if he doesn't confess!"

"Mr Leeson is a known crook. He is a fraudster and a serial liar. Why would you believe anything he says?"

"As I have said, Mr Holmes, I can spot truth and lies. Besides, why would he lie about this? If he helps us fix Smythe for the murders, it may count in his favour when he gets his comeuppance."

"By all means take Smythe to Leicester, Inspector. Indeed, if you would take my advice, I recommend that you do not let him out of your sight for one moment. Could you indulge me in one small matter? Could you keep your men at the school, just until tonight?"

The Inspector nodded, grabbed his hat and hurried from the room.

"What do you think of the Inspector's theory?"

Holmes shook his head. "Smythe's cricket bat was found beside Dolman. The school's knife was found beside Bushey. A school rifle was used in the attempt on Leeson and abandoned at the scene. The behaviour of a murderer is inexplicable, of course, but they usually act in ways which serve their twisted interests. In the horror and fright of their terrible crime, they can behave in ways which make no sense, even allowing for the fact that to take another person's life makes no sense to begin with. The Inspector's theory relies on the belief that Smythe committed all the crimes and left readily identifiable weapons beside the two dead men and at the location from where a shot was fired from towards the next intended victim. He also believes that

Smythe took the shot at Leeson and made it back to the school in time for his interview with you. All of this is possible, I grant. But it seems unlikely."

A maid knocked and entered the room. "The newspapers you asked for, Mr Holmes." She presented him with a pile: the Leicester Evening Mail, the Nottingham Evening Post and the Derby Evening Telegraph.

"Ah. Thank you, Margaret. Now, Watson, let us see what the gentlemen of the fourth estate have made of events around Pickvale Hall." We passed the papers around so we could each read what all reported. The Leicester Evening Mail had the most complete account, so I reproduce it here.

Pickvale Hall Mystery Deepens

Teacher arrested – School forced to close

Mystery continues to surround the deaths of two teachers at the Pickvale Hall Preparatory School in the north of the county. Miss Elsie Sandling, who was arrested on suspicion of the murder of the school's geography master Mr Peter Dolman, has been released. No new suspect has yet been named. Neither is any suspect named for the second murder, that of French master Mr Reginald Bushey. Mr Dolman was found beaten to death in woods near the school last Monday morning and Mr Bushey was discovered stabbed on a path between the school and the nearby village early on

Tuesday. It is thought both killings occurred on the evenings before the discoveries of the bodies.

However, an arrest has been made. Sources inside the school report that Mr Matthew Clearly, history master at the school, has been detained to answer charges of fraud in the colonies.

Despite the lack of arrests for the murders, the police are optimistic about solving the mystery. On being contacted by telephone, Inspector Underwood informed this paper that new events were being studied and that the official investigation was proceeding at a normal pace for a case of this nature. He declined to give further details. On being directly asked whether the man suspected of fraud abroad was also suspected of murder at home, the Inspector flatly refused to comment.

What parent would wish to entrust their young gentlemen to such an establishment as Pickvale Hall? The school has already lost members of staff to war service. With two more now dead and another languishing in gaol, it seems the school can no longer operate. This newspaper has been told that the school is to be wound up forthwith. The headmaster will lead a private service of thanks and remembrance in the village church (which is within the school

grounds) at seven o'clock this evening
before the school is disbanded and the
remaining staff go their separate ways.

The paper also carried news of a German prisoner,
who had escaped from Donington Hall, being
recaptured at Liverpool docks. However, no connection
between the stories was made.

"The headmaster said nothing about the school
being closed at the meeting last night," I observed.

"That is because he does not know about it."

"What? How could the headmaster of the school not
know it is being closed? There must be a board of
governors who would have made the decision. They
would not have made it without consulting, or at least
informing, the head of the school!"

"Watson, my dear fellow, one should not believe
everything one reads in the papers. Especially in a local
rag which might not have experienced reporters."

"But however did they get hold of this story, if it's
not even true?" Then it struck me. I looked again at the
newspaper article. "'Sources inside the school'. That
was you, Holmes." I looked at the article for a few
moments more. "You planted this story, including the
part about a church service before the staff disperse."

"Very good, Watson."

"You expect someone else to come to this service?
Someone who may see it as their last chance to finish
what they have started?"

"Precisely."

"A disgruntled former pupil, I suppose. Someone who suffered the cruelty of these school masters and has been exacting revenge."

"An excellent theory, Watson. My hope is that we shall get the truth this evening. I suggest you take a rest now; we made need your energy this evening. I have some further telephone calls to make, then I too will take some restorative time."

At church

Later that afternoon we made the now familiar journey from the village, across the meadow to the school and found the establishment in a state of turmoil.

Inspector Underwood had not taken Reverend Smythe to Leicester. Instead, they had been closeted in his office upstairs for the past two hours; none of the staff knew why. They had all seen the news of the school's closure in the newspaper, or had it pointed out to them, and so gathered in the staff room to find out what was going on: Anna Harting, Eric Wheatfield, Simon Yarding, Mona Hood and George and Sarah Evans. As soon as we appeared, they pumped us with questions: did we know why the Inspector was with the headmaster? Had anyone been charged with the murders? Did we think they were safe?

"Ladies and gentlemen, please relax," said Holmes. "I am confident that none of you is in any immediate danger."

"The paper said there's a service of thanksgiving in the church soon; is it safe for us to attend?" asked Miss Harting.

"I'm not going in any event," said Mrs Hood.

"Is it true that the school is closing?" asked Mr Yarding.

"That is a false report, so far as I am aware," said Holmes. "However, in view of all that has taken place, I would think it prudent for you all to consider the opportunities available to you for your next steps in your careers."

This time there was only a short silence before Miss Harting spoke. "That's a relief to me, Mr Holmes. I've long wanted to join up but felt disloyal in leaving the school at this time. I'll go to Leicester tomorrow and sign up for the Voluntary Aid Detachment."

Mr Yarding spoke next. "You'll make a great nurse, Miss Harting. As is happens, I've been offered a job working for the Royal Engineers."

"Thank you, Mr Yarding, and well done to you for joining up. They will take you, even with your foot?"

"Oh, no, not as an active soldier. They want me for my mathematics. I'll be working for Doctor Bragg. You might have read about his Nobel Prize last year. I can't talk about what they are working on but they need someone to help with the numbers. I'll be what's called a computer. A small part but it could make a big difference."

We all shook hands with the future nurse and computer. Eric Wheatfield spoke next. "Actually, Major Dee has tentatively enquired of me, once or twice, whether I would be interested in working with him full time. There's much useful intelligence to be had from the prisoners and I do seem able to win some of them over pretty well. I did not like to leave the boys in the hands of people like Clearly, but now that he and the others have gone... and I think the school has to close, after all these scandals. I doubt many boys will return after this holiday." He looked across to Mr and Mrs Evans. "I don't know what will become of Pickvale Hall but the military are always commandeering buildings and estates. Someone's going to take this place on and they'll need people to look after it. You will both have my recommendation."

"That just leaves you, Mona," said Anna Harting. "What will you do?"

"Don't fret about me, I'll find something. I read about a new women's land army which is taking over farming work while the men are away. I think that's for me. We'll show the country what women can do."

Eric Wheatfield spoke again. "Mr Holmes, you said you thought the report in the newspaper about the school closing was premature, although it does seem to have been an accurate prediction. What about the line saying there will be a private service in the church, led by the headmaster? Is that really going to happen? Because, if so, it will start in about an hour."

"There is no private service, Mr Wheatfield," said Holmes. "Indeed, I think it is not possible to hold a private service in a public church. That aspect of the story was intended to keep people away and I ask that you all remain here for the time being. As I have mentioned, I do not believe any of you is in danger while you are gathered here but I advise you all to stay away from the church this evening. The final act of the drama will soon unfold."

Holmes and I left the staff in the staff room and set off down the long central corridor towards the main staircase.

"Holmes, slow down old chap, you're expecting the murderer to come to this supposed church service?"

"I think it possible. It offers him a last chance to complete his mission. I'm sorry, Watson, but we cannot afford to slow down. We must collect the Inspector."

We climbed the stairs and, by the time I caught up, Holmes was already in the headmaster's study.

The Inspector was looking morose. "It's no use, Mr Holmes. He has an answer for everything and it does appear as if he might not be the person we are seeking."

The headmaster looked very relaxed for someone being questioned about murder. He almost looked as if he had been enjoying himself. "I'm not the person you are seeking. As I have explained, I was with my wife in our cottage while these dreadful events took place. I still see no evidence that anything that has happened has any connection to my school."

"Right and wrong, headmaster," said Holmes. "You are right that you are not the person who committed the crimes but you are wrong about the connection. Your school is at the heart of these tragedies. Inspector, I think we may be able to close this matter now. Can you gather your men in the hall? Headmaster, I must ask you to stay in your study for a time. Please close the blinds, lock the door and only open it to one of us."

A few minutes later, we were gathered by the main school entrance. The Inspector had four bobbies with him. Holmes addressed us. "Gentlemen, I hope all will become clear soon. But we have no time for explanations now; we much go to the church and see what awaits us."

As we walked down the path that crossed the swathe of lawn which stretched between the hall and the church, the bell struck six o'clock. The sun shone and the scents of early summer drifted across the English landscape. Not for the first time, I sensed the strangeness of the contrast between the natural environment in which I found myself and the mission I was on with my illustrious friend.

The churchyard was surrounded by tall trees and the temperature dropped as we came into their shadow. The church had white-painted walls, a pitched tile roof and a squat tower of grey stone. When we reached the porch, Holmes held up a hand to stop us, then made a close examination of the floor of the porch and the church door. The door opened with a latch and the sound of it echoed around the interior: white walls, windows of small, diamond-shaped panes streaked with green and grey, and plain pews facing a simple altar. Above us and to the right was an organ loft. The church felt very cold and was full of a slightly sickening earthy smell. Our footsteps rang on worn slabs as we approached and then moved slowly up the aisle, the policemen and I looking around curiously, cautiously but seeing nothing untoward.

Holmes halted halfway to the alter and we, who were following, stopped in our turn. Holmes turned around and addressed the organ loft. "Good evening. I believe you entered the church shortly before us, judging by the mud deposited in the porch." There was a moment of silence before Holmes spoke again. "My name is Sherlock Holmes. I hope I do not flatter myself

231

by suggesting the possibility that you may have heard of it. The headmaster will not be coming here this evening. No one in this church has any association with the school, other than yourself." Another long pause. "Do I need to ask one of these police officers to climb up to find you or will you save him that disturbing duty and reveal yourself?" There was another pause, then a creak from behind the organ, which became a series of creaks as a man emerged from a cavity behind the instrument. He was a pale, refined-looking man in his middle thirties, with coal black hair and moustache and dark eyes which seemed to twinkle; his thin red lips were curved in a slight smile. He grasped the rail of the organ loft with both hands and looked down on our little party.

"Sherlock Holmes? The famous detective?"

"I am he. And I believe I am addressing Captain Norman Lighterman, former science teacher at this school?"

"You are living up to your reputation, Mr Holmes. Can I ask how you knew my identity?"

"A process of elimination. I thought it could be a former pupil, but the actor in this drama knew more than a former pupil would: where the key to the rifle range was hidden, how to get in and out of the school when it was locked and where to find items that suited his purpose. I have been able to clear the current staff of the school so a former employee was the remaining possibility. This school is riven with hatred and bitterness so it had to be someone who took the side of masters like Wheatfield and Yarding, and despised the approach of Dolman, Bushey and Clearly. That pointed to you. A simple enquiry found that you have been on home leave since last Friday. You are due back with your unit this evening."

The man gave a mirthless laugh. "Oh my, am I absent without leave? I hardly think that will be of significance now. But you're right: I despised those sadistic bullies. They loved to hurt boys, both physically and mentally, and covered their crimes by fabricating the idea that such suffering was somehow good for them."

I had to speak up. "But you have killed two of them!"

He looked at me. "Could you be Doctor Watson?" I gave a nod. "I have killed many people, doctor. The difference between my two former colleagues and the rest were that Dolman and Bushey deserved it. The world is a better place with them gone from it."

"Why, who else have you killed?" I asked, and almost immediately wished I had not, as I guessed the answer.

"I don't know their names. I am not even sure how many I have killed. I think I can claim two for certain at Le Cateau. My platoon killed three or four at the Marne, but I could not say exactly which of us fired fatal shots. At Messines I called down artillery on a concentration of Germans we spotted. It looked on target but we'll never know how many we bagged. The one that sticks in my mind was at Ypres last year. I led a night raid on the trench opposite. We'd been told to snatch some Huns for interrogation. We got over well enough and surprised a couple of sleepy chaps. They seemed quite happy to come over. Well, it means they're out of it. We're just getting them out of their trench when round the corner comes another of their number. Just a boy. Looked like he'd never even shaved. He dropped the mess tins he was carrying and looked at me, just shaking. I remember his little lip going up and down."

He paused. The memory was obviously upsetting him. I asked another stupid question. "What did you do?"

"I shot him, of course. He didn't have a gun but he could have raised the alarm and we'd have never made it back. We had some whizz bangs going off to hide any noise we made. He gave me a strange, sort of disappointed look and just crumbled. One more mother who won't ever hug her son again. I do that to a poor German child and I'm a hero. I kill thugs like Dolman and Bushey and I'm a criminal."

"You planned to kill Clearly as well," stated Holmes.

"Oh yes, another really nasty individual. I was going to finish him as he walked back from the pub on Wednesday night, as I had done for Bushey two days before. But he had some ancient old man with him, almost clinging to him, so I decided not to risk it."

"I was that elderly gentleman," said Holmes.

"Oh, that was you? Acting as a bodyguard, very clever. And I suppose it was you who shouted out when I took a shot at him from the old church tower the next morning? And it was you, Doctor Watson, you were the other fellow, who threw him to the ground?" We both gave nods of agreement. "Well, if you knew the sort of man you were protecting, the monster you were risking your lives for, you might have thought again."

"I don't think so," said Holmes, who continued, "You went to some effort to implicate your former employer, Reverend Smythe, for these crimes. Why did you want to see him hanged for what you had done?"

"He's not a savage like some of his teachers were but he allowed their cruelty to go without check in his school. He knew exactly what went on here. I told him. I had challenged my colleagues several times over their cruelty. They spun their lines about beatings and bruising being in a boy's best interests, but I'd seen their faces light up whenever they came across an excuse to indulge themselves. I threatened to report their mistreatment to the headmaster and, eventually, I did. But he did not want to hear about it. He is too great a coward to challenge the bullies he employed. He likes to pontificate about being a headmaster and a leader but we all despised him. He did nothing to stop what happened here. In some ways, that's worse."

"You came here tonight to kill him," stated Holmes.

"Certainly. It said in the papers that he was going to lead one of his boring, maudlin services here tonight and I decided it was my last chance to finish him. I knew he was bound to have an alibi for at least one of my executions." He paused for a moment. "Although the thought of a hangman's noose slipping under that greasy beard of his does have some appeal."

The man disgusted me. "Instead, it's going to be your neck that feels the rope," I barked.

He shrugged. "Not so bad. To die quickly and painlessly while warm, dry and fed. There's many who would settle for that." He looked down at our faces. "Have you really no idea what's going on over there? I've sat in my dug-out and listened to men strung out on the barbed wire take all night to die."

There was another painful pause before Inspector

Underwood finally broke it. "Where have you been staying this past week? I've had enquiries made, locally, about anyone connected with the school and nothing showed up."

"I have been at The Castle Inn. Your search won't have turned me up as I've got the identity papers of a Lieutenant Chambers."

"Where is the real Lieutenant Chambers?" asked the Inspector.

Lighterman shrugged again. "I imagine he is still where I last saw him, face down in the mud at the bottom of a shell crater."

I felt the cold of the church running right into me as I looked up at this man. The Inspector spoke again. "Well, that's mighty sad, but it makes no difference to what I have to do. Now, are you going to come along with us?"

"I don't really see any point in that," said Lighterman, and in less than a moment he had pulled out a revolver and shot himself through the head.

Holmes and I sat in silence on the train to London. It was the following day. After all we have seen in our many adventures together, and all that is going on in the world, we had spoken little since the events in the church. Neither of us had felt like eating after witnessing the end of the Pickvale Hall mystery, although I had managed to eat a little breakfast before we began our journey home.

Suddenly Holmes spoke. "Give me an honest criminal every time."

I did not understand. "What do you mean by an honest criminal?"

He looked at me and I was reminded of our advanced years when I looked into his eyes. "I mean one who acknowledges that what he does is a crime. One who is honest, at least with himself, that what he does is wrong. Better that than a criminal who creates a myth that his crimes have justification."

"You mean Lighterman, killing former colleagues and believing he is distributing justice."

"Lighterman, yes. He is damaged by his experience of the war but I cannot see that as an excuse for his actions. But not just Lighterman."

"Who else, then?"

"Dolman, Bushey and Leeson. They like to bully children. They take pleasure in causing pain and suffering. Therefore, they create their absurd myth in which this is of benefit to their victims. I don't know what good or ill comes from their approaches but I do know they did it for their own pleasures, not for any benefit to their charges. As well as them, the weak headmaster, Smythe, creating the myth that he is an inspiring leader while ignoring the cruelty, factions and in-fighting in his school." The train rattled over a set of points before Holmes continued. "I wonder if a true measure of a person's evil is not merely in their actions, but as much in the excuses they contrive to justify those actions to themselves."

"Entire nations are creating myths to justify unprecedented evil which serves their interests."

"That we, who have devoted our lives to fighting

crime, should live to see crime on a world-wide scale."

I was alarmed by this maudlin attitude in a man who had always risen above emotion to address the facts of a situation. "Holmes, you have done so much that is good. My small part has been to record what you have achieved. I expect people will be talking of your great works for generations to come. You will inspire people to goodness and greatness. Even this, which may be our last adventure together, will provide an illustration of how intelligence and determination can prevent evil and shine light on a dark mystery."

He looked up at me. "What makes you think this may be our last adventure together?"

"Why, the big push is coming. The war should be over soon. Let us pray that Christmas 1916 will be a true celebration of peace on Earth. I will be needed at Challis House for many months, perhaps years, as we help the wounded recover. But we can hand criminal investigation to the next generation once peace is restored."

"Yes, peace. I hope you are right Watson, and that our contributions will soon no longer be needed."

THE ADVENTURE OF THE LAND SHIPS

Warning: this adventure contains spoilers about one of the original Sherlock Holmes stories – but you don't need to have read it to follow this story.

A visitor

Over the course of my adventures with Mr Sherlock Holmes I have collected the principal facts and essential details of several hundred cases. When choosing which of these cases to lay before the reading public, my first concern was to select those which are interesting in themselves, and which most clearly display the great skills which make my friend unique in my experience. I have also chosen to select only those cases which led to a successful outcome and which, I feel sure, no one else could have been relied upon to provide. Remaining in my files will be notes of puzzles which another detective might eventually have been able to solve (such as the Bishopgate jewel case) along with those related to cases which even Holmes's great powers had not been able to bring to a conclusion, such as the disappearances of both the cutter *Alicia* and of Mr James Phillimore.

Other notable adventures were made known to the public by newspaper reports at the time, and to which I have nothing further to add — such as Holmes's famous investigation of the sudden death of Cardinal Tosca.

The next criterion I have applied in selecting tales for publication was whether I ought to make the story known. Some cases, such as that of the giant rat of Sumatra, or the events surrounding the House of Silk, are so shocking that the world may not be ready for them for many years. Others, such as that of Colonel Warburton's madness and the story of the Grice Patersons in the island of Uffa, would reveal private information which no changes of names of places would be adequate to protect. Those who have sought Holmes's assistance on matters which should remain confidential have nothing to fear.

Similarly, the story concerning the politician, the lighthouse, and the trained cormorant will remain locked in the vaults of Cox and Co. for many years to come, all being well. I am certain that our adventures during the Great War, of which this tale is one chapter, will also have to remain hidden until long after the conflict is won.

I have been able to publish some adventures after a few years (occasionally with changes of names and other adjustments) with the permission of Holmes and the clients he represented. Others I hope to make known to the public in years to come; if I still have life and strength once this war is over, I hope to narrate the service Holmes was able to provide to Sir James

Damery, which led to terrible injuries being inflicted upon Holmes, and the extraordinary story of the Sussex vampire.

Then there were adventures which I was free to publish soon after they occurred, either because they contained no great secret, or because events meant a secret no longer needed to be kept. I was reminded of one such example, one forenoon in June 1916.

I had returned to Challis House, the auxiliary hospital in the north-western outskirts of London, after our adventure in Leicestershire. I was slow to recover from the exertions and the excitement, as well as the tragedy, and even after several days of no more than light duties at Challis, I still required regular breaks to recover my strength. In particular, I found my knees became uncomfortable after just an hour on my feet. A painting class had been arranged in the mess hall and I was sitting in the rear where I could see the patients' work being created under the supervision of a Gunner who had been an artist before losing his hand at Loos. Most were creating bucolic, peaceful scenes of farming life or rural villages. A couple were working on portraits of each other. Two men, however, were painting horrific scenes of the front: one showed a group of men cowering in a filthy trench, the other a view of no-mans-land, with black smoke rolling over a landscape of barbed wire and shell holes, illuminated only by flares and explosions.

One of the VAD nurses came in, saying, "Ah, there you are, doctor. You have a visitor."

"Oh, who is it?"

"He wouldn't give his name, just asked us to find you

and ask you to meet him in the entrance hall."

"Do you think you could ask him to come here? I'm feeling a little stiff and would prefer to greet visitors somewhere more comfortable than that draughty hall."

"He said he didn't want to come in, doctor. Just asked us to fetch you."

I started getting to my feet and said irritably, "And he wouldn't even give his name?"

"No sir, he just – well, he just asked us to tell you that Tadpole was here."

Tadpole? Tadpole... the name rang a distant bell which was becoming clearer as I made my way to the entrance hall. It came to me just as I arrived and caught sight of my old schoolfellow, who was skulking in the shadows by the main doors.

"Phelps! My dear ch..." I began, but he waved me into silence. "Shh! Watson, please, not here!" He pointed outside to the grounds, so I followed him into the sunshine. Percy Phelps, Tadpole Phelps when we were at school, and many years later our client in the Adventure of the Naval Treaty. That was an example of a case which, while involving a secret of national importance at the time, I had been able to publish just two or three years after the event: the existence of the treaty ceased to be a secret after a few months; Lord Holdhurst retired unexpectedly a few months later and Phelps and his wife moved to take up a position in the Indian administration shortly after that.

Phelps did not speak until we were clear of the buildings and away from any trees. Even so, he kept looking around as if we might be spied upon from any shrub or bush nearby.

At last he relaxed a little and smiled. "My dear Watson," he said as we shook hands. "It is good to see you after all these years." Phelps was of much the same age as me and, indeed, he looked it. I cannot hide my age, and see no need to, but I hope I am not being unduly vain to suggest that Phelps showed the years even more than I. His face was heavily creased with lines that suggested anxiety rather than laughter, his shoulders were stooped and no more than wisps of white hair were scattered across his head. On top of that, he looked exhausted. But beneath it all, I could readily see the little boy I knew as a child.

"It is a delightful surprise for me, Phelps! How did you know where to find me?"

"I was able to track down Mrs Hudson in Frinton. She had your address here from your card last Christmas."

"But why did you not telephone to say you were coming? I might have been away."

"I couldn't risk it, Watson. No one must know I am here. I regret that I even had to give Mrs Hudson a false name."

Phelps always had something of a sensitive and nervous character. I recognised it again in his strained tone of voice and his continued looking around for eavesdroppers.

"Phelps, old friend, I can see you have something on your mind. Why not unburden yourself right away?"

"Watson, oh dear me, a most terrible event has occurred, so like the tragedy which befell me before, when the naval treaty went missing from my room at the Foreign Office. I hardly slept last night, after what happened yesterday, and took the first train to London this morning. I fear that, once again, I must ask you to seek the assistance of the great man who saved my honour, and indeed my life, more than twenty years ago."

"If you need Holmes, you could have contacted him yourself. Mrs Hudson has his address as well as mine. I am sure he would be delighted to hear from you."

"No, no, that would never do! If I rang him, a telephone operator, making the connection, might wonder why I was calling him. If I was seen travelling to his home in Sussex, rumours would start! No, you must call him and ask for a meeting. What could be more innocent than two old friends getting in touch to arrange a reunion? But do not mention my name. We can meet in London. I know an hotel which will let us have a private room. We must meet as soon as possible and then travel north."

My legs were starting to ache, so I pointed to a fallen tree and suggested we sit on the trunk while he told me about this terrible event which had led him to me.

"Very well. To begin with, you must know that I retired from the Indian civil service the year before the war started. Annie and I returned to England and settled in Lincolnshire, where our daughter lives with her husband and baby. Last year, I was approached and asked if I would consider coming out of retirement. So many young men are now in uniform. All government departments are short of men but have enormous volumes of war-related work, on top of what they previously had to do in peaceful times. Many retired civil servants and officials have received the call and, of course, any that can have put away their slippers and dressing gowns and picked up pens and ink once again. As I live near Lincoln, I was put to work on a special project there. We're building a secret weapon, I must say little about it, but it is something to help us break through the German lines and win."

At this, a memory of a few months ago stirred; a café in Folkestone and a Colonel saying, 'imagine steel bunkers, mounted with guns and motorised so they can drive across no-mans-land.' Could this be the secret weapon? I decided to say nothing and allowed Phelps to continue. But he refused to give more detail, insisting that I call Holmes and ask him to meet me as soon as possible at the St Pancras Hotel. I started to mention that I knew the hotel and had lunched there recently but Phelps interrupted, "Please, Watson, ask him to meet us there as soon as he can, and bring what he needs to stay away for a few days."

The Hospital Supervisor allowed us to use his office, so I rang Holmes and asked him to meet me at St Pancras as soon as he could.

"It would, as ever, give me enormous pleasure, Watson. But it is less than a week since we said our farewells at that very railway terminus after our adventure in Leicestershire. I am sure that, like me, you are still recovering from exertions that were rather unbecoming for gentlemen of our age."

"Yes Holmes, but I have, ah, a friend with me. Someone also known to you." Phelps made frantic gestures to indicate I must not give any clues to a telephone operator. So I nodded to him and continued

"Holmes, I am sure you recall a night spent in Surrey that ended with you getting a cut on the knuckles of your left hand?"

"Yes... followed by a surprise at breakfast?"

"That's right! Well, our companion at that breakfast is with me now, saying a similar situation has arisen to that which troubled him then. He hopes we could come with him for a few days."

"Indeed... I do hope our friend is not suffering as badly as before. Do I take it that the levels of confidentiality and urgency are of a similar nature as last time? Very well. Let me see... I will have to make a few arrangements but I will be able to join you for dinner at the station hotel."

"He can come no sooner?" hissed Phelps.

"Yes, Holmes, I am sure that will be ideal. I shall see you this evening."

Immediately after I had hung up the telephone receiver, Phelps was showing signs of   nervous illness, worrying that someone would have overheard the telephone call, that I had given away too much information, and that a meeting with Holmes this evening was too late. As we had a much shorter journey to London than Holmes, I hoped to be able to distract him with a tour of our humble establishment, but the sight of so many wounded and maimed men seemed to distress him further. Instead, I packed my bag and informed the Hospital Supervisor that I was again going away for a few days. He gave a knowing smile and asked, "Will I ever be told what you are really doing on these little breaks you take?" I hated telling him a falsehood, especially when he had clearly guessed the truth.

"I hope to tell you, one day, after the war."

"We all look forward to that day. *Bon voyage*, Doctor Watson."

I decided we should walk to the Metropolitan railway station. The weather was fine and I felt a little exercise would benefit us both, although my knees were uncomfortable. As we walked and, later, rode a rattling train into London, I tried to distract Phelps by talking about his life since the Adventure of the Naval Treaty.

"I imagine you got to a senior position in the Indian Administration?"

"Not a senior role. A medium level position was right for me."

"Really? But you were one of the brightest at school. I can't remember how many prizes you won."

Phelps gave a wry smile. "Yes, I had the brain power, I suppose, but I rather lacked the assurance to take high office. I was happier devoting myself to a set area of work, attending to numbers and reports. In truth, I never fully recovered from the illness brought on by the loss of the treaty all those years ago. Holmes recovered it and, without him, I would probably never again have been able to work at all. But I don't have the confidence that I can make big decisions and I don't think I can be relied upon in a crisis."

The conversation had not taken a direction that was elevating Phelps's mood, so I changed tack and asked him why he had not returned to his house in Woking, which was the scene of the Adventure of the Naval Treaty.

"Briarbrae? Oh no, we sold that when we went out to India. Too many bad memories, not just for me but for Annie. We experienced a terrible betrayal there. It's long gone now. Woking has changed beyond recognition. I recall you described it as 'fir woods and heather' in your account of the events there. Where the old house and grounds were there are now streets of new houses. Watson, did you ever read Mr Wells's book 'The War of the Worlds'? It is set in Woking and the surrounding area and was written only a few years after we were there. Even then, Wells described a largely rural area with just a few houses near the station. Now..." He shook his head. "If the Martians wanted Woking now, I think we should let them have it."

Despite his joke, he seemed to be getting down again, so I decided to move on to happier matters. "You said you settled near Lincoln to be near your daughter and grandchild?"

This brightened him up. "Yes, we had just the one child who lived to adulthood. We sent her to school in England, where she met a young man called Adrian Wenderton. His family owns land in Lincolnshire, near a place called Welton, so that is where we have all ended up. A lovely part of the world."

Having found a pleasant topic for conversation, we kept to that until we arrived at the St Pancras hotel. Phelps had had a very early start so he took a room and retired for a rest. I gave him a small sedative to help him sleep.

It was evening by the time Holmes arrived. He was pleased to see us and Phelps was positively afire to see him: "Mr Holmes, my dear Mr Holmes, you saved me once before, I put all my faith in you, once again, to come to my aid at a moment of crisis."

The three of us sat down to dinner. Phelps wanted us to miss the meal and make directly for Lincoln but Holmes insisted he had travelled enough for one day, there would be little we could do in Lincoln by the time we arrived, and the hotel had comfortable rooms and good food. Phelps agreed, putting his trust entirely in Holmes, but still complained about the delay.

He refused to speak of the matter which had brought him to us while we were in a public room. It was only after the meal was complete, and we were enjoying brandy and cigars in a private room, that Phelps felt able to tell us his tale. Even so, he twice jumped up and pulled open the door to make sure no one was listening. He also spoke in a sotto voice, which meant I had to strain to hear him.

"Gentlemen, I have the honour to be working on an endeavour of national importance. We are creating a new, secret weapon which has the potential to end the war. Experimental models have been built and tested and the device is now being produced in numbers at Lincoln, ready to be shipped to France and used against the enemy in a few weeks' time. The army has such hopes for this weapon that a second site for production is being started, at Birmingham." He took a gulp of brandy. "I manage a small team of administrators. We work on procurement of materials and financial control of the project. When a need arose to deliver some plans to the Birmingham manufacturers, I suggested one of my officials to take them. They're top secret, gentlemen! Even the smallest idea of their content would be of immense value to Germany!" Poor Phelps began to tremble. "Attacked and robbed, gentlemen! My man, name of Jonah Bass, was knocked unconscious in the lavatory at Nottingham station. When he recovered himself, the briefcase containing the plans was gone!"

"It was hardly your fault, old man," I said.

"Not entirely, no," agreed Phelps. "I was not the one in charge of the plans when they were stolen, as I was with the naval treaty. But it was I who suggested Bass as the messenger. I thought that a mission of such responsibility would be beneficial for him. I was wrong, he's in the hospital now, in a state of brain fever that I recognize all too well. Not only did I put him in danger, but I have also put the country in danger by allowing the plans to be stolen."

"Come now," said Holmes. "Your choice of courier is no grounds for your taking any of the blame for this event. Any other courier might have met the same fate. Now, we will be up early to catch the train north. Before we retire for the night, I have a few questions for you. My first is: do you have any reason to suppose that the assailant who attacked your man Bass knew what he was taking?"

"Well, no," admitted Phelps. "It could have been what they call an ordinary 'mugging'."

"Very well. My second question then. How many people knew what Bass was carrying when he left on his mission?"

Phelps had to think for a moment. "I cannot be

certain of that. Some of the directors of William Foster & Co – that's the factory building the weapon in Lincoln – will have known. Perhaps some of the draughtsmen as well. Also, directors and engineers at Metropolitan Carriage, that's the factory in Birmingham, which is also to begin production; they knew the documents were to be delivered to them. I think it cannot have been a very large number of people. We keep everything very secret in Lincoln. Even in the city, few know what we are building there."

"What were the documents carried in?"

"One of our standard secure briefcases. Black, couple of straps and a lock. We have a stock of them. We use them all the time."

"Hard to open if you don't have the key?"

"Not hard at all. A sharp knife would open them, they're only leather. Even the locks would probably be no barrier to a thief who knows his business. The cases look ordinary, that's the idea."

"Hmm. Finally, then, why did you say that this task of carrying the plans would be beneficial to Bass?"

"Oh that," said Phelps. "No special reason. He's had problems recently. Domestic arrangements. Led to some ragging from some of the men in the factory. I thought that asking him to carry the plans would give him a bit of dignity. Now I have a question for you, Mr Holmes. Early tomorrow, do you think we should travel first to Lincoln, where the factory is, where Bass's journey started and where he is recovering now, or to Nottingham, where the robbery took place?"

"We will have an early breakfast and then board a

train to Lincoln," said Holmes. "And with that, I wish you good night."

The tank factory

The next morning, an hotel porter told us that there were delays on the Great Northern line from King's Cross. Fortunately, the man seemed to know the Bradshaw's Railway Guide by heart. He advised us to take the eight twenty-five Midland Railway train from St Pancras and change at Nottingham for Lincoln. This gave us a longer time than planned to have breakfast, which pleased me, although Phelps could not hide his impatience.

We had fifteen minutes to change trains at Nottingham. We emerged onto a grimy platform and Holmes stood still for a while, surveying the scene. The train driver and fireman came past, wiping soot from their faces, and Holmes stopped them. "Excuse me, gentlemen, I understand a poor fellow was found knocked out here yesterday?"

The two engineers were very happy to discuss the news. "Yes, sir, gentleman found hurt in the lavvy, begging your pardon, sir, up by the booking office." He pointed up the stairs to where the main station building straddled the platforms. "Shocked, we all was." Holmes nodded and asked for the Lincoln train. "Cross over to the other platforms, sir." One our way, Holmes paused again to take in the features of the station.

Another journey, and we pulled into Lincoln Midland station at twenty minutes to twelve o'clock. Phelps wanted to go to the factory right away, to discover any events since his departure the day before. Although there was a light drizzle he assured us it was a short walk. We crossed the river and in a few minutes arrived outside the factory gates, among a clutter of bicycles and a few motorcycles. The commissionaire on duty at the gatekeeper's lodge knew Phelps, so we were admitted through the gates and along to an open yard surrounded by industrial buildings. There was a scattering of strange pieces of metal, a number of oil drums and other industrial scraps. The sounds of hammering and shouting came from all around. I was looking about to see whether there was a works canteen where we could take some refreshment when suddenly the level of noise rose enormously. It began with the rumbling of a giant engine, followed by a fearsome clattering and clanking which, combined, drowned out all other sounds.

"Well, gentlemen," shouted Phelps, "I think we are about to see an example of the new weapon." The huge doors to the largest building were pulled open by workers and a monster emerged from the gloom within. It was a metal colossus, at least eight feet high and perhaps thirty feet long, rattling along on two continuous tracks which rotated around the edge of its giant rhombus-shaped body. The barrel of a large gun protruded from the side of the beast. Although we were standing on a concrete floor I could feel the vibrations made by the contraption, not just through the ground, it also felt as if the air itself was shaking. It performed a few forwards and backwards manoeuvres and then shuddered to a halt, although its sound was still ringing in my ears as three men, presumably drivers, clambered out of a hatch at the rear of the side protrusion and started talking to their colleagues about oil pressures and a problem with the large wheel that was attached to the tail of the machine. I noticed engine fumes drifting out of the open hatch and the tick-tick sound of cooling metal coming from inside.

"It's called a land ship, mark one, but the locals all call it the tank. That's not a name that will catch on, it's just a nickname which also adds an extra level of secrecy to the project. Workers can tell their families they are building water tanks, you see." Phelps looked at our aghast expressions. "Horrific, I know, but this war is horrific. If these beasts can bring hostilities to a quick end, imagine the lives it will save, on all sides. It has a six-cylinder Daimler-Knight engine, built in Coventry, and an armour-plated body, made from steel forged in Glasgow and Sheffield, although we have a small foundry here for specialist work. This is what we call the male variant. That's a Hotchkiss six pounder gun at the side, and there's another on the other side. There's also going to be a female type, armed with four point three-oh-three Vickers machine guns. Weighs about twenty-eight tons, has a crew of eight when in action and, while not fast, it only needs to move at walking pace so infantry can come along behind."

I tried to picture a fleet of these 'land ships' sailing across the image of no-mans-land that I had seen being painted the day before.

Phelps continued. "I can tell you more about it another time, but we must make a start. Please, come with me to the office. Every moment matters. Haste and secrecy, my dear friends. May I remind you that very few people know what we are building here and fewer still know of yesterday's disastrous loss. If anyone asks, I will introduce you as old friends who are here on a social visit. Now, we will go to my office to see if there are any messages."

We entered a small brick building, to one side of the huge hall from which the land ship had emerged, and climbed a flight of stairs to a large, airy, well-lit room filled with various desks, work benches and drawing boards. Men were working at most of these and did not look up as we passed though and entered a smaller, darker room at the back. It contained just three desks, a number of filing cabinets, a large floor safe with a combination lock and one person: a man of many shades of pale grey. He had grey hair, grey skin, a wispy grey beard and wore a shabby grey suit. The bags under each eye completed his ashen palette. He looked up at us with no sign of pleasure in seeing his manager arrive with visitors.

"Gentlemen, this is my colleague Mr Portman. Portman, here are some friends of mine, Holmes and Watson, come to visit." Portman's dull eyes roved over us both as he shook our hands but still his face showed no expression.

"You're Sherlock Holmes," he said and continued after a pause, "I suppose you've come here because that oaf Bass lost our tank plans."

"Now, come, come, Portman," said Phelps. "Don't be so hard on him. How did you hear about the plans going missing anyway? That's meant to be a closely guarded secret."

"All factory knows, Mr Phelps," said Portman. "There's a message from the hospital. Bass is still under sedation. Military Police want to see him as soon as he's able to say anything useful. Might have a long wait, if you ask me. You won't be able to see him until after lunch earliest." Finally, Portman's face showed the slightest sign of pleasure as he was able to deliver what he saw was bad news.

"Not until after lunch? Even the MPs have not been able to speak to him about what happened!" Phelps started to pace up and down at the news of this further delay.

"Well, well," said Holmes. "It cannot be helped. Maybe we could use the time to see the factory? I am sure it will be of great assistance to understand something of the endeavours being undertaken here."

I would have much preferred a chance to sit down and take some tea but Holmes seemed to have the boundless energy which was a hallmark of his younger days whenever he had a challenge. So we went back into the larger room, through a door to the side and down a different flight of stairs which led directly into the large building from which the mechanical monster had emerged. My senses were overwhelmed. Sounds of hammering, smells of hot metal and engine oil, light from red-hot rivets and movement everywhere. A great number of the land ships were laid out in two long rows, all in various stages of construction. It was fascinating to see the internal structures of the tanks and the components which were being fitted. There were people crawling all over the assemblies and, as my eyes became used to the light, I noticed most of them were women. Women were riveting and hammering, fixing pieces into the body of the tanks, discussing plans, giving and taking orders.

"It was the Admiralty which came up with the name 'land ships'," shouted Phelps over the commotion. "It was their idea, originally. Winston Churchill, First Lord of the Admiralty at the time, pressed for the production of some experimental vehicles. They were tried out, which led to the design of the mark one, and here it is in production."

"I see a great many ladies are contributing," I observed.

"Indeed, with their men in military uniform, the munitionettes are proving very capable."

"They'll be wanting the vote next," said Portman, who had followed us on the tour. "Not all their men are in uniform either. Mrs Bass is a riveter here. I used to make fun of him, an office pencil pusher while his wife actually builds the tanks."

"Is someone looking after Mrs Bass?" asked Phelps.

"Oh, she's up at the hospital now. Her shift ended this morning and she's not due back on until Monday night."

"The factory works through the night?" asked Holmes.

"We need to get as many machines built as is possible," replied Phelps. "We work round the clock on three shifts, six days a week. We close around seven thirty on Saturday nights to give everyone a decent break on Sundays. Most of the workers would carry on, but the government insists that all factory workers get a complete day of rest once a week. You're looking at the last shift of this week, then we'll close until early shift on Monday."

We had to step out of the way as a gantry crane moved down the construction hall, carrying a gun which was to be fitted to one of the tanks. A woman in factory overalls approached us and said, "Mr Phelps, I was sorry to hear about what happened to Mr Bass. Do you know if he is recovering and whether the stolen plans have been found?"

"I have no news, Mrs Johnson," replied Phelps, "and no one is meant to know about that!" Mrs Johnson smiled, shrugged her shoulders and returned to work.

We progressed to the end of the hall and passed through a workshop where men and women were engaged in all sorts of noisy tasks using all manner of equipment, from small spanners to a huge steam hammer. Next we passed through the paint shop, where completed land ships were being given coats of camouflage paint in four colours. Finally, we reached a quieter room where three men sat at desks working through correspondence.

"Gentlemen, allow me to introduce you to our gallant allies," said Phelps. It transpired that there was some degree of co-operation between the allied nations in the development of this new weapon. We were introduced to the Russians first, starting with Baron Konstantin Khitry, a tall man, probably in his thirties, with a cadaverous face framed with black hair and whiskers. He was frequently smiling and laughing but he had the rare quality of a smile not improving his appearance: his moustache seemed to crawl under his large nose and an unusual pattern of wrinkles appeared all around his face. His laugh was humourless: it sounded like a motorcar engine being turned over but failing to start. He explained he was attached to the Imperial Moscow Technical School and was nearing the end of a tour of British manufacturing establishments, offering insights where he could (again his grinding laugh) and collecting whatever "my English friends feel able to share that could benefit my country in our shared struggle against the common enemy."

He certainly had a rich and flowery English vocabulary, which is more than can be said of the man introduced as the Baron's secretary and assistant, Ivan Bedny. This man was very much shorter and stouter. His skin looked stretched over his wide countenance and had a number of red blotches. It would be hard to estimate his age. The extent of his stomach, combined with his short stature, meant he had to lean backwards slightly to address us. He could speak some English but in a basic form and a with heavy Slavic accent.

The third man was Monsieur Mathis Janot of the Renault company of France. He was only slightly younger than Holmes and me, probably in his late fifties, with dark, wavy hair, piercing blue eyes and an extraordinary grace of movement. Although no shorter than I, he had a habit of lifting his chin when he spoke, which meant he looked at us through half-closed eyes. On being introduced as Mr Holmes and Doctor Watson, he immediately knew who we were. "The great detective and the great writer! An honour, my dear gentlemen," he said as he shook our hands, and the unfavourable opinion I had formed on seeing him began to dissolve.

A young woman hurried into the room. "Mr Phelps, sir! Major Elles is on the telephone, asking for news about the recovery of those plans that were stolen." Phelps immediately broke into a sweat. "Does the whole world know? At least I can tell him that you are here to investigate, Mr Holmes. I'm sorry I have to go, but I'll leave you with our foreign friends."

With that, he hurried away. Monsieur Janot indicated a corner of the room where some easy chairs and a settee were arranged around a coffee table. He said to the young woman who had summoned Phelps, "Enid, my dear young lady, could you arrange some coffee for our little group?" It was a great relief to me to sit down and enjoy a hot beverage, although the coffee had a distinct flavour of engine oil.

Baron Khitry was looking concerned. "What is this about plans for the land ship being stolen?" So not everybody already knew. Janot looked delighted to be 'in the know' and was happy to explain the detailed technical nature of the drawings and specifications which had been on their way to Birmingham. Indeed, I felt he was going into far too much detail but, being there as a guest, I could not think of a way to suggest he was saying too much. Holmes, however, found the words: "Monsieur Janot, is it wise to be discussing such details of what is, clearly, a highly secret endeavour?"

Janot waved the objection away. *"Nous sommes tous amis ici!* We are all friends here, Mr Holmes. And anyway, knowing the existence of the drawings is just like knowing the existence of the tanks, which I consider a first-degree secret."

"I am not sure I understand," said Holmes.

"Donc, the existence of the machines is a secret that we must keep for now, but it will cease to be a secret as soon as the first tank goes into action. As soon as a Hun sees a tank, he will run away and tell his superiors about our new weapon. So their existence is very quickly no longer confidential. That is what I mean by a first-degree secret. Second-degree secrets are what the

Germans will immediately want to know next: how fast can they go, how much ammunition can they carry, how thick is the armour? These questions will help them prepare to fight the tanks. If they know how they are armoured, they can determine what sort of gun can stop one. These secrets are in the documents which have been lost, but these details will also cease to be secret as soon as the Germans capture a tank. I hope that will not happen soon after they start being used, but it will happen. One will break down or become stuck, German infantry will move forward and capture it and then it will be in Berlin being taken apart. The lost plans will give a great deal of this second-degree information, of immense value to our enemy, but only in the shorter term."

"Do you think they will build their own land ships once they know how they are built?" I asked.

"With what?" responded Janot. "Your Royal Navy's blockade of Germany means they have a desperate shortage of iron and steel."

The Russian Baron had been following the conversation with great interest and now asked, "What would be a third-degree secret, if there is such a thing, Monsieur Janot?"

"Ah, yes indeed, my dear Baron, the biggest secrets, and ones which the Germans will not find from capturing a tank, or even capturing a crew. What they will desperately want to know is the future of the tank. How fast can we build them? What improvements in design are in development? How many tanks, and what nature of tanks, will they face if the war continues? This type of information will be true gold to the Kaiser and his rats."

"But this type of information is not what has been lost?"

"*Non, non.* Such third-degree information as is held here is locked in the safe in Mr Phelps's office. It would never have been entrusted to a person such as Bass."

"Bass?" asked the Baron. "Jonah Bass was the person entrusted to carry the plans to Birmingham?"

His countryman Bedny spoke for the first time. "Bass? But is he not…"

The Baron silenced him with a glare, then turned back to Janot and made his smile, with the centre of his moustache actually disappearing under the hook of his nose. "It is a great relief to me to know that you, Monsieur Janot, are not so greatly concerned about the loss of these documents. I am sure they will be recovered anyway. A common theft, I am sure. No doubt the thief will either destroy them or hand them to the authorities, if he realizes they are matters of war. You can be a criminal and still be a patriot. Who could a thief sell the plans to anyway, in Birmingham?"

"Nottingham," corrected Janot, and he related the story of the robbery.

Phelps and his grey colleague Portman returned. Phelps seemed relieved, saying his superiors were finding ease in their distress from knowing that the great Sherlock Holmes was here. "Do you have any ideas yet about who might have taken the plans?"

"I have no data yet," said Holmes. "It is a capital error to start developing theories without adequate data. However, I do suggest you place advertisements in the Nottingham press, describing the lost briefcase and offering a reward for anyone who finds it and takes it to the police. The thief could always claim he found the briefcase abandoned in a public park and decide a reward would at least bring some profit."

"We will place advertisements in all the newspapers and have some hand bills printed," said Phelps. "Mr Portman, could you see to that right away?"

"How much should the reward be?" asked Portman.

Holmes answered, "Enough to make a thief keen to secure it, not so much that it seems an unlikely amount for a case of papers. I suggest fifteen shillings."

Portman smiled, nodded and hurried off. "An excellent idea, Mr Holmes," said Phelps. "At last I feel that we have taken an active step. Now some more good news. First, we have hotel rooms available for you. Second, I am told that Bass is awake and being interviewed by the Military Police. They will want an hour at least, so I suggest we take your bags to the hotel, where we can have some lunch and then take our turn with Bass."

The case is closed

It had been many hours since breakfast and the idea of lunch seemed to me an excellent one. We said goodbye to the Russians and the Frenchman, collected our bags and went, with Phelps, to the White Hart, an ancient coaching inn set between the cathedral and castle. It was a steep uphill climb but fortunately one of the factory directors had a pony and trap with a driver. We were allowed to borrow it, although we were rather crammed in and the unfortunate animal looked quite spent when we arrived.

The hotel and bar were very quiet when we arrived. As we checked in, the landlord said, "Holmes and Watson! Gentlemen, this is an honour indeed. Are you here to investigate the robbery of the tank plans?"

"Goodness, man, however did you know about that?" asked Phelps, with great exasperation.

"I'm sorry, sir," said the landlord. "But you should know the whole city's talking about it. Old Johan Bass was a regular here, and some of the other city bars as well. Can't keep much quiet in a small place like Lincoln, especially when so many are working on building the things."

I was delighted with the establishment. Considering wartime shortages, the lunch was excellent. We were the only diners and the landlord was pleased to make every effort for us. Phelps hurried us along and so soon we made our way to the Red Cross auxiliary hospital which was established in the Old Palace building. The walk from our hotel, through the Exchequer Gate and along the south side of the imposing mass of the great cathedral, took just a few minutes.

There was a Military Policeman standing guard outside the room which had been set aside for Bass. The MP told us that his superiors had just finished their questioning of him for now, that his wife had gone in moments earlier and would need some time alone with him before we could go in. But almost immediately Mrs Bass, a florid-faced women with long grey hair, hurried out of the sick room. She said she needed to get some supplies for her husband and we could go in. Holmes suggested that Phelps wait outside as Bass might speak more freely in the absence of his manager.

The room had four sick beds but only one was occupied. Mr Jonah Bass was forty-two, according to the medical notes on a clipboard hanging at the foot of his bed, but he looked much older. There was a faint yellowish tinge to his skin while his nose and cheeks showed a pattern of blood vessels. His eyes were bloodshot. Although I detected no tremor, the signs of an alcoholic were unmistakable. If I had spotted them, I knew Holmes must have as well.

We sat on wooden chairs beside the patient and introduced ourselves. Holmes began very gently. "Mr Bass, I am sorry that you have suffered an assault, and I further regret that I must ask you about that unpleasant episode, even after you have just had to narrate it to the Military Police."

Bass licked his dry lips. I poured a glass of water and handed it to him. "Thank you. Well, gentlemen, I was given the papers by Mr Phelps. They were locked in a secure briefcase and I was instructed to deliver them to Mr Wells at the Metropolitan Carriage works in Birmingham. There's no direct trains from here so I got the first train I could as far as Nottingham, where I had to change. There was a forty-minute wait so I went to have a cup of tea in the refreshment room. Well, after that I had to go to the necessary. I was just washing my hands when – I don't exactly remember, next thing I'm waking up and the Station Master and all are there. I tell them what happened, they call the police. I felt well enough to travel back here, to Lincoln, and report the robbery to Mr Phelps. But then I'm told I need to be questioned and it all gets a bit much. They give me some medicine and I had a sleep. Then I've told the story to the monkeys, sorry, I mean the Military Police and now you. There's really nothing more to say. Sorry, gentlemen."

"Thank you Mr Bass. It would help me to get a precise account of your movements. Which refreshment room did you go to for your tea?"

"Oh, um, the one by platform six, where the Lincoln trains arrive."

"Doctor Watson and I were at Nottingham station yesterday. That refreshment room has been commandeered by the army for military use only."

Bass's face seemed to crumble and the yellow tint was replaced by red. "Ah, yes, that's right, I meant to go there, I've been there many times before but, as you say, closed to civilians now. I think I, yes, I headed to the other refreshment room instead, the one between platforms one and three."

"Then why not use the lavatory which is also between platforms one and three? You were found, as I understand it, upstairs in the main station building."

Bass gulped some more water. He was now sweating and shaking as he stammered out his answer. "Yes, yes, I remember now, I was crossing from one set of platforms to the other. Well, if you've been there, you'll know there is a station bar in the main building. Seemed a bit pointless to walk past one place of refreshment just to get to another." He tried to smile but it faltered.

There was a pause before Holmes asked, "When did you realize you no longer had the briefcase?"

Bass grew redder and began to tremble. "What do you mean? You know that. When I came around, after I was coshed in the lavatory."

"The doctor here found no injury to your head," I said, as I flipped through the medical notes.

"He said they must have used a soft cosh," gasped Bass.

"Mr Bass, I am only interested in the discovery of the documents. How they became lost is of no direct concern to me, but I must know precisely what occurred in order to be able to secure their recovery and bring this saga to a close. I am going to give you one chance to give us a true account of events. Start by answering this question: is it true that you were attacked and hit over the head?"

The trembling got worse. "I... I..." At that moment the ward door opened and Mrs Bass came in, saying, "I've got what you..." She saw Holmes and me and stopped talking. The bag she was carrying gave the unmistakable clink of glass bottles.

"Mrs Bass, could you give us a few minutes more?" asked Holmes. The lady left the room and Holmes turned again to Bass, his face set.

Bass began to weep. "I just wanted a drink. That's not a crime, is it? I forgot the case, I left it on the train, anyone might make such a mistake, it was just one moment of forgetfulness. I was at the bar when I remembered it but by then the train was on its way to Leicester. What was I to do? I went to the lavatory and lay down. After a few minutes someone came in, saw me and called for help. I told everyone that my bag had been stolen, I didn't know what else to say. Then one thing led to another and it's all just got into this big mess. I never meant it to, I'm sorry, so sorry."

We called his wife in and left them together. Holmes

briefly told Phelps what had transpired. He was shocked by Bass's lie but relieved to learn that the plans had not really been stolen.

We were offered the use of an office to telephone the railway companies. We soon learned that all lost property in the Midlands was being sent to an office in Derby. On calling there, Holmes spoke to a Miss Postlethwaite, who confirmed that a briefcase matching the description of the one we sought had been found by a railway employee at Leicester and was now at the Derby Lost Property Office, which was open today until half past five.

"Is the case undamaged?" asked Holmes. He held the earpiece away from his ear so Phelps and I could hear Miss Postlethwaite make her reply as she examined the briefcase, "Yes... the case is closed... the buckles are done up and the lock seems intact... it certainly feels like there is a great number of papers inside it."

Phelps began to dance around the room, just as he had all those years ago. We informed the Military Police that the missing case had been located. They immediately lost interest in the event and seemed to think their time had been wasted.

Holmes and I offered to go to Derby to fetch the case so that Phelps could return to work. The next train did not leave until a quarter past three, so we decided to return to the White Hart for a rest while Phelps returned to the factory in a very bright mood.

From having been deserted less than an hour earlier, we found the pub packed. "Here they are!" someone shouted as we came in and instantly we found ourselves surrounded by all manner of people who wanted to greet us.

"Welcome to Lincoln, Mr Holmes!"

"Have you solved the case, Mr Holmes?"

"Was the injury you had in Afghanistan to your shoulder or your leg, Doctor Watson?"

"Is the panic over, Mr Holmes? The missing papers have been found?"

"Loved the stories since I was a boy, now my young lad loves them just as much."

It seemed that the news of our arrival at the White Hart had spread across the city like wildfire. Our opportunity for a relaxing break before more travel quickly evaporated. Everyone wanted to buy us drinks and talk with us. An informal queue system emerged, in which groups had a few minutes with us before the next set ushered them along with a "Now, now, you've had your time with our distinguished visitors, time to let someone else meet them." It was all done with great politeness and in good heart, so I was able to forget my weariness and relax. After all, the case was as good as closed.

A jolly husband and wife who worked at the factory wanted to tell us about the land ships. "Mr and Mrs Ilett. We were on the night shift last night so should be resting but as soon as we heard you were here... Have you seen our land ships? What do you think? Going to scatter the Huns in short order! They're riveted together, like ships, because it's naval engineering that's gone into them, and naval guns..."

Following in turn were two men in their fifties. "Too

old to fight, so we've been told," said one of them, who introduced himself as Frank. "But Pete and I, we do our bit. We guard the tank factory over the weekend when there's nobody there, except a few maintenance lads who come in to get jobs done. We give them a hand sometimes, fixing lights, cleaning out, all manner of work. Turn our hands to anything."

Next a pair of junior officers from the Royal Flying Corps took their turn. "Lieutenants Copely and Parker, gentlemen." They both looked too young to be in military uniform. Copely had managed to grow a moustache in the style of a pilot; Parker was trying to but not succeeding. Copely continued, "We're stationed at Waddington, less than five miles down the road. We're going to open a new Royal Flying Corps training base there. I know the metal bashers here think their land ships are the new thing in war that's going to end it all, and I hope it will, but real the future of war is in the air. We've got to train hundreds of pilots, air gunners and observers. We're even going to be teaching fliers how to drop bombs on the enemy when we get going. You must come and visit us while you are in the area, gentlemen. We have just had our first kites delivered, the de Havilland B.E.2, a two-seater, ideal for training. We'll have ten of them eventually, lovely aeroplanes."

"It is the engine which makes the aeroplane," said Monsieur Janot, who arrived at this moment. "Built by Renault! Our sixty horsepower, air-cooled V-8 engine."

The RFC officers were very pleased to meet Janot and discuss engines, so our attention was taken next by a group of engineers who all wanted to tell us about this supposedly top-secret weapon.

"They are amazing machines, Mr Holmes, but just as terrible inside as they are outside. The noise, fumes, vibration and the terrible heat!"

"You can't see, you can't hear, you can't breathe, you're cooking and being shaken apart!"

"We say that if you drive a land ship over a penny, you can tell if it's heads or tails! It's a joke, of course, but you do feel every bump."

"I heard that the first meetings about the land ships were held in secret, upstairs in this very hotel!"

Finally Holmes announced, to general disappointment, that we had to leave to catch a train. Monsieur Janot said he would walk with us to the railway station.

"Your Russian friends did not come with you?" I asked him as we made our way down the very well-named Steep Hill.

"Not my friends, Doctor Watson. They only arrived in Lincoln the day before yesterday and I overheard them discussing going to Gibraltar next. Quite the tour they are getting! They might have already left; I do not keep track of them. Now, you will send a telegram to let us know when you have acquired the briefcase? Do not keep us waiting, I beg of you."

I assured him that we would inform the factory as soon as we could after recovering the case. We said goodbye outside the station and boarded our train. As we steamed through the countryside I felt delighted with our success and the welcome we had received at the White Hart.

"One of your easiest cases ever, Holmes!"

"Yes, Watson, so it would seem. I will be glad when we have recovered the papers and know for certain that all is well."

"Of course, of course. It is going to take us a couple of hours to get to Derby and collect the briefcase, then a similar journey back to Lincoln, but we will be in the White Hart in time for dinner. I noticed they have fresh fish, landed at Grimsby this morning, on the menu."

I dozed off thinking about fresh whiting in a creamed sauce. We changed trains at Nottingham and arrived at our destination fifteen minutes late but in enough time to get to the Lost Property Office before it closed.

Derby station was extremely busy. It is an important junction and had been busy when I had spent an hour there, between trains, on my journey to Pickvale Hall less than two weeks earlier. On this Saturday afternoon it was even busier, with troop trains in addition to normal traffic. There were some Tommies coming home on leave and many more returning to duty. I could not help thinking that they were on their way to take part in the big push: our summer offensive which was expected to begin at any day. We witnessed countless joyful reunions and tearful farewells; it was very moving.

Less affected by these dramatic events was the official at the Lost Property Office. He was a large man, who might have been athletic once but was now just bulky and clumsy. When we entered, he was complaining to a boy, his underling, "Why does army give hats to officers if they can't hold on to them? If they're so stupid they leave all their bits on trains what hope have we got? I bet Germans don't leave hats on trains." He looked round and saw us. "Well, gentlemen, what have you lost? Umbrella? Walking cane? It's almost five thirty, we're closing soon."

"A black briefcase," said Holmes. "We called earlier and spoke to Miss Postlethwaite."

"She's off now. You'll have me to deal with. If you want her ladyship, she'll be back Monday."

"Not at all, not at all, Mister?"

"Beeston."

"Mr Beeston, I am here on behalf of a colleague who mislaid a briefcase. Miss Postlethwaite said one answering the description had been found and was here."

"Black briefcase, carrying handle, two buckle straps, lock?"

"That's right."

"To be kept for a Mr Holmes who called about it earlier today?"

"Indeed."

"Holmes has been here and got it."

My mood of elation evaporated but Holmes remained perfectly calm. "I am Mr Holmes."

Beeston barely troubled to hide his ire. "Oh, now, don't you give me any of that! I've followed the regulations. Gentlemen came here, described the lost item in detail, gave the name Holmes, now you come along making accusations."

Holmes made a calming gesture. "It is no matter, and I have no complaint. It is clear you have followed your

273

instructions perfectly. It was assuredly one of my colleagues who collected the bag. He gave the name Holmes because he knew I had telephoned. Did he discuss the reward with you?"

Beeston's ire cooled immediately. "Reward? No... but we're not supposed to accept rewards. How much is the reward?"

"Call it a tip, no one need know. It's fifteen shillings." Holmes pulled six half-crowns from his pocket but did not hand them over. "But I am annoyed that my colleague did not discuss it with you. I will need to have words with him. Was it the elderly Scotsman with a ginger beard?"

"No, there were two of them. Will they both be in hot water?" I could not tell if Beeston was more delighted at the prospect of the coins or the idea of getting people into trouble.

"I am afraid I will need to have stern words with them if I can work out who they were. It was not the two very young lads we use as messengers?"

"No, sir, two foreigners. Spoke strange. Tall one with a big nose and a moustache, and a short fat one with a spotty face. I didn't like them. Do you think they plan to claim the reward?"

"They will be in even more trouble if they attempt such a thing." Holmes clinked the coins together. "Did you notice anything else about them?"

"They seemed to be in a tearing hurry to get along. The fat spotty one kept tugging at the tall one's sleeve and saying something in foreign. But he definitely said Gibraltar, so I reckon that's where they're off to. He was waving his watch in front of his chum's face so I think they were due to be heading off pretty soon."

"Thank you, Mr Beeston, you have been most helpful." Holmes handed over the coins and for a moment I was back in Covent Garden Market on a cold December evening.

Outside the Lost Property Office, the crowds were starting to thin. Those who were welcoming heroes home on leave had gone to their homes or to find somewhere to celebrate. Those who were still weeping after making a farewell were being comforted by friends, family and small, bewildered children.

"So it was the Russians. Why did they come? How did they know?"

"They guessed," replied Holmes. He stopped a passing porter and, asking for the next train to Lincoln, was told to take the train leaving in six minutes, changing again at Nottingham. Further enquiries informed us that there was no public telephone in Derby and that the nearest Post Office was a few minutes' walk away. Holmes scribbled a note on a scrap of paper and gave it to the porter, with a generous tip, urging him to send the message, by telegram, as soon as he could. The porter complained that he wasn't a messenger and that it wasn't his job to dispatch telegrams but he took the note and the tip.

We scrambled onto the train as the whistle was blowing.

"We may as well relax for the journey, Watson. Lacking pigeons, we have no means of communicating with anyone from a moving train."

"What do you think about the Russians finding the briefcase?"

Holmes lit his pipe and puffed at it for a minute. "They knew Bass, so were able to make an educated guess that he would put getting a drink before his duty. They tried their luck with the Lost Property Office and got there before us. When asked for a name, they gave mine, which was another clever guess."

"It seems incredible that a government employee would be so incompetent as to leave important documents on a train. Anyway, they have been found now. I suppose the Russians want to return the documents to strengthen relations with their hosts?"

"I hope so."

"What else would they do? There will be no point in taking them with them to Gibraltar. I am sure we would share the design with our Russian allies anyway. But if they are leaving for Gibraltar soon, will they have time to return the plans before they go?" A thought struck me. "Holmes, what if they stopped in Derby on their way to their departure port? Maybe they were on their way to Liverpool?"

"We shall see."

Taking flight

At Nottingham, we had time before our connection to Lincoln to send more telegrams. Holmes sent one to Phelps and another to his assistant Portman, telling them the Russians had the missing documents and urging them to locate the pair. He also sent telegrams to Monsieur Janot and to Adrian Wenderton, Phelps's son-in-law, although we did not have the complete address. We waited in the telegraph office in the hope of a reply but none came before we had to leave to catch our train.

It was due to arrive in Lincoln at a quarter to eight but this train was also fifteen minutes late. As is now normal, there were no cabs at the station but we knew the route. It is a short walk but Holmes ran and I struggled to keep up with him. At the factory gates, most of the bicycles and motorcycles were gone and the gates were closed, but we shouted and rattled them until Frank, one of the weekend guards we had met earlier, ambled out of a side building.

"Evening gents. What brings you here at this hour?"

"Is there anyone still in the factory?"

"The workers finished up half an hour ago. They've all gone now for the weekend."

"What about Mr Phelps, Mr Portman or Monsieur Janot?"

"Funny you should ask that, we've had a bunch of telegrams arrive for them. They're piled in the post tray in the lodge. I don't think any of those gents can be here or the telegrams would have been delivered to them."

"Have you seen the two Russian gentlemen?"

"Ah, now, yes, they are here. They said they had to collect some of their things and wanted to check that we would be here to let them out of the gates when they were done."

Holmes interrupted, "Do you have weapons?"

Frank looked surprised. "There's a couple of Lee–

Enfield rifles in the lodge."

"Anyone on guard apart from you?"

"Yes, my chum Pete, he's just making a brew if you'd like a cup?"

Holmes instructed Frank to lock the gates behind us and went to the lodge, where he told Pete to get the rifles ready and loaded as fast as he could. While he was doing that, I asked, "Holmes, what do you think is going on?"

"I am not certain, Watson, but if it is the worst, the Russians want to add to their collection of stolen documents by taking the papers on the future of our tanks – the coming improvements and production plans. You remember Janot talking of them as third-degree secrets, those of the greatest value to our foes?"

"But they are locked in the safe in Phelps's office!"

"An old Hassenforder. I could open it myself in a trice." He thought for a moment. "But it needs silence in order to hear the tumblers. I don't think even a proficient thief could open it while there was hammering in the factory. So they have not had much time."

"But the Russians are on our side!"

"The Tsar is on our side. That does not mean we can trust every Russian."

By now Frank and Pete had their rifles ready. Holmes told them to grab all the keys they had, led us into the small brick building and told Frank to lock the door behind us. We hurried up the flight of stairs, through the drawing office and into the dark office at the back.

The safe was open and empty.

"They can't have passed us the way we came," I said, stating the obvious.

"They might have heard us coming and taken the other stairway," said Holmes. "Hurry, all of you."

We took the second stairway and emerged into the huge production hall and saw the Russians hurrying towards the far end.

"Stop or we open fire!" called Holmes. They glanced round at us but carried on. Pete did not wait to be instructed but fired a warning shot. The Russians immediately took cover behind a partly-built land ship and opened fire at us. We, in turn, took cover behind the hulk of a land ship at our end of the hall.

"Mr Holmes!" It was Baron Khitry. "We both have revolvers and considerable ammunition! You retire away now and leave us to go about our business!"

It transpired that Pete, despite his years, was a hot-headed man who was furious at anyone who challenged the security of the factory it was his job to guard. He leapt up and fired two rounds in the direction of the Russians. The bullets clanged into metal and the noise echoed around the hall.

There was a pause and we heard some whispered Russian conversation. Then a volley of shots rang out, some whizzing past our land ship and some crashing into it. As soon as the shooting stopped, Pete was on his feet again and opened fire. "One of them got away," he said. "The tall one. I saw him going through the back way. There's an emergency fire exit back there."

The echoes of the shooting had died away. "Mr

Bedny!" called Holmes. "The Baron has deserted you! You have no escape. Give yourself up."

"No, Baron has gone for help. He come back with more men, more gun."

"What more men? Who in Lincoln will take up arms for you? He has gone and left you to your fate."

"No, is not true. He go for help. He have more gun. He find men. Then we go together. We have all British land ship plans. We will be rich men and you will die in this place."

"Give yourself up, Bedny. If you do not, the factory guards here will shoot you as soon as you show yourself."

"And I shoot if I see any of you!"

It was a stand-off. Each side could peer around their sheltering land ship to watch the other with little risk of being hit, but any attempt to flee the scene would have been fatal. Time passed but there was little we could do. Occasionally Holmes would repeat his calls to Bedny to surrender but this was always refused, as he continued to believe that Baron Khitry would reappear at any moment to save him. Pete and Frank (I am ashamed to say I never caught their surnames) kept a close eye on Bedny and he would occasionally fire a round at them.

"Well, well, Bedny, it seems we are all stuck here until the Baron returns with his promised help. In the meantime, you may as well confirm to me that your intention is to sell all the documents you have gathered to the Germans?"

"Of course! We have been collecting information all

along our tour of England. But these papers about your land ships are the main prize. We will be well paid by our German friends."

"It does not trouble you that you betray your motherland?"

"Russia? Why must I be loyal to Russia? I own no land, no property, nothing in Russia. Neither does Baron. We are gentlemen, we have noble blood, but we poor and our government says we must work. What does Russia do for us? We do not have vote, like you English. We have to obey weak and cruel Tsar, we are to come to England to run errand, why? This war gives us chance, we have chance to be rich men, like we deserve! You English, you never understand why... uh..."

His speech ended in a grunt. There was a thud and then a different voice called out, "I say! Are you chaps all right?"

I knew the voice at once. "Phelps! Is that really you? Is it safe for us to come out?"

"Yes, I should say so." We hurried out of our shelter and down the hall to where Phelps, holding a large wrench, stood over the unconscious Bedny. "I'm sorry I seem to be late to the party. I thought all was well so I popped back to see the family. I was out on the farm, helping bring the cows in for milking, when your telegram arrived. Well, we all need to help where we can, eh? So I didn't get your message until about half an hour ago. I borrowed Adrian's car and drove here right away. I saw that some fool had left the emergency exit door open so I came in that way. I heard enough of what Bedny was saying to decide what to do. I picked up this wrench and clubbed him. I think he'll be out for a few minutes. Frank and Pete, can you cut a length of cable from that reel and tie him up?"

I shook Phelps warmly by the hand. "Phelps, my dear, dear friend. Never again say that you cannot be relied upon in a crisis. Your quick actions and decisions have saved the day."

"Not yet, Watson. The Baron has the documents and has half an hour's start on us. Now, in which direction will he have fled?"

"They've been heard talking of going to Gibraltar," I said. "But I don't know why they would go there; it's hardly going to help them get to Germany."

"They may have meant Gibraltar Point," said Phelps. He looked at our expressions and continued, "Gibraltar Point. On the coast, just south of Skegness. About fifty miles from here."

"And they clearly had an appointment," said Holmes. "Yes; it is possible they were due to rendezvous with a German vessel."

"Sailing a ship across the North Sea would be risky for the Germans – the Royal Navy rules the waves."

"A submarine, then," said Holmes. "But even a U-boat belonging to the enemy would not risk surfacing off our coast in broad daylight, given that they still lack the Bruce-Partington adaptations of our boats. What time is dusk?"

"Sunset is at nine thirty, sir," said Frank, who had made the unconscious Bedny secure.

"Do any of you know when the next high tide will be?"

"A little later, sir – about ten tonight," replied Pete.

"Come with me everyone," said Holmes, and he led us at a surprising pace out to the factory gates. Frank unlocked them and Holmes hurried over to where the few cycles and motorcycles were parked. "There were three motorcycles here when we arrived, now there are only two." He thought for a moment. "A Triumph Type H, petrol tank painted green, wicker basket on the back. That's what he's taken."

"However did you notice all the motorcycles, Holmes?"

"Habit, Watson. We all see, some of us observe and I am in the habit of remembering. Does anyone know what speed such a motorcycle can achieve?"

"It should get up to fifty miles per hour on straight, flat stretches, sir," said Pete.

"How fast is the car you've borrowed, Phelps?"

"Ah, I need to keep it below thirty. There is a problem with the oil pressure, the engine overheats and the brakes are ropey."

Holmes looked at his watch and thought for a moment. "Almost nine o'clock. The Baron could arrive at Gibraltar Point within forty minutes. It will be starting to get dark by then. We don't know what time the rendezvous is exactly, but we need a faster way to get there than by car, even one in top shape." He thought for a moment. "Faster than a car... Frank, Pete, there is a telephone here in the factory?"

"We have two, sir," said Frank with pride. "One in the lodge and one in the director's office."

"Here is what I need you to do. Frank, call the Royal Flying Corps at Waddington. See if Lieutenants Copely and Parker are available, but whoever you can get through to, tell them what has happened, that we are on our way and that they must get aeroplanes ready for flight. Pete, call the police in Skegness and alert them. Describe Baron Khitry and the motorcycle and tell them they must mobilize every officer and man they can rouse to intercept him. Once you have made those calls, ring anyone else you can think of. Start with the army and navy. Tell them we have reason to believe that a German submarine is going to pick up a spy off Gibraltar Point tonight. Use my name, tell them you are acting on my orders and that I take full responsibility. Now go!" As the two guards set about their missions, Holmes continued, "Phelps, I ask that you drive us to Waddington."

We had been through a long day of travel, timetables, trains, meetings and adventure but there was clearly more to do. It did not take us long to get to Waddington and we were pleased to discover that Frank had got through on the telephone, but that there were not many men at the RFC aerodrome to assist us. The base consisted of little more than a few huts and four aeroplanes, although work had begun on a number of larger buildings. Inside one temporary hut, Lieutenant Parker explained, "Copely and I were just finishing up for the day when the call came through. Apart from us, there are just a couple of ground crew and a few men guarding the base. The message we have received is scarcely credible! Something about a Russian who is spying for the Germans and being picked up by a submarine?"

"Some certainly true, some conjecture for now," replied Holmes. "So you are both pilots. Do you have any observers, or anyone else who can go up with you?"

Copely replied, "No trained observers, Mr Holmes. We could take the ground crew once they have got the engines going but I don't know how good they would be at looking out for what you are after – they both happen to be rather short-sighted. We cannot take the others as we cannot leave the base unguarded."

"Hmm. Do you have any bombs or flares?"

This time Parker answered, "We have two flare guns and a few mills bombs – hand grenades, they are known as. We don't have much as we're not operational yet."

"Tell the ground crew to get two aeroplanes ready to fly. Gather the flare guns and grenades. Tell the ground crew that, once we are in the air, they are to telephone the Skegness police. They should already know about the fugitive Russian. Tell them we will drop flares if we see him." He turned to me. "Well, well, Watson. We have seen many adventures together. Are you ready for something new?"

I gave my assent, not without considerable trepidation, but our duty was clear. We hurried out of the hut as the two RFC officers called over the ground crew and a guard to give them a rapid briefing. In no time we were each wrapped in a sheepskin jacket and I was standing with Parker in front of an aeroplane. I could see why they referred to their craft as a 'kite': it looked like little more than an oversized variant of a box kite of the sort that we all flew as boys. The canvas that covered the frame and wings looked like tissue paper and the overall impression I had was of a flimsy construction held together by struts and string.

Parker looked me over and said, "It's a training aircraft so it has controls in both cockpits. I think I'll have you in the rear seat, it's a little less uncomfortable, you will have a better field of view and, er, it will help the aeroplane's centre of gravity. Just don't touch any of the controls."

I needed a little help from one of the ground crew to climb the short ladder up to the edge of the cockpit and then lower myself into the narrow seat. He strapped me in and handed me a pair of goggles, a Webley flare pistol and two Mills bombs. He removed the ladder and some blocks under the aeroplane's wheels and, after shouted orders from Parker, he gave a great push to the blade of the propeller. The engine lurched into life and the great machine began to move. It was a bumpy ride as we turned onto the grassy strip and started down it, getting faster and faster and the engine louder and louder until suddenly the bumping and shaking stopped as we took off. The ground fell away, revealing a patchwork of fields and network of roads, looking very narrow from above. I had seen pictures taken from the air, of course, but nothing prepared me for the full panoramic view. The bumping and shaking were replaced by the occasional lurch as we roared across the sky.

The breeze was coming from the west, so we took off in that direction. To turn us around, Parker dipped the aeroplane to the right (or perhaps I should say starboard) and I was alarmed to find myself looking directly down at buildings, trees and cows which looked like models, all casting long shadows. Then, any trepidation I felt vanished with a spectacular view of the mighty Lincoln Cathedral, once the tallest building in the world, atop its escarpment and the ancient city. The immense building shone in the last rays of the setting sun.

The air was driving into my face, so I quickly put on the goggles and wrapped my jacket around me as it was desperately cold. Being now thousands of feet high, we were still in sunlight, which lit the aeroplane carrying Holmes and Copely ahead of us.

I found myself gasping for breath, from a combination of euphoria, alarm, cold and the power of the air hitting my face. I was able to remain calm and remember the work we had to do. Then it struck me that it would take some time to fly to our destination so decided to enjoy the ride for the time being.

"We'll fly east by the compass until we reach the coast, then turn south," shouted Parker above the noise, and I was alarmed to see he had a Bartholomew Touring Atlas, by which he was navigating.

By the time we reached the coastline, over half an hour after leaving Waddington, the sun had set but the skies were clear and there was still enough light to see objects on the ground. The aeroplane again dipped to the right to make us turn.

"I'm going to patrol up and down, close to the shore, as low as I dare," shouted Parker.

"I see police," I shouted back, pointing at a horse and trap on the coast road below us, the police helmets of the driver and three passengers easily seen in the half light. The ground between the coast and the road looked marshy, with large areas of open water. There could not be many routes between the road and the sea. But then the green light of a flare shone ahead of us – Holmes had seen something. Parker steered us towards the light and took us even lower. Sure enough, on the narrow strip of sand was the figure of a tall man and a motorcycle lying on its side. I could make out the path he must have taken, it was wide enough for a motorcycle but not for a horse and trap. We circled over him and I fired my flare pistol as well.

"Skiff!" shouted Parker, pointing out to sea. Looking out, I could see a small boat being rowed by four oarsmen with one other person on board. It was still a mile or so from the shore so we turned towards and flew over it. I caught a glance of uniforms. We circled around again, Parker pulled out a revolver and started taking shots at the small craft. Parker had a very narrow field of view to shoot in, between the lower wing of our aeroplane and the propellor (which I feared he might hit). He circled around again and fired again but it would have been an extremely lucky shot to hit a small boat from a moving aeroplane. However, the crew had seen our flares and now, with the gunfire, they rapidly turned about and began rowing back, away from England's shore.

The aeroplane carrying Holmes and Copely roared past us and a minute later there was a flash, followed by a colossal bang. They had found the submarine and had dropped a Mills bomb on it. We flew to the point of the explosion and there was no mistaking the long grey shape in the water. I was getting a Mills bomb ready to drop on it when men on the boat opened fire at us.

"Now!" shouted Parker. I pulled at the ring and threw the grenade over the side. A few seconds later there was a huge whooshing sound. Looking back, I saw a mound of water erupting from the surface, sadly at least twenty yards from the boat. Holmes and Copely were circling around to drop their second bomb. I could see the flashes from the machine gun mounted on the submarine, then another large flash, followed by the sound of the explosion, as their second bomb exploded close enough to the boat to send a spray of water over the men on deck.

As we turned for our second run, Parker shouted, "When I shout 'one', pull the pin out. When I shout 'two', throw the bomb." I later found out that the Mills bomb has a seven second fuse – long enough for it to land in the water if dropped from two hundred feet. At the time, I was not happy at the prospect of being in a flying aeroplane while carrying a Mills bomb with the pin removed.

"One!" shouted Parker and I pulled at the ring to remove the pin. At the same moment, a hail of machine gun bullets ripped through the fabric of both our wings on the starboard side of the aeroplane. "Two!" shouted Parker, and I dropped the bomb over the port side, where I could see the flashes of gunfire below. As soon as I had thrown the bomb, Parker surged the aeroplane skywards and veered to starboard. I saw bullets flashing past us, then there was a flash and a bang as the bomb detonated.

"A hit, well done doctor!" shouted Parker. "But I do not imagine we have done a great deal of damage. We've no more bombs. We will take a look at what is happening on the shore, then we had better head back to Waddington. I think we have taken a bit of damage ourselves!" Indeed, one of the struts between the lower and upper wings was broken and there were holes in the canvas of both.

Circling over the shoreline we could see, in the last of the daylight, the policemen running onto the beach and the Baron standing still with his hands raised and a number of document cases at his feet.

It became fully dark as we flew back over the Lincolnshire countryside. I sat back and admired a view of the stars that one can never experience in London. I lost track of time. Then we were descending and landed with a hard bump, followed by rattling and shaking as we slowed to a halt on the grass, near a small bonfire that the ground crew had lit to guide the pilots home. The engine was shut off and then all was stillness and silence. I do not recall ever experiencing a sense of stillness such as that moment. Then there was the sound of running feet and someone was shaking me.

"You're not hurt, Watson? For God's sake, say you are not hurt!"

"No, Holmes, just a little shaken and very cold. Do you think we could now return to our hotel and see if we are not too late for a little supper?"

We spent a week at the White Hart in Lincoln, recovering from our exertions and taking in the sights. I spent an entire morning searching the cathedral for the famous Lincoln Imp. We viewed the Magna Carta in Lincoln Castle, a symbol of the freedom for which we were fighting. We watched land ships being tested on open land south of the factory and more being driven onto railway low-loaders for transport to Norfolk, before being taken across to France.

We did not hear any reliable news of events surrounding our adventures for the first days. The whole story had been made officially secret but that did not stop the whispering. We heard many rumours; all we told people was that all was well. After a few days the stories died away as people lost interest.

Phelps was away in London making a report to the Admiralty. It was only on Tuesday evening, three days after we had landed at Waddington aerodrome, that Phelps came to find us at the White Hart. He was as relaxed and happy as I have ever seen him. He began, as is his custom, by reminding us that everything was secret and that no word of the recent events must be allowed to become known to the general public.

There were written commendations from the Admiralty for Phelps, Frank and Pete. The War Office had awarded similar citations to Parker and Copely. There were letters for Holmes and me from the Prime Minister and there would have been medals awarded, were it not for the need for complete secrecy.

The Russians had been captured and handed over to officials from their embassy. Their prospects were not thought to be good.

All missing documents had been recovered and the damage at the factory was repaired. Production of land ships was going at top pace in Lincoln and production in Birmingham was to start very soon. Phelps had heard that land ships were expected to be used against the enemy for the first time within three months.

Although Frank and Pete had convinced the Skegness police to come out, they had a harder task with the navy. They had simply refused to believe the story. Even after Phelps rang from Waddington (after we had taken off) they were still doubtful. However, by the next morning they had alerted their patrols in the North Sea to the possibility of a submarine being in the area. Nothing was seen of it and we would never know if the boat had been damaged.

The following evening we had dinner with Monsieur Janot. He was shortly to return to France where, he told us, Renault planned to build a fleet of smaller, faster tanks which would overcome the enemy "like a swarm of mosquitoes."

After lunch on Saturday 1st July, we packed our bags and were driven to the Lincoln Central railway station. When we arrived at King's Cross there were crowds around every news stand and the shop of W. H. Smith. The evening newspapers were published and the news was historic. The big push had begun. That morning, the British army had launched an offensive along a twenty-mile front north of the River Somme. The reports told of parts of the German front line being taken and many prisoners being captured.

"Maybe it will all be over before those terrible devices have to be used," I said.

Holmes looked over the news reports. "Little detail for the newsmen to report yet. Still, this is certainly an event of great significance." He shook my hand. "Here is where I leave you for now, my great friend. I return home to Sussex and you to your vital work at Challis House. Let us hope that we will meet again soon, for no other purpose than to celebrate the arrival of peace.

Real Events Used in the Stories

There were auxiliary hospitals across Britain in the Great War, providing care for servicemen.

Bees do a 'waggle dance' to communicate the location of food to their hive (this was first fully proposed by Karl Ritter von Frisch in 1927).

Folkestone was a major departure port for troops and equipment heading for the battlefields in Europe and large areas of northern France were home to the military forces of Britain and what was then the Empire. Troops were stationed in holding areas in the build up to the 'big push' (the Battle of the Somme).

German troops facing an Australian trench did erect a sign reading 'Advance Australia – if you can' but not until a few months later than suggested in this story.

The British General Headquarters in France moved to Montreuil-sur-Mer at the end of March 1916.

Winston Churchill ordered plans for a blackout of coastal towns in 1913; these were implemented in August 1914. A partial blackout of London and other cities followed and there was a general blackout in England from February 1916.

The Duchess of Westminster did open and run a hospital in the Le Touquet casino and it did have an x-ray machine.

Gaining information of the movement of enemy troops was of immense value to both sides; the Allies build an elaborate organization of train watchers in occupied Belgium and Luxembourg, with many brave people risking their lives to get information to the

British and French.

There was a Private Nigel Bruce who was wounded by machine gun fire in 1915. He went on to star as Doctor Watson, alongside Basil Rathbone as Sherlock Holmes, in more than a dozen films. I know it was indulgent to include him, sorry.

The Secret Intelligence Service (MI6) did have an office in Kingsway and used the cover of Messrs Rasen, Falcon Limited, an invented firm of 'shippers and exporters'. The Adventure of the Absent Spy makes references to some real member of the service, such as 'the Captain' (Sir Mansfield George Smith-Cumming, also known simply as 'C'), to the real Room 40 (the department for breaking enemy codes, a forerunner of the more famous Bletchley Park) and to common British beliefs about the Germans, such as the value of a fencing scar.

The German navy bombarded Great Yarmouth and Lowestoft in the early hours of 25th April; eight Zeppelins had bombed Norwich, Lincoln, Harwich and Ipswich earlier that night. At Lowestoft, a serviceman and three civilians were killed.

Captain Charles Fryatt of the *SS Brussels* really did attempt to ram the German submarine U-33 when it ordered him to evacuate his ship in March 1915. The Germans captured Captain Fryatt in June 1916 after five destroyers surrounded the *SS Brussels*. They executed him on 27th July.

The Netherlands was neutral throughout the first world war. Travel between Britain and Holland was possible but (obviously) risky. I found the most useful books for describing Rotterdam at the time were 'Spynest' by Edwin Ruis and 'The Secret Corps: A Tale of "Intelligence" on All Fronts' by Ferdinand Tuohy. All manner of activities were under way. Refugees and deserters mingled with criminals and spies. The Germans did build an electric fence along the Belgian border. The Grand Hotel Coomans did prosper as a result of all the comings and goings – no trace remains of it since the German bombing of Rotterdam in 1940 but the Hotel Mastbosch in Breda is still there.

During the Second Boer War (1899-1902) the British built concentration camps: at first to provide for the civilian population, later to contain them. Boers, black people and others were imprisoned. Altogether around 45,000 people died in these terrible camps, mainly due to neglect, poor conditions, disease and inadequate diet.

German naval intelligence was known as 'N'.

The town of Baer-le-Duc, also known as Baarle-Hertog and as Baarle-Nassau, includes many enclaves of Belgian territory. The complex borders run through streets, buildings and even houses. The Allies did keep a wireless station there. The Germans could see it from the 'main body' of Belgium and intercept everything it transmitted, although it was always in code. The Germans protested to the Dutch about the petrol which was supplied to the enclave of Belgium to power the transmitter; eventually it had to be smuggled in.

Donington Hall, now best known for the motor racing circuit, was used as a prison for German officers in the Great War. There were all sorts of rumours about the luxuries enjoyed by the prisoners there. Some did escape but only one made it back to Germany: Lieutenant Gunther Pluschow escaped with Oberleutnant Oskar Trefftz in July 1915. Trefftz was recaptured at Millwall but Pluschow arrived in Germany later the same month. The Kaiser awarded him the Iron Cross First Class and, after the war, he moved to Argentina.

Simon Yarding says he will become a computer; this term was sometimes used for people who made mathematical calculations by hand, before the advent of electronic devices. He says he will be working for Doctor Bragg; Sir William Lawrence Bragg was an Australian-born physicist who won the Nobel Prize for Physics in 1915 at the age of 25. The prize was shared with his father Sir William Henry Bragg for their work on X-ray crystallography, the technique which would later reveal the structure of DNA. During the Great War, Bragg led a team that developed the hot wire air wave detector. It was used to detect the sounds from enemy artillery. When recorded by an array of microphones, the location of the artillery piece could be identified – and attacked.

With three exceptions, the adventures Watson lists at the start of The Adventure of the Land Ships (the Bishopgate jewel case, the disappearance of the cutter *Alicia* etc) are all mentioned in the original Sherlock Holmes stories but never published as actual stories. The exceptions are, firstly, the story of The House of Silk, which is a Sherlock Holmes novel published in 2011 by the brilliant Anthony Horowitz. The final two referred to are The Adventure of the Illustrious Client and The Adventure of the Sussex Vampire which were published by Sir Arthur Conan Doyle in 1924 but set in the nineteenth century.

The War of the Worlds, the early science-fiction story by H. G. Wells, was published as a novel in 1898. In it, the Martians begin their invasion of Earth in and around Woking, Surrey, which seems an odd choice. Today you can see a sculpture of a Martian tripod vehicle in the town centre.

The idea of mobile armoured vehicles is old; Leonardo da Vinci drew one in 1487 and several ideas were in circulation in the years leading up to the Great War. The first prototype of what we now call a tank was commissioned by the Admiralty, under Winston Churchill. That prototype (called 'Little Willie,' possibly because that was a suitably disrespectful name for the Kaiser) and the last remaining mark one 'land ship' are on display at the Bovington Tank Museum, where the staff are friendly, enthusiastic and very well informed. Both were built by William Foster & Co in Lincoln. Production later expanded at Metropolitan Carriage in Birmingham.

Lincoln had two railway stations in 1916, less than a mile apart. The Midland Station (used by the Midland Railway) was later renamed Lincoln St Marks, and it closed in 1985. The modern Lincoln Station is on the site of the station used by the Northern Railway.

RAF Waddington originally opened as an RFC flying school in 1916. The B.E.2 two-seat biplane was in production from 1912 and was used throughout the war, both for training and in action. There is a full-size replica of a B.E.2b at the Royal Air Force museum in

Hendon, although the version I have used in the story is the B.E.2d, which had dual controls.

Tanks were first used in action by the British at the Battle of Flers-Courcelette on 15th September 1916. The tank model produced in the greatest numbers during the war was the Renault FT, with over 3,000 built and used by the armies of France, the United States and other countries.

The Battle of Flers-Courcelette was part of the Battle of the Somme, which began on 1st July 1916.

Author's Note

As a long-time fan of the Sherlock Holmes stories, I had often wondered what Holmes and Watson might have done in the Great War. Conan Doyle wrote one adventure for them set just before the conflict began but I imagine the horrors of the war were too recent for him to use them in a work of fiction.

I often thought of writing an adventure for my heroes set in the war but never seemed to have the patience to sit down and work at it. Then came Covid. I wrote 'The Detective at War' while we were all forced to stay in. The other three stories followed over the next couple of years.

What next for Holmes and Watson? What did they get up to in 1917? If you think I should write more Great War adventures for them, please write a review of this book, give it some stars, tell your friends and share a link on social media.

Thank you for reading my tribute to the immortal characters of Sir Arthur Conan Doyle. I hope you liked it (just as I love modern Germany).

Finally, apologies to certain French and Dutch friends whose names I pinched.

Richard Barton, Canterbury, UK.

https://www.youtube.com/fivemtc

Printed in Great Britain
by Amazon